ANGEL

A DCI RYAN MYSTERY

LJ ROSS

ISBN: 978-1-912310-04-3

First published in 2016 by LJ Ross

This edition published in June 2020 by Dark Skies Publishing

Author photo by Gareth Iwan Jones

Cover layout by Stuart Bache

Cover artwork and map by Andrew Davidson

Typeset by Riverside Publishing Solutions Limited

Printed and bound by CPI Goup (UK) Limited

For my sister Rachael, whose beautiful red hair was the inspiration for this story.

With all my love, now and always.

"I was a strong lad and survived; but the poison was in the wound, and the wound remained forever open."

~ Vladimir Nabokov

PROLOGUE

Easter, 1990

The hallway was quiet as the grave.

Early morning light shone through the grubby window panes and sent dust motes dancing on the air, which smelled of old wood. The floorboards creaked as the girl tiptoed along, as quickly as she dared. She counted off the nuns' quarters as she scurried past, keeping to the shadows.

One, two, three, four.

Reaching the doorway at the end, she twisted the old brass knob and slipped inside the communal bathroom. She cast furtive glances to either side and dropped to her knees to peer underneath the rickety stalls. When she was sure she was alone, she made directly for the end cubicle and climbed on top of the cracked toilet seat, then pushed her spindly legs onto the peeling window sill above it. Layers of old paint had sealed the window permanently closed but over the past weeks she had chipped away at it.

When she shoved her weight against the dirty brown pane, it began to crack open.

Sweat beaded her forehead as she struggled with the window but eventually it swung wide open, letting a rush of cold air into the stale cubicle. The girl raised her face to the wind, like a caged animal scenting freedom.

It was intoxicating.

Eager for more, she eased her skinny body through the gap and onto the sloping roof beyond. Her bare feet clutched at the mossy tiles and she began to crawl towards the guttering. A loose tile broke away and clattered loudly over the roof, landing distantly on the ground below. In the silent morning, the noise seemed deafening. She froze until she could be sure it had not disturbed the people inside, but she heard only the rush of her own frantic heartbeat drumming in her ears.

She shuffled towards the edge and peered over, jerking back at the sight of a fifty-foot drop to the hard ground below.

Struck by doubt, she glanced behind her, back towards the tiny bathroom window. For a moment, the window became a dark, angry eye.

Come back!

She shivered and turned away from it to look out at the fields and woods lying beyond the perimeter of the grounds. She crouched there, surveying the landscape of her birth and hope bloomed at the prospect of a brighter future, one she had never allowed herself to imagine until now.

Carefully, she swung her legs over the stone wall and wrapped them around a drainpipe, which strained against her weight and let out a long metallic whine, as if it were crying out a warning to those who still slumbered inside.

Her body was shaking with fatigue by the time she managed to shimmy halfway to the ground. Her legs were cut and bleeding, and the first wave of adrenaline was wearing off, leaving her chilled and hungry. She faltered, her muscles shaking as she fought to hold on. Her fingers scraped at the old metal and a sob escaped her, echoing out into the quiet morning.

With a slow inevitability, her grip loosened. She let out a strangled gasp as her body fell backwards, down and down until it crumpled onto the tarmac far below with a sickly *crunch*.

In the east, morning had broken. Sunshine burned through the mist, casting warm rays over the hills and glades of Northumberland, illuminating the girl's body where it lay twisted and broken. Her pale arms were outstretched, and long strands of red hair fell in a tangle around her head in a bright halo, like an angel.

Twenty-six years later

Like the shutter of a photographic lens, the man's eyes closed but the memory of her face was imprinted upon him forever; the soft skin of a girl blossoming into a woman.

Tears clogged his throat and began to fall down the man's face. The pain was still fresh. It followed him as a constant, unrelenting ache that festered and fed off his flesh like carrion.

His angel.

All these years later, she still walked beside him. Each day he saw her—a reflection in a shop window, a glimpse in the face of a passing woman—and each night when he slept, they were together again.

As he thought of her, his hands began to relax their tight grip on the woman's neck and he realised she had stopped struggling a while ago.

His vision cleared and he stared in wide-eyed fascination as the woman's body slumped to the floor at his feet. He watched her soul depart her body, rising up to meet her Maker, and he was filled with contentment. He had saved her; he had redeemed her.

God was good.

With two trembling fingers, he made the sign of the cross.

CHAPTER 1

Friday, 25th March

Good Friday

There was an eerie hush among the gravestones at the West Road Cemetery. Fog swirled, snaking its damp tendrils across the man's face as he tugged on a neon-yellow safety jacket and prepared to head out across the uneven ground. Above, the sky was a leaden grey, but the sun fought its way through the blanket of thick cloud to shine a trickle of weak light upon the city of Newcastle upon Tyne. Beyond the cemetery gates, people were awakening all across the city. They yawned, stretched and looked forward to a long Easter holiday weekend without the drudgery of work.

But for Keith Wilson, today was a day like any other. The dead still required burial, even if the living would rather not be burdened on what would usually be their day off. Keith made his way along the worn pathways and fired up a mini digger. The sound of its engine jarred with the quiet solemnity of the enormous cemetery but that didn't trouble him. His hearing wasn't what it used to be after twenty years operating heavy machinery—and only ten of them using protective headgear. Even now, it felt silly to don a hard hat and ear muffs just to operate what he considered to be little more than a glorified golf buggy.

He steered the digger along the perimeter of the cemetery past the plain lawn graves and then turned along a wide central avenue lined with expensive tombstones decorated with effigies of the Virgin Mary and angels cast in white granite. He supposed that long, solitary hours surrounded by monuments to dead people who lay under the ground, their bodies spent and wasted, was not an obvious career choice for many people. But then, Keith had always preferred his own company. He didn't put much stock in ghost stories and he didn't bother much with the church, either.

Once you're dead, you're dead.

The digger wheezed along, running parallel to the outer wall of the cemetery. The sound of traffic carried over it to remind him that life went on, but Keith didn't hear it. Under his breath, he whistled a football chant and looked forward to chewing the fat with his mates down at the Hope and Anchor at the end of the day.

He steered his machine down a row of fresh graves until he reached the spot earmarked for some old bloke who had popped his clogs at the beginning of last week.

He turned off the engine and leaned over the gear sticks to stare down at the ground.

The earth had already been freshly turned.

It wasn't a very neat job, certainly not up to *his* standards. The edges were ragged and didn't follow the clean lines of a digger's shovel but there was certainly a fresh mound of soil where there should have been none.

Keith huffed out an angry breath and looked back across the acres of ground he had covered, over to a cluster of stone buildings and the crematorium in the far distance. The council administrator had probably made some simple 'computer says no' error between episodes of *Geordie Shore*, he thought peevishly. Now, he was left standing like a prize muppet waiting to dig a hole that had already been dug.

He looked down at the map again, then at the note he had made in thick biro beside it which clearly stated this was the correct spot. He chewed the inside of his cheek as he considered what was for the best and then retrieved his old brick of a mobile phone to key in the number for his supervisor's office with one chunky index finger. When that didn't work, he tried calling the Council directly.

The number went straight to the messaging service for Newcastle City Council, reminding him, *"Our offices are now closed. Ordinary hours of business are between nine and five..."*. He barked out a request for them to call him back, pronto, then stepped down from the digger to stretch out his aching back while he waited. He happened to know that messages were automatically forwarded to the Bereavement Services team and, from there, to the bunch of limp-wristed morons in charge of his section. Most likely, they were still tucked up in bed and he wouldn't hear a peep out of them. Keith's heavy, steel-capped work boots squelched into the grass underfoot and he thought absently of the rain that had fallen the evening before. The turf smelled of dew and he inhaled deeply.

Much to his surprise, the mobile phone in his pocket began to vibrate and he fumbled around to answer it.

"Keith? It's Kayleigh. I got your message. What's up?"

"Somebody's stuffed up royally, here, love," he said forthrightly, with just enough condescension to imply that the 'somebody' was *her*. "I'm standing here ready to dig a grave, but the site already has somebody in it."

There was a brief sigh and a pause while she booted up her laptop and logged into the work system remotely, keying in the reference number he gave her.

"Okay, Keith, I've got the database in front of me here." *Another pause.* "Are you sure the site is already in use? I can't see any record of a burial there."

Keith rolled his eyes and glanced over at the small mound of earth.

"Aye, pet, I'm sure. I'm standing here looking at a fresh pile of muck."

There was a long pause.

"Alright, listen, I'll try to get a hold of the ground staff and see if we've missed something. I'll speak to Suzy, too, because she might have forgotten to update the system."

With an upbeat 'cheery-bye!' she rang off, telling him to stay put.

Keith stared at the phone in his gnarled hand and then shoved it back in his pocket. The sun was winning its battle against the clouds and it burned through the vapour to shine a comforting light over the quiet graveyard. There were worse places to be, he thought, and leaned back against the hood of his machine. He scratched at the stubble on his chin and ran a hand over his head, which sported thick blond hair that was just beginning to grey at the temples. Women were always surprised to find that he dug graves for a living, somehow imagining it was only sinister-looking, balding old men who needed to earn a crust—not somebody who looked vaguely reminiscent of Alan Shearer when he made the effort.

Smiling at the thought, Keith cast his eyes downward and focused properly on the messy, upturned soil. It was a rich, dark brown, interspersed with tufts of grass. The rain had dislodged it overnight and there were tracks in the mud where the water had run in rivulets on either side. Idly, he daydreamed, tracing the path of the lines.

Then his heart ground violently to a halt, slamming against his chest in one hard motion.

He crept closer and his heart restarted, this time skipping and skidding frantically while his mind processed what he could see, very clearly now.

It was a single dead eye, peering sightlessly at him through the soil.

A few miles further south, Detective Chief Inspector Maxwell Finley-Ryan examined his bedroom floor with a similar kind of bemused horror. Wedding magazines were strewn across the carpet and a small cork board was propped against the dresser, bearing all manner of paraphernalia. He was reliably informed this was something known as a 'mood board', which every bride must have. Naturally, people couldn't just head down to the nearest registry office, say a few words and live happily ever after. No, no, *no*. There needed to be suits and ties, frocks and hats and—God help him—*fascinators*. He could only presume these magical items of headwear were designed to fascinate those who looked upon them, otherwise he would be sorely disappointed.

Ryan took a hasty slug of strong coffee from the mug in his hand and told himself not to panic. He was a murder detective, after all. He had toppled a cult circle; he had diced with death and survived to tell the tale.

But he hadn't seen anything like this.

The author of his present misfortune sashayed into the room. In her arms, she clutched another pile of magazines and a stack of unopened envelopes. Her dark hair was bundled into a ponytail and she wore a red jumper over jeans and bare feet. Through the open door, he heard the strains of an eighties ballad and surmised that, once again, the radio had found its way back to her preferred station.

Catching sight of him, Doctor Anna Taylor stifled a chuckle.

"I was thinking we could look through these together, maybe decide on some of the final touches for the wedding."

Ryan's face remained admirably calm as it drained of colour.

"What else can there be?" He was dumbfounded. "We've been planning this state event for nearly seven months—"

"We need to think about wedding favours," she said, with a glint.

"Favours?"

"Mm hmm," she said cheerfully, dumping the pile of magazines on the bed. "Then, there's some of the late RSVPs to open and sort—"

That clinched it. Ryan could see the rest of his day stretching before him in a haze of stationery and spreadsheets and decided that enough was definitely enough.

"Ah, you know, whatever you choose is fine with me," he said, edging towards the door. "I was thinking of taking a drive out."

Anna's lips twitched.

"Well, if you're sure."

Ryan was nearly out of the door when his mobile phone began to shrill out a tinny rendition of the *Indiana Jones* theme tune and the number for the Control Room flashed on the screen.

"Work!" he exclaimed, gleefully.

Detective Sergeant Frank Phillips yawned widely and dipped under the police tape which hung across the imposing iron gates at the entrance to the West Road Cemetery, raising a hand to greet the two constables who stood guard with a log book to record everybody entering and leaving. The West Road itself was steep and a line of traffic made its way upward with an angry jerk of gears as people continued their slow journey into the city from the west, no doubt disgruntled at the prospect of having to go to work on a day earmarked as a national holiday.

Much like himself, he thought, imagining the sleepy-eyed redhead and crispy bacon sandwich he had sacrificed to be here.

Best not to dwell on it.

Ahead of him, two stone chapels were linked by a cloister and clock tower whose large wrought-iron hands told him the time was now half past nine. Behind the cloister, he knew, there was a Garden of Remembrance where his father's remains had been scattered, years earlier. Phillips' mind wandered back to that windy morning in the late eighties and he could see himself clearly; a man with considerably more hair and less paunch, dressed in a beige anorak and clutching a small urn under his left arm. It had been a cold day in January, colder than it was now, but he had been numb to the frost. Hastily pushing the memories aside, he glanced around the main complex, noting the CSI van and the ambulance which was turning around to give easier access to its double doors at the back.

Phillips found his Senior Investigating Officer standing on a carpet of thick plastic sheeting that had been laid over the damp ground, several feet away from the site of an open grave on the far side of the cemetery. Ryan cut a striking figure; a tall man standing perfectly still while the wind occasionally ruffled the shock of black hair against his brow. Beneath it, calm grey eyes surveyed the scene and missed very little. Tom Faulkner, the senior CSI, hovered nearby brandishing a hefty-looking camera as he prepared to record his initial walk-through of the crime scene.

They heard his heavy footsteps approaching.

"Morning Phillips," they said in unison.

"Gents," came the easy reply. "What's the craic here, then?"

"Take a look for yourself," Ryan said, stepping aside and gesturing towards an opening in the large forensics tent which had been erected to preserve the site. Phillips dipped his head inside.

"Oh, for pity's sake," he muttered, as his stomach did a slow flip. He watched the CSIs begin the slow, painstaking process of excavating the body of a woman. Their overalls crackled as they brushed away the layers of soil to reveal a contorted face, its expression fixed into a shocked grimace.

But it was the eyes that had the most impact. They were open and staring, clouded over with the milky-white film that death brings, and no less penetrating because of it.

"It's always the lasses," Phillips managed, his throat working again.

Ryan said nothing and continued his silent observation of the CSIs, who checked the fine grains of soil for evidence, storing samples and taking swabs as they went.

"Who called it in?"

"A man called Keith Wilson rang it in about an hour ago." Ryan glanced back towards the entrance and the small collection of police vehicles with their neon yellow and blue banners. "He's employed by Newcastle City Council as a grave digger. As far as I can tell, Wilson arrived for work at eight and headed up here to dig a grave for a funeral due to take place tomorrow. He found this waiting for him instead."

Phillips nodded sombrely.

"Interesting they chose this particular spot, alongside everybody else in the row."

"Yes, it is. I don't think I've come across a killer who actually buried his victim in a cemetery. Have you?"

"Nope," Phillips said roundly. "I've only seen the ones dumped in rivers, in woods, in bin bags and all that. This feels like a treat."

Ryan smiled grimly.

"I take it the Council have no record of a burial?" Phillips asked.

"None whatsoever. Apparently, there have been instances where people have snuck into the cemetery to bury their dead grandmother, but it's very rare."

Phillips pursed his lips and watched as the CSIs brushed away the soil around the woman's face to reveal long strands of red hair, caked with mud. The sight of it sent an uncomfortable prickle racing up his spine as he thought of his partner, Detective Inspector Denise MacKenzie, whose long red hair had lain across his chest earlier that morning.

He cleared his throat.

"She doesn't look like anybody's grandmother."

They stood in silence for a few minutes until the woman was fully revealed to them and it was as if a shroud had been lifted. She seemed to rise from the earth, her jaw wide open and gaping. Ryan thought briefly of *The Lady of Shalott* and then watched in dismay as a long earthworm made its journey from the inner crevices of her throat and began to crawl along the side of her neck.

"Faulkner?" he said sharply. "Thoughts?"

The man in question snapped another picture and then sat back on his haunches, slipping slightly on the plastic underfoot before righting himself again. He adjusted his glasses and looked down at the body with sad, puppyish brown eyes.

"Far too soon to say what happened to her and, in any case, I'm no pathologist. But if I were a betting man,

I'd say she was strangled. Look here," he said, as he gestured a gloved hand towards a thick, purple-black line around the woman's neck, then stood up with a rustle.

Ryan absorbed the information, noting the fine cobweb of broken blood vessels beside the eyes.

"What's that?"

The other men turned to follow the direction of his gaze and watched one of the junior CSIs brush off a stiff piece of card, grubby and curling at the edges, before transferring it into a transparent evidence bag.

Ryan held out a gloved hand to examine the stained note. It read:

Et ego te absolvo a peccatis tuis in nomine Patris, et Filii, et Spiritus Sancti.

"What does it mean?" Faulkner queried.

"It's Latin," Phillips explained. "It's what the priest says when he's giving absolution: 'I absolve you from your sins in the name of the Father and of the Son and of the Holy Spirit.'"

Phillips looked up and caught the surprise on Ryan's face.

"My ma and da were Catholics," he added. "I went to Mass every Sunday when I was a nipper."

"But not now?"

"No, not now."

Ryan did not enquire further. He had never ascribed to any organised religion, so he wouldn't pontificate on the many and varied reasons why people followed or relinquished their faith.

"I doubt she wrote this note herself," was all he said, handing it back to Faulkner to be logged.

Phillips glanced at the note and grunted.

"He used a permanent marker."

Apparently, they had a practical killer on their hands.

"Whoever did this chose to bring her here, to this exact spot, rather than somewhere she was less likely to be found. It's a shallow grave and he left a note."

"You think whoever it is *wanted* her to be found?" Phillips asked.

"Maybe. On the other hand, he could be sloppy." He took a sweeping glance around the area, then remarked, "Either way, it was risky. Opening hours are between nine and four forty-five on weekends and bank holidays. I'll venture to say that our perp came outside of those hours, under cover of darkness, in which case he needed an access point. This is a built-up area and there are no signs of forced entry at the main gates, so let's look at how he let himself in. Get the PCs to canvas the vicinity. Surely somebody saw something."

Phillips nodded his agreement.

"I'll ask about CCTV," he added.

Ryan turned, preparing to leave Faulkner to his task and then paused mid-step as another scene began to unfold. The CSIs worked quickly to uncover the woman's body and a sickly feeling began to roll in his stomach. The woman's arms rested above her head in a coarse rendition of a ballerina's pirouette, the skin a stark grey-white against the muddy ground. The material of her blouse had been torn at the arms and had been smoothed out in a fan around them. Her legs, still clad in navy-blue trousers, were drawn together neatly with the toes of her plain black shoes pointing forward.

No, he realised, looking at the scene again and thinking of the note. Not a ballerina.

Whoever did this had given her wings.

CHAPTER 2

In the neighbouring county of Northumberland, Detective Inspector Denise MacKenzie and Detective Constable Jack Lowerson stood outside a small pebble-dashed bungalow which nestled in a cul-de-sac on the edge of the picturesque town of Rothbury. It was a stately, upmarket corner of the county, a few miles to the north of Newcastle and accessible via a pleasant drive along the A1. Riders astride glossy-coated thoroughbreds *clippety-clopped* along streets lined with attractive stone buildings redolent of the Victorian era, which soaked up the sun and blended nicely with the freshly-harvested fields.

Several pairs of inquisitive eyes followed their progress from the windows of neighbouring bungalows, shaded behind a swathe of lacy blinds and chintz. MacKenzie reflected that local busybodies were both a blessing and a curse in her line of work. If she had a pound for every well-meaning neighbour who had given a falsely embellished report to 'help' an investigation, she would be a rich woman indeed.

They exchanged a brief word with the police constable on the door and then headed inside the house to see what awaited them. A quick glance around the interior betrayed a love of cleanliness and order bordering on the obsessive. Books and CDs were arranged in alphabetical order, cushions were plumped and free of creases, and the oven held not a speck of grease.

All was pristine except the lady of the house, whose decaying body littered the floor of her immaculate living room. MacKenzie came to a standstill just inside the doorway, careful not to go any further and risk contaminating the scene.

"What do we know about her?" Lowerson said, training his eyes towards the ceiling to allow his system time to recover.

MacKenzie gave him credit for maintaining control over his stomach. You got used to it, after a while.

"Barbara Hewitt, aged sixty-five. No obvious signs of aggression that I can see but the body's well into decomposition, so it's hard to tell."

"Who reported it?"

"The cleaning lady," MacKenzie replied, while her eyes tracked over the details of the room. "She has a key to the house and let herself in as usual this morning. Apparently, Barbara promised to pay extra if she came to work on the bank holiday."

"Really?" Lowerson was surprised. "I thought she lived alone. How much mess can one person make?"

MacKenzie looked meaningfully at Barbara's corpse.

Lowerson found the courage to look down at the mass on the floor and felt his stomach revolt at the sight. The woman's bloated body had obviously been lying there for some time. It held an unnatural blue-green tinge and the skin was blistered, providing a fertile ground for the swarms of pre-pupae maggots which festered in the crevices and the flies which circled the stagnant air. Blood and fluid pooled around the body in an island, seeping into the carpet and beginning to crust as it dried. The stench of putrid death was palpable.

"Yeah, it's not pretty," MacKenzie said, breathing hard through her teeth. "Control Room thought this was a case for CID. It's a nasty sight but I can't see anything particularly unusual. Am I missing something?"

Lowerson frowned and cocked his head to one side, but was careful to remain standing in the doorway.

"I agree with you. I can't see anything out of the ordinary, nothing that would usually alert us to a suspicious death, at any rate." He gestured a hand towards Barbara's remains, curled in a foetal position on the carpet. "This lady might have had a heart attack and keeled over, for all we know. I'm surprised she wasn't found earlier."

MacKenzie shrugged.

"Faulkner is sending over a couple of CSIs but most of his staff are working the crime scene over on the West Road."

Lowerson raised an enquiring eyebrow.

"Ryan and Phillips caught one earlier this morning," she explained. "The body of a woman found in a shallow grave at the West Road Cemetery."

Lowerson pulled a face.

"Two bodies on the holiday weekend? No rest for the wicked, is there?"

They retreated back outside the house into the watery spring sunshine. The smell of death followed them, clinging to their clothes and invading their nostrils.

"Nice enough place," Lowerson commented, though it was too quiet for his taste.

MacKenzie nodded as she cast a sharp eye over the Arcadian scene.

"You're thinking something's off?"

MacKenzie smiled again.

"I'm just naturally suspicious."

"Want to have a word with the cleaning lady?"

"Let's do that."

They found Carole Dudley sitting inside a squad car being comforted by a police constable. Her rounded face was puffy with tears and she clutched a sodden tissue in her fingers. MacKenzie opened the door and smiled a greeting.

"Mrs Dudley? My name is Detective Inspector MacKenzie and this is my colleague, Detective Constable Lowerson, from Northumbria CID. If you don't mind, we need to ask you a few questions. Would you like to take a walk and get a breath of fresh air?"

Lowerson held out a gallant hand to help her from the car.

"A-alright then."

"I understand you must have had a terrible shock this morning."

"It was awful. Just awful. The smell—"

MacKenzie steered her away from the trauma and back to the facts.

"Why don't you tell us how long you've been working for Barbara?"

"Um, well, I started working for Miss Hewitt and her mother about ten years ago. They liked me to use their last names, they didn't like to be too familiar," she explained.

"That's a bit stuffy, isn't it?" Lowerson commented, from his position on her other side.

Carole clamped her lips together and adopted the reserved expression of one who would not speak ill of the dead.

"What were your usual hours?"

"Every Friday, eight-thirty till one," she said. "Miss Hewitt liked to stick to a schedule, come rain or shine."

"I see. How did you find the house?"

"What do you mean?"

"Well, was it messy, dirty? Did you find anything out of place recently?"

Carole screwed up her homely face in concentration, then let it fall again.

"Not that I can think of," she said apologetically. "She just liked things how she liked them. A place for everything, if you know what I mean."

"I understand. Do you happen to know who we should contact, in terms of next of kin?"

Carole's lip quivered again.

"She didn't have anybody, as far as I know. Her mother died last year and her father died back in the nineties. She didn't have any brothers or sisters."

"I understand she wasn't married—how about children?"

"None that I know of."

"Alright. Was there anybody special in her life?"

"You mean like a feller?"

"Yes, or a good friend."

"No, nobody. Although—"

MacKenzie waited.

"She always went out on Fridays, while I did the cleaning. I never knew where she went," Carole confided. "It's not as if she had any friends or family. I don't think she had anybody. But she always had her hair done on Friday mornings then went off in the car for a few hours, all dolled up."

"She never told you?"

"No, we didn't have that kind of relationship," Carole said, stiffly. "She was a very private person."

MacKenzie nodded.

"When was the last time you saw Miss Hewitt alive?"

"Last Friday morning, same as usual. She let me into the house at eight-thirty, then headed out in time for her hair appointment at nine."

MacKenzie made a mental note.

"Did she seem troubled or unwell?"

Carole sniffed and blew her nose again.

"She, well, the thing is…" She trailed off and MacKenzie gave her an encouraging smile. "The thing is, she wasn't a sociable person. She didn't go in for small talk. She left a note with a list of the jobs she wanted doing, then left me to it."

"Did she ever complain of ill health?"

"No, she seemed as fit as a fiddle. I never heard her talk about any ailments; oh, a bit of stiffness in the joints from time to time but that's to be expected at her age."

"I see. How about when you found her this morning: did you notice anything out of place or anything unusual?"

"I didn't really notice anything except…except the body." Carole swallowed. "I suppose the curtains were drawn, which I thought was a bit odd because she's an early riser and, like I say, she's normally at the door to meet me. When there was no answer, I thought she must have left a bit earlier than usual for her hair appointment."

"Had she done that before?"

"No," Carole said decisively. "She always liked to be there to let me in. I have a key, but I've never known her not to be at home to open the door."

"Would anybody else have had access to your key?"

The woman drew herself up to her full height, cheeks flaming.

"Certainly not! The key is right here, in my bag." She retrieved a jumbled key ring and pointed to a brass key with a red sticker on the edge. "I colour code them, so I'm the only one who knows the address they belong to. I keep them in a locked box at home."

"Alright." MacKenzie drew on a pair of nitrile gloves and deposited the key inside an evidence bag which she kept in her pocket. Then she steered them back towards the squad car, walking at an even pace which had the desired effect of calming the woman's taut nerves. "One final question, for now, Carole. Did you see anybody else hanging around, anybody who seemed out of place, today or even last Friday?"

"No, nobody."

It took another hour for the CSIs to arrive and longer still until Barbara's body could be transferred to the mortuary. MacKenzie and Lowerson spent a tedious couple of hours canvassing the area, knocking on doors to speak with Barbara's neighbours to record their preliminary statements. It was early afternoon when they emerged from the final house on the street, their ears ringing with local scandal and their stomachs sloshing with an excess of instant coffee and custard cream biscuits.

"I need an aspirin," MacKenzie muttered darkly.

"I need a pint," Lowerson shot back.

She grinned.

"There are no cameras here on the street and nobody remembers seeing Barbara any time after last Friday night. Mr Owen at Number 12 thinks he remembers hearing her car turning back into her driveway sometime around five-thirty because he heard the engine. Apparently, it needs servicing." MacKenzie looked across at the little electric-blue Citroen C1 sitting on the driveway in front of Barbara's bungalow. "We'll take a wander along the main high street and speak to the local businesses. Carole says that Barbara was in the habit of doing certain things on certain days. We'll check she didn't go to the supermarket as usual last Saturday morning—it might help us to narrow down a timescale when we speak to the pathologist."

Lowerson resigned himself to a long afternoon and made a mental note to cancel his date for the evening.

"It seems to tie in with what we thought," he said. "Barbara has lived in Rothbury for over twenty years, but she kept herself to herself and didn't bother much with her neighbours."

MacKenzie nodded.

"She may not have been popular, but I can't imagine somebody offing her just because she wasn't the chatty type."

"Seems like it's probably death by natural causes?"

It was on the tip of MacKenzie's tongue to agree with him, but some instinct held her back.

"Let's wait to hear from the pathologist, Jack. I can't put my finger on it, but something doesn't feel right. She was a woman in good health, with a particular routine." She took a slow survey of the street. "It could be something or nothing."

"I guess we'll find out."

Ryan and Phillips entered the Northumbria Criminal Investigation Department's Headquarters on the western outskirts of the city and instantly felt at home in the squat, sixties building with its perpetual odour of stale sweat and cleaning detergent. They made directly for the coffee machine outside their open-plan office on the second floor but were intercepted in the corridor by the Chief Constable's officious personal assistant before they'd had a chance to fortify themselves.

"Ryan!" Donna Peters greeted him with her usual hauteur and ignored Phillips completely, which he accepted with good grace.

"The Chief Constable wants a word with you."

Ryan held off a sigh. "Is it urgent?"

Donna raised a single, tattooed eyebrow. "Have you got more important things to be doing?"

"Don't answer that," Phillips murmured, under his breath.

"Not at all," Ryan smiled winningly. "Just trying to find a killer, nothing heavy. Tell the boss I'll be with her in a moment."

Donna flipped her hair extensions and stalked away.

"Charming woman," Ryan drawled. "Frank, I want you to get straight on to the handwriting expert—"

"Graphologist."

Ryan paused mid-breath and eyed Phillips with suspicion.

"How do you know these things?"

"Common knowledge," Phillips beamed.

"Right. Well, get onto whatever *ologist* you can find and ask them to spare a couple of hours to look over that note. You never know."

While Phillips made his escape, Ryan tapped on the Chief Constable's door and waited for a response.

"Come!"

Sandra Morrison was a deceptively able person. Over the years, her diminutive height and unglamorous approach to policing had led many to assume she owed her present position to a combination of positive discrimination and good luck. In truth, Morrison was a student of human behaviour; a keen observer of people and their foibles and that insight had enabled her to progress through the ranks. She believed in the law, in its due process, and she had her own firm ideas about what constituted 'right' and 'wrong'. Her devotion to her work had cost her several relationships and a brief bout of alcoholism but you can't make an omelette without breaking a few eggs.

She looked up from a stack of paperwork as Ryan entered the room and indicated for him to take a seat in one of the uncomfortable visitors' chairs. He folded his body into a foamy lounger and crossed one long leg over the other.

Elegant, Morrison thought. He was an elegant man, something you didn't see too often nowadays.

She turned her mind to the matters in hand, preferring not to beat around the bush.

"I heard you've caught a new case?"

Ryan rolled his shoulder slightly and prepared to deliver his report.

"Yes, ma'am. DS Phillips and I responded to a request to attend the West Road Cemetery earlier this morning. One of the Council's grave diggers discovered a body left in a shallow grave."

Morrison waited patiently for more.

"There are several interesting factors to this discovery, which I have determined to be a matter for CID given the injuries and manner in which she was found."

"Interesting factors?" she prodded.

"Yes. Firstly, a shallow grave was dug—we believe manually—on a site which follows the existing Council map of grave sites at the cemetery. Second, the body may have been arranged before she was covered over."

He thought briefly of other bodies at other times.

"Initially, ma'am, I considered the arrangement of the body to be a cruciform formation, or something similar, but the victim's arms were drawn above her head and bent sharply at the elbow with her blouse torn around it, suggestive of something like a wing."

Morrison frowned but remained silent as he continued.

"Finally, and perhaps most revealing, a note was left with the victim. It consisted of one line of text, written in Latin, giving absolution. For these reasons, our current thinking is that we have a religiously-motivated crime."

Morrison leaned back in her chair and sighed deeply, her sharp brown eyes looking weary all of a sudden.

"Do you feel there is any connection?"

Ryan knew the question she was really asking him. Last year, they had brought down a band of fanatics who had taken lives and spread their malice far and wide, all in the name of warped belief. Morrison wanted to know if they had resurfaced.

"No, ma'am, I don't. There was ritual in the Circle's crimes but not like this. For one thing, we appear to be dealing with someone who attaches significance to church dogma, rather than the other way around."

"True enough," she acknowledged. "What steps have been taken?"

"We're working on finding out her identity. The lady was discovered fully clothed but without any identifying markers, so we'll be looking into that as a priority. Meanwhile, the pathologist will be performing his post-mortem and we'll await the results. We've requested all available CCTV and a canvas of the local area is being conducted as we speak."

Morrison nodded. It was no less than she had expected.

"What about the grave digger—Wilson, did you say?"

"Yes, Keith Wilson. We've taken a statement from him and we'll be checking it out. According to him, he spent last night in a couple of bars followed by a club in the Bigg Market area. He tells us he got lucky at the end of the night but was unable to provide either a name or telephone number for the aforementioned lucky lady, ma'am."

"I see." Morrison's lips twitched.

"We can check the bars and the club to compare his movements with the post-mortem interval of the deceased, once we know it."

Morrison gave a satisfied nod. "I don't need to tell you what the outcry will be, once the media gets hold of this."

It was Ryan's turn to sigh. "No, ma'am."

"I want a press statement ready and on my desk by three o'clock. I want to get ahead of this and take charge of the direction early on. I won't make the same mistake as last time."

Ryan didn't respond.

"Ryan? Is that understood?"

He raised icy grey eyes. "With respect, I won't be releasing any statement until we have identified the woman and contacted her next of kin."

Morrison stopped her mouth falling open, just. "I don't think you appreciate the sort of backlash—"

"I'm more than aware."

She acknowledged the hit and took a mental step backwards. Ryan had seen his fair share of media intrusion, both personally and professionally.

She gave a brisk nod.

"As soon as you've spoken to next of kin, then."

Ryan inclined his head. "Was there anything else, ma'am?"

Morrison leaned forward again, all business.

"Actually, there is. Ryan, as you know, there's a vacancy available in the department."

There was a short pause.

"Yes."

"Have you given any thought to it?"

Ryan looked away for a moment, then back into her watchful eyes.

"I thought about it, briefly."

"You're young for the post but I believe you've earned it. More importantly, you would make a good job of it."

Ryan shifted in his chair and re-crossed his legs. He wasn't ready to talk about the possibility—it seemed too soon.

"We have a surplus of highly-qualified men and women who could easily fill Gregson's shoes," he said eventually. Their former Detective Chief Superintendent had fallen from grace in spectacular fashion, a few months before.

"We need good people at the helm," Morrison said. "You're one of them."

Ryan found himself taken aback.

"I—thank you, ma'am."

"Don't thank me, just tell me you'll give the matter serious thought."

"Alright."

Morrison searched his face and assumed correctly that was all he was going to give her for now, so she turned to the final item on her agenda.

"As you know, the trial is coming up." She steepled her fingers and met his eyes across the expanse of her beech desk. "The CPS are satisfied that we put together a solid case, that we dotted the i's and crossed the t's."

"That's gratifying to know," Ryan drawled. In his experience, there would always be a defence lawyer eager to find some technical loophole to enable his client to wriggle off the hook. Well, not in this case. Arthur Gregson, former Superintendent of Northumbria CID, would not be going anywhere except prison. He would personally slam the door shut behind him.

"They want you to give evidence," she continued. "Are you prepared to do that?"

Ryan's eyes turned flat.

"I have no qualms whatsoever in setting out, in detail, Gregson's many and varied crimes. When the call comes, I'll be ready."

Morrison nodded her approval.

"That'll be all."

"Thank you, ma'am."

Ryan escaped the confines of Morrison's office and returned to the relative comfort of his open-plan office space further down the hall. He found Phillips sitting at his desk with a telephone handset wedged between ear and shoulder, while his hands completed the intricate task of unwrapping a steaming hot beef and onion pasty. To Phillips' consternation, Ryan wasted no time in appropriating it for himself, throwing his sergeant a breezy smile as he fled to his own desk with the stolen goods.

A few moments later, Phillips ended the call and hurriedly looked across to where Ryan was dusting the crumbs from his shirt.

"You thieving—"

"Now, now," Ryan admonished. "What's a bit of beef pasty, between friends?"

"Aye, well, you can buy me another on the way to the hospital."

"I take it that was the pathologist on the phone?"

Phillips nodded.

"That's a bit quick, isn't it?" Ryan cast a glance in the direction of the large white clock on the wall and noted that the time was barely three o'clock. "It usually takes him a while longer to do a post-mortem."

"He hasn't finished but he wants to show us something."

"That man loves an audience," Ryan muttered, but rose from his chair and made a grab for his coat.

They found Doctor Jeffrey Pinter shaking his bony hips to a compilation of seventies disco classics. The music filled the wide, windowless space of the basement mortuary at the Royal Victoria Infirmary and managed to offset its inherently depressing atmosphere. A bank of metal drawers lined one wall and a row of metal gurneys had been placed at intervals in the centre, three of which were presently occupied by veiled bodies of the recently deceased. They spotted Pinter at the head of the room—a tall, spindly man whose grey pallor and narrow, sagging face matched his profession perfectly. He turned at the sound of footsteps against the tiled floor.

"Afternoon, Jeff." Ryan chose not to accept the outstretched hand, fearful of where it had been. Beside him, Phillips studiously avoided looking at the row of bodies and shivered at an icy blast from the air conditioning system whirring overhead.

"You look busy," Ryan commented.

Pinter made a *clacking* sound with his gums which Phillips instantly disliked.

"No such thing as a bank holiday in this business," Pinter complained, moving towards the first gurney in the row. With a theatrical flourish, he whipped back its paper covering to reveal the stiff body of the redheaded woman they had found a few hours earlier.

"Cleaned her up a bit," Pinter began matter-of-factly, as if he had just returned from the car wash.

"What can you tell us?"

"Well, first and most importantly, I'd say she'd been dead for somewhere in the region of twelve to fourteen hours when she was first brought in, accounting for ambient temperatures being colder overnight and her body having been exposed to the elements. I might have suggested a consultation with a forensic entomologist but, frankly, I don't think it's necessary at this stage. The body carries all the signs consistent with that timescale."

"So, we're looking at something in the region of nine p.m. onwards, last night."

Pinter nodded, then drew on a pair of gloves and pointed at the underside of the woman's body. It was a deep, ugly purple, in comparison with her face and torso which was an almost translucent grey.

"Here, you can see that her body has undergone post-mortem hypostasis—"

"Speak English, Jeff," Phillips grumbled.

"The blood has congealed and succumbed to gravity, which tells us that she has been lying on her back for at least six hours. Factoring in rigor mortis, the core temperature... yes, I would say she had been dead anywhere up to fourteen hours when we found her. Nineteen hours, by now."

"You're certain?"

Pinter held both hands out defensively.

"It's your job to find out the 'whys' and the 'wherefores'. All I can do is give you my medical opinion."

"Alright, Jeff, keep your hair on," Ryan muttered. "How did she die?"

"Ligature asphyxiation. There is clear evidence of violent compression around the windpipe; both the trachea and larynx have been crushed."

"In other words, she was strangled," Phillips said, a bit testily.

"Exactly. You can see the ecchymoses on her neck, just here—" He took out a retractable pointer and held it in front of the woman's neck, where lurid bruising circled the hollow skin in garish shades of purple and black. "These bruises were sustained ante mortem."

Ryan forced himself to look and to muster the detachment he needed to do his job. He stared down at the shrunken body of what had once been an attractive woman of around forty and pity stirred in his chest. Despite the early stages of decay, he saw even features and high cheekbones. Her eyes were taped closed and her hands had been encased in plastic bags to preserve any remaining evidence. Dismally, he noticed they were starting to balloon as natural gases oozed from the woman's pores and began to collect inside the plastic folds.

"How about defensive wounds?"

"I've swabbed the skin and nails; they're with forensics now. I'm also waiting for the blood and toxicology reports to come through but it's the bank holiday weekend, so we can't expect miracles."

"Tell them I'll authorise the overtime," Ryan interjected.

Phillips raised an eyebrow but said nothing. Resources were always stretched and paying for the 'express service' was a luxury reserved for urgent cases.

Then again, he was inclined to think that every case was urgent.

"Right you are. Even without the results, we can draw certain inferences. Three of her nails are broken, for instance, which would be consistent with a struggle. However, I will venture to say that the scratches you can see on her neck were self-inflicted."

"She fought to survive."

"Yes."

They fell silent as they imagined a woman fighting for her life, but their reverie was interrupted by the unpleasant sound of skin being drawn together as a mortuary clinician stitched together the open folds of a man's torso on the other side of the room.

"Any signs of sexual assault?" Phillips asked.

Pinter shook his head.

"No evidence of trauma in the vaginal or anal tract but, again, I've taken swabs to be sure. I found the vestiges of some chicken and bread or similar wheat-based food substance, alongside a quantity of white wine in her system, which appears to have been her last meal around twenty hours ago. That's all I can really tell you at the moment, but I'll know more when the results of the tests come back."

Ryan turned to his sergeant.

"Frank, get on to the Control Room and see who's been reported missing this morning."

Phillips shook his head sadly.

"No need, boss." He tapped the edge of his work phone. "I've got a message here from Missing Persons. I think we might have found our Jane Doe."

CHAPTER 3

"Her name was Kristina, but everyone called her Krista."

Ryan sat on the edge of a plush green velvet sofa, having completed the unenviable task of informing Krista's next of kin that she wouldn't be coming home. A small, cowardly part of him wished he could have delegated it to somebody else, but that wasn't his way. So he and Phillips had trudged the long journey from the car to the front door of a smart, newly-built townhouse in an area of Newcastle known as Spital Tongues.

You couldn't make up a name like that.

"We've only just returned from our honeymoon," Nina Ogilvy-Matthews was saying. She swiped a hand over her eyes, which were red-rimmed and raw as the tears continued to flow. "We were together for years, ever since university, you know?"

She looked up at Ryan, desperate for him to understand.

"We decided to use a double-barrelled surname after the wedding." She was prattling, and she knew it.

"Kristina Ogilvy and Nina Matthews became Mrs and Mrs Ogilvy-Matthews. Everyone said it has a posh ring to it."

She laughed, a bit hysterically, then her eye caught a silver-framed wedding portrait on the window ledge and she let out a long, low sound, like an animal in pain.

Nina's mother was seated beside her, saying nothing but holding her daughter's hand as her own tears fell. Her father stood silently in the corner, looking shell-shocked.

"I'm very sorry for your loss," Ryan murmured, though the words felt like sawdust on his tongue and he hated himself already for the questions he was bound to ask. "I need you to help us piece together Krista's last movements."

"You said she had been…had been…"

The woman buried her face in her hands and sobbed, the harsh sound of it reverberating around the small sitting room. Her mother raised a hand to rub soothing circles over her back, murmuring quietly.

Ryan gave Nina another minute to compose herself.

"Mrs Matthews, is there anything we can get for you?"

The woman scraped her fingers through shoulder-length blonde hair, drawing it tightly away from her scalp while she fought to stay lucid.

"No, no, I'll…I suppose I'll need to call Krista's mother," she whispered. "They didn't get along but—"

"We can do it, if you prefer?"

She shook her head, bearing down on the waves of grief.

"It will be better coming from me," she said, looking up at Ryan as if seeing him for the first time. "I seem to recognise you."

He said nothing and waited for her to make the connection.

"You're the detective who brought down the cult circle, aren't you?" Her voice was stronger while she focused her mind elsewhere. "I couldn't believe it when I heard about it on the news last summer."

"It's my job to seek justice for the dead," Ryan said simply.

Tears swam in the woman's eyes and she nodded, trying to organise her jumbled mind so that she could help him.

"Krista went to work as usual yesterday. She rang me at lunchtime to say that she might stay for a few drinks with her colleagues to celebrate the long weekend, but she'd be home by nine-thirty."

"Did Krista say where they planned to go?"

"She thought they would head into town, maybe try out the *All-American Diner*."

Ryan and Phillips exchanged an eloquent look as they thought of the man who owned that particular establishment—a notorious gangster called Jimmy 'The Manc' Moffa. He was like a bad penny, turning up in one form or another in their investigations and no amount of man-hours had elicited sufficient evidence to charge him with any crime.

"Was that the last time you heard from her?"

"No, I had a text at around nine o'clock to say that she would be heading home soon. I texted back, then put the kettle on." She looked down at the tissue in her hand, now torn and shredded.

"Would you mind if we looked at the messages?"

Nina gestured to a smartphone sitting on the oak coffee table between them and recited the passcode for him in a dull voice. Ryan spent a minute or so flicking through the text messages and found that the timings matched Nina's story, with the following text received at 21:08:

Hi babe. Heading home now, will probably get a taxi or walk. See you soon! Love u. xxx

The tone was that of a contented woman, looking forward to returning home to her wife. Nina's reply, sent a couple of minutes later, was equally loving:

Oky doky. Will put the kettle on! Love you too xx

With a heavy heart, Ryan thanked her and moved on to the next question.

"When did you begin to worry?"

"When it got to ten o'clock and she still wasn't home," Nina whispered. "I tried calling her mobile, but the number was disengaged. I started to panic, so I rang a couple of her colleagues and they told me she left the pub around quarter past nine, just after she texted me. I tried her number a few more times and then I rang the police."

Ryan had already listened to a recording of her frantic 999 call.

"They told you to wait a bit longer, to be sure?" It was protocol in Missing Persons cases.

"Yes." She nodded helplessly. "I was beside myself. I rang mum and dad." She turned to her mother, who nodded her agreement and continued to rub slow circles on her daughter's back.

"We came over straight away," she agreed.

Ryan ran his tongue over his teeth and prepared to ask a trickier question.

"I'm sorry, Nina, I have to ask. Can you account for your whereabouts last night?"

The woman paled but answered without a qualm.

"I finished work at about six. I-I'm an architect, at Vaughn & Rodgers, on Grey Street. You can check with them. I walked home and let myself in at around six-thirty, then put a frozen pizza in the oven. I had a quick shower and then watched television mostly. After...after Krista didn't come home, I told you what happened then. Mum and dad came over and stayed here all night. I'm sorry, that's the best I can do."

Ryan continued to hold her gaze for a moment longer, then nodded his satisfaction. If necessary, they could triangulate her location from her phone usage. Besides, every instinct was telling him this woman was genuine.

"Did your wife have any enemies? Anybody who gave you cause for concern?"

Nina shook her head miserably.

"Nobody. Everybody liked her."

"Not everybody agrees with gay marriage. Did you experience any bigotry?"

Nina closed her eyes and re-opened them slowly.

"We were lucky. Friends of ours have had people shout at them in the street, a few scuffles, but that never happened to us. Everybody has always been supportive and I suppose we surround ourselves with good people. I don't know anybody who could possibly do this to Krista. She is— was—the gentlest woman. All her students loved her and so did I.

"So did I," she repeated, as the tears began to flow again.

MacKenzie and Lowerson were getting to grips with the small, close-knit community of Rothbury. They made their way along the high street, taking their time chatting to passers-by and noting down their idle comments concerning the death of Barbara Hewitt. They nodded at appropriate times and tried not to grind their teeth as they heard the same thing, repeated in different ways, from different mouths.

"We're getting nowhere," Lowerson burst out eventually. "If I have to hear one more person telling me that Barbara was a *miserable woman, God rest her*, I'm gonna kick off."

MacKenzie cast an amused glance in his direction.

"This is the boring part of the job and there's no escaping it. You got a taste for the action, after all the fun last year.

Now everything is back to normal and you're finding it hard to adapt. Besides, we *are* getting somewhere. For instance, we've confirmed that Barbara didn't go to the supermarket last Saturday morning as she usually would. Nor did she go to the bakery for her regular croissant at eleven o'clock. Both places said that was highly unusual behaviour, which means our process of elimination is bringing us closer to understanding the dead woman and gives us a better timescale of when she probably died, which the pathologist can hopefully confirm. After our next stop, we'll start looking more closely at her activities last Friday 18th.

"See? That's plenty of legwork to be getting along with, Jack."

Lowerson scuffed his new shoes along the pavement.

"Wasn't Rothbury the centre of a manhunt, back in 2010 or '11?" he asked.

"That it was, Jack," MacKenzie replied. "There were guns and helicopters and even an ex-England footballer turned up to give us a hand negotiating the suspect's surrender."

Lowerson looked around at the quaint buildings and heard only the tinkle of the River Coquet as it passed through the town and made its way through the surrounding hills.

"I can't believe it," he said eventually.

"Real life is often stranger than fiction," she chuckled. "If it's action adventure you're looking for, this place isn't a bad starting point. It's got a long history of bloody battles, being so close to the old border with Scotland."

MacKenzie lifted her heavy red hair away from the collar of her suit jacket, surprised to find that she was overheating in the afternoon sun which shone down upon the quiet little northern town.

Lowerson thought briefly of men and women waging their battles on the windy hilltops, then sighed.

"Maybe I do miss a bit of action sometimes," he confessed. "What do I do about it?"

"You remember that every suspicious death is important, no matter how it comes about. That's why we signed up to do this job. We'll give Barbara Hewitt the same effort, the same concentration and legwork as we would a film star. Death is a great leveller."

"We don't know that her death was suspicious at all yet," Lowerson moaned.

MacKenzie gave him an owlish smile and they stopped in front of a tiny shop built into a long stone building which looked like a former stable. A hand-painted sign declared it to be Sally's Snips—Barbara's hairdresser of choice.

"This is the place Carole Dudley was telling us about. Apparently, Barbara came here every Friday morning without fail."

MacKenzie threw her partner a look of sufferance and pushed open the door, which jingled to announce their arrival.

Inside, the tiny shop had evidently stuck a cheerful two fingers up to the sages and beiges favoured by its neighbours. Clashing bold colours and reggae music complemented a beachy mural painted on one of the walls and bright spotlighting flooded the room in a jarring yellow light. The shop was brimming with people; so many that MacKenzie concluded that almost the entire resident population must have migrated there for a cut and blow-dry. Every inch of space was in use: styling gadgetry was stuffed into pots and bundled onto shelves; imposing sales racks touted hair-related products and neon cardboard signs advertised '2-4-1' deals to the savvy purchaser. Banks of chairs and washing stations filled the floor space, all occupied by women of a certain age who chattered happily to one another. The remaining walls had been painted a garish shade of magenta and were plastered with faded posters of hair models from the eighties and nineties. Perhaps most eye-catching was the Cliff Richard calendar hanging above the front desk. He was sporting cowboy chaps for the entire month of March.

"Mac." Lowerson's throat bobbed up and down. "It's a bit busy in here, isn't it? Maybe it would be best if I waited outside—"

"Leave me alone, boyo, and I'll demote you quicker than you can say 'short, back and sides.'"

A buxom woman in a glitzy top hurried across the room to greet them.

"Can I help you, lovelies?"

"Ah, we'd like to speak to the manager, please."

"You've found her!" The woman cast an assessing eye over MacKenzie's mane. "What are you looking to have done, flower? I wouldn't change that lovely colour, if I were you, but I might think about updating the style, maybe have a few layers cut in."

MacKenzie opened her mouth and then closed it again.

"We're from Northumbria CID," she recovered quickly and retrieved her warrant card. "We'd like to ask you a few questions about Barbara Hewitt."

The woman—who turned out to be Sally—tutted and shook her head meaningfully.

"Eeh, terrible to hear about what happened to her. Wasn't it, Gladys?"

One of the elderly ladies sitting nearby with her hair in rollers looked up from where she had been pretending to read a magazine.

"Didn't come as any great shock to me," the woman sniffed. "Always was a—"

Miserable woman, Lowerson mouthed silently.

"—very miserable woman," Gladys finished.

Sally heaved her generous chest.

"I wouldn't like to say that she was a *skinflint,* or that she complained about *everything*. Not now that she's dead."

"Of course, we understand." MacKenzie tucked her tongue in her cheek and decided to let the conversation play out. It was amazing what you could learn if you let people talk.

"She never showed her face at a single one of my coffee mornings," another woman called out from her reclined position at the basins. "For years, I made the effort to invite her. She never came—not once! I ask you!"

"I know, Penny, I know," Sally sympathised, then turned back to the two detectives who were watching the byplay as they would a soap opera. "She hardly showed her face anywhere, to be honest, though she always kept her appointments here."

"Oh? When did she usually come in?"

"Fridays at nine o'clock sharp," Sally answered without a pause. "She liked to have the first available appointment on Fridays."

"She never came in on other days?"

"No, never," Sally replied, then laid a conspiratorial, manicured hand on MacKenzie's arm. "You have to understand that Barbara was a finicky woman. She had her own ideas about what she liked, and woe betide anybody who suggested otherwise."

Sally pouted, remembering a past altercation.

"How did she like her hair?" Lowerson looked up from his inspection of the calendar. "I'm just curious," he added quickly.

"I did her hair for years." Sally leaned against the front counter and turned her assessing gaze onto the young detective, approving of his generous use of hair gel on his voluminous quiff. "She always had the same style: a cropped bob around her face, trimmed neatly, blow dried with a bit of body in the crown. I suggested that she dye it after the greys came in, but she wouldn't have it."

"Ah. Right." Lowerson said, inadequately.

"I said to her, 'Barbara, God wouldn't have invented hair dye if he didn't want us to use it,'" Sally finished, to nods of approval from her comrades. "That made her even more irate."

MacKenzie's ears pricked. "Why?"

Sally shrugged. "Common knowledge that Barbara hated the church. If anything ever came up about religion, she always liked to have a good rant about it."

"She was an atheist?"

"She was certainly something," Sally snorted. "*Rude*, for one thing. Only last week, I saw her arguing with Father Healy outside St Agnes'. Now, that man is kindness personified, but I can tell you he looked as if he wanted to wring her neck."

MacKenzie raised a finely-arched brow.

"Last week?"

"Mm hmm," Sally said, distracted by a tap on the shop window and a wave from one of the locals. "It was right after she left her appointment here, last Friday, because I remember she'd forgotten her purse and I ran after her, to give it back. It felt really awkward, I can tell you."

She paused for breath and then seemed to remember why they were there.

"Anyway, what did you want to speak to me about?"

MacKenzie couldn't say what it was about the town of Rothbury that set her teeth on edge. On the face of it, the setting was idyllic. Its old stone buildings gleamed silver-grey in the late afternoon sun and the landscape undulated in a blanket of green and gold, all the way to the misty outline of the Cheviot Hills even further on the horizon. It was middle-class heaven, populated by people who could afford to live a commutable distance outside of the city. Its strategic position allowed the residents to take advantage of the nearby amenities of larger settlements, not least the swift and personal service of the Northumbria Police Constabulary, whose headquarters lay a few miles further south.

DC Lowerson bade a polite farewell to the hill farmer who had engaged him in a long discussion about the changing economics of his profession and strolled across to where MacKenzie stood waiting for him.

"Feels like it's been a long day and it's not even over yet," he remarked, with a longing glance in the direction of his car.

MacKenzie said nothing at first and continued to watch the townsfolk of Rothbury gathering in groups of two or three to chatter about the 'goings on' in their quiet, ordered world. She looked back across at Lowerson. He was thirty, but his face was smooth and unlined, his hair cut into a sharp style to match his tailored grey suit and shiny shoes. His eyes were wide and hopeful, betraying a lingering optimism that human beings were essentially good, despite all he had seen to the contrary in his short years working as a murder detective.

MacKenzie envied him that look in his eye; the idealism she had lost somewhere along the way. Still, she couldn't bring herself to lie to him, not even to preserve the fairy tale. She thought about saying something flippant to lighten the mood, then she spied a man walking down the high street wearing the quintessential garb of a priest.

"Sally says she saw Barbara having a steaming argument with Father Healy last Friday morning, around quarter to ten. Let's go and see what the local cleric has to say on the subject."

Father Simon Healy was a seasoned man, well used to the various eccentricities of his parishioners. He stood tall and commanding with salt-and-pepper grey hair smoothed back from a handsome, strong-boned face that belied his advancing years. Though the number of people who would identify themselves as 'Catholic' continued to fall nationally, the figures remained strong in his parish thanks in no small part to Healy's own natural charisma.

He was exercising some of that charm upon a group of local volunteers when he spotted MacKenzie and Lowerson strolling along the pavement towards him and—just for a second—he faltered. He blinked twice but was careful to keep a smile pinned on his face for the benefit of his audience.

The likeness was uncanny, was all he could think, before they were upon him.

"Father Healy?"

"Yes?"

"DI MacKenzie and DC Lowerson, Northumbria CID. I wonder if we might have a word in private?"

His face fell into aggrieved lines and he excused himself from the gaggle of admiring women.

"I was very saddened to hear the news about Barbara."

He raised a hand to greet a passing local, then tucked it back inside the pocket of his tweed blazer. They walked in the direction of the small church of St Agnes and the shelter it would provide.

"How long had you known her?"

He calculated the dates swiftly in his head.

"Goodness, it must be over twenty years. I believe she moved to Rothbury in the mid-nineties to join her parents and help to care for her father, who was ailing at that time. I have been a priest at St Agnes' since the mid-eighties, although I serve other parishes." He gave them a rueful smile and added, "Even the church has to make cutbacks, in this modern world."

"What were your impressions of her?"

"Barbara was a self-contained person, as I'm sure you've heard. I must tell you that I rarely spoke to her, or saw her, for that matter. She preferred her own company."

They crossed the main square and made their way towards the church, tucked along a side street.

"We understand that Barbara was not a religious woman. Is that correct, to the best of your knowledge?"

He stopped outside the doors to the church and spread his hands, laying it out for them.

"Actually, Barbara was brought up as a Catholic and both of her parents were regular churchgoers until her father's stroke, after which he was unable to make the journey. I fell into the habit of stopping by their house to hear confession, give communion and so on." He paused. "Barbara tended not to be present at those times but, when I did see her, she was perfectly cordial."

Lowerson interjected.

"One or two people have told us that Barbara had some animosity towards the church. Would you agree with that?"

Father Healy smiled genially at the young man.

"God granted us free will and Barbara certainly exercised that from time to time in conversation with me. I always enjoy a healthy theological debate, an opportunity to allay concerns, clarify a point of doctrine..." He trailed off.

When he looked back, Lowerson was watching him closely.

"We understand there was an argument. Last Friday?"

Healy looked taken aback.

"I don't remember any argument...perhaps you're mistaken."

MacKenzie and Lowerson exchanged a look.

"Are you sure she didn't stop to...speak to you, at all?"

"Not that I recall." The priest was adamant. "Detectives, I don't know what caused Barbara to lose her faith, but it certainly didn't trouble her overmuch, certainly not enough to strike up arguments with me. She might have spent more time alone, she might have liked things a certain way, but—"

"Her routine was well known, then?" MacKenzie slipped in the question.

"I suppose so, yes," he replied. "She shopped at the supermarket on certain days, went to the post office on others, that sort of thing. In a community like this, people talk."

MacKenzie continued to regard him.

"Yet despite all that, nobody reported her missing," MacKenzie observed.

The priest made an expansive gesture.

"It's true that she wasn't a popular member of the community. But who would want to hurt her? She lived an ordinary, solitary, life. I'm sure you will find a reasonable explanation for her death, inspector, and I'm only sorry that she wasn't discovered sooner."

MacKenzie looked back at the main square where people went about their business and then back up at the priest's contrite face.

"I hope you're right, Father. Thank you for your time."

He bade them a smiling farewell and retreated indoors, whistling a hymn. MacKenzie and Lowerson began to stroll back towards the cul-de-sac where Barbara had lived, until they were well out of earshot.

"It's a sin to lie, isn't it?" Lowerson said, eventually.

CHAPTER 4

The sun was setting by the time Ryan's team of detectives reconvened. It dropped low into the horizon, spreading wide arcs of flaming light over the city while stars began to pop in the cardinal-blue sky far above. The temperature had fallen so that the air was crisp and cold, wiping away the clouds to leave a blank canvas for the night sky in all its splendour.

The beauty of the natural world was lost upon the occupants of CID, whose minds were collectively engrossed by the more prosaic question of murder. Ryan hitched a hip onto the corner of his desk and began to swing a leg idly back and forth as he skim-read MacKenzie's report. Phillips took the trouble to water the dying plants on the long window sill, which some thoughtful soul had arranged in an effort to brighten the place up a bit. MacKenzie watched him potter about with an indulgent smile, thinking that he was a man who liked to nourish living things. Beside her, Lowerson slouched in one of the uncomfortable plastic tub chairs while he fiddled with his shiny new smartphone. Judging by the number of times he was swiping his screen to the left, he was not having a successful day in the world of internet dating.

Eventually, Ryan looked up again.

"Sorry, Mac—you'll probably have to wait another day for the pathologist to get around to looking at Barbara Hewitt, unless you want to draft in someone from Durham or Teesside. We monopolised Pinter's time today," he explained. "I have to say that, on the face of it, you seem to have a straightforward case of a lonely older woman who died in her own home. Pretty standard, don't you think?"

MacKenzie rolled her shoulders while she considered her answer.

"I know that's how it looks. The locals all agree that she was—"

"—a miserable woman," Lowerson interjected smoothly, with a smirk that was met by a green-eyed glare from his superior.

"—an *insular* lady, who preferred her own company," MacKenzie corrected him, then turned back to face Ryan. "There's something about it that doesn't sit right with me, boss."

"Suffering from a bout of intuition again?"

"Call it my sixth sense as a murder detective," she said, with a lopsided grin.

Ryan looked down at the report in his hand and thought quickly of the workload and resources at his disposal.

There had been an influx of serious crime over the past few weeks, so he needed to be pragmatic. On the other hand, MacKenzie had a nose for the business and he trusted it.

"Alright, listen. If nothing turns up after Pinter's post-mortem, I need you to close it down. There's too much going on at the moment and I don't know how this cemetery murder is going to pan out. We might need to re-allocate your time."

"Understood," she said. "Lowerson has been looking into Barbara's next of kin but so far we've been unable to find anyone. By all accounts, she was an only child—and no marriages, divorces or children on record."

"Another windfall for Her Majesty's Treasury," Ryan pronounced.

"That's just sad," Phillips couldn't help but remark. It had been his great pleasure to love three women during the course of his fifty-two years: his mother, his late wife and the delectable redheaded Irishwoman who was seated beside him. It was hard to imagine a life without having formed any lasting or meaningful relationships, but then, not everybody was as fortunate as he.

He leaned across and gave MacKenzie's fingers a quick squeeze.

Ryan fiddled with a biro while he thought back over the events of the day.

"Phillips and I have made decent progress identifying the woman found up at the West Road Cemetery this morning. Her name was Kristina Ogilvy-Matthews—she went by

'Krista'. Thirty-eight years old, long red hair and blue eyes. She was found strangled early this morning, buried—no, *arranged*—in a shallow grave."

"Arranged?" MacKenzie queried.

Ryan took out an enlarged copy of one of the crime scene photographs which he handed to her. As she looked down at the image of a woman around her own age, with hair and eyes of a similar shade, MacKenzie felt the hairs on the back of her neck stand on end.

"She looks…"

"I know," Ryan said flatly. "A bit like you, but don't let it get under your skin. Focus on the facts. Phillips and I are taking care of this one for the moment."

MacKenzie nodded and tried to get past the superficial similarity between herself and the dead woman. Looking with fresh eyes, she began to see what Ryan had seen that morning.

"She looks like a dancer, with her arms looped above her head."

She passed the image to Lowerson, who took his turn to scrutinize it.

"Maybe her arms fell into that position accidentally when she was laid out?" he suggested, and Ryan had to admit it was a possibility.

"It's a good thought, Jack, but her clothing was torn at the arms and the material spread out deliberately. And there's something else to consider." Ryan reached into his box file and withdrew a photocopy of the note they had found buried with the body. He watched them pore over it and waited to see if they followed the same thought process he had.

"Roman Catholic?" MacKenzie began. "Absolving her of sin? Not very original, is he?"

Ryan shrugged.

"Religion, sex, money, jealousy...same old justifications, brand new victims."

"What sin did she commit, in his eyes?"

Ryan pointed the biro, as if to capture the thought.

"As far as we know, Krista had no criminal record, an exemplary employment history as a teacher, a concerned group of friends and a loving wife."

"Wife?" Lowerson's eyebrows rose all the way up into his gelled quiff.

"That's what the man said." Phillips sent him a mild look. "What's the matter, lad, has it offended your sensibilities?"

"No, I mean...no," he finished lamely, and wondered if he could ram his foot any further down his own throat.

"Good," Ryan said smoothly. "It would hardly be worth mentioning, except for the small matter of same sex relationships having been viewed unfavourably by certain traditional factions in days gone by, Roman Catholics included."

"It still happens," MacKenzie said.

"Which is why we need to treat this as a potential hate crime. Krista Matthews was a happy, well-regarded woman. The circumstances of her death suggest a degree of premeditation; a person who planned ahead, wrote their little note, dug the grave and knew how to enter the cemetery without drawing too much attention. The note suggests that the killer considered Krista a sinner, but we don't know *why*. We need to look deeper into her life to see if there's something we're missing but who's to say she wasn't stalked and selected because she had the temerity to fall in love with a woman?"

"It's a definite maybe," Phillips said, unrolling a fresh stick of nicotine gum without much enthusiasm. Over a year since his last cigarette and he still missed the little tar-infested buggers. "On the other hand, it could have been a purely opportunistic kill. Let's not forget that it's Easter either."

Ryan nodded slowly.

"The timing could be significant for him, if we presume that he or she is a religious fanatic—"

"We'll live dangerously," Phillips put in.

"Let's hope it *isn't* significant," MacKenzie sliced through the banter. "There are a hell of a lot of dates on the Catholic calendar."

"Let's just deal with the here and now." Ryan was determined to keep morale high from the outset. "Krista's wife, Nina, tells us that she was due to have some social drinks with her workmates and was expected to be home by nine-thirty last night. We've spoken to Krista's colleagues, who confirm they all left work together. They made their way into the centre of town to the

All-American Diner, where she left them at around quarter-past nine."

MacKenzie's head snapped up.

"*The Diner?*" They all knew the man who owned it. He was currently being investigated by a team of forensic accountants regarding his association with their former Detective Chief Superintendent Gregson.

"I'll be asking for copies of the CCTV footage. It's all we can do without disturbing the ongoing investigation into his actions last year."

He wouldn't allow past events to divert them from the needs of the present.

"The pathologist thinks that Krista died somewhere between eight and ten p.m. Factoring in what we know about her movements, it's looking more likely that she was picked up or snatched sometime shortly after nine-fifteen, when she left the Diner."

Phillips linked his fingers over the paunch just visible through his baby blue shirt.

"I've requested footage from the cameras in the local area. I also had a word with the local taxi firms and they're going to ask their drivers about it, but that's a bit of a needle in a haystack until we know whether she walked or hailed a cab."

"It's a good start," Ryan said.

"The cemetery has a few cameras, but they're mostly trained around the main entrance and none of them actually work," Phillips added, with a note of apology.

"Wait—what?"

"Budget constraints." Phillips grimaced. "Apparently crime rates around council-run burial sites are low, so it's not high on their list of priorities."

Ryan swore loudly and threw the biro back onto his desk in disgust. Financial constraints were a fact of life and there was nothing he could do about it. He knew it; they all knew it. Yet when he looked down at the picture of Krista Ogilvy-Matthews smiling happily into the camera on her wedding day, he couldn't help but think of his own wedding which was due to take place in the summer. The thought of Anna ever being taken from him was like a knife in his chest. He wanted to believe it could never happen and that he could promise to keep her safe, always, but life had taught him not to make promises he could not keep. He knew that there were people out there who acted without mercy—sometimes without rational thought and at other times in full awareness of their actions. All the while, he was usually powerless to stop them until it was too late.

Krista continued to stare back at him and Ryan added her face to the catalogue of others he kept locked in his mind.

When he looked up again, his eyes were a fierce silver.

"We might not have any helpful footage of our perpetrator coming and going but he's already made his first mistake. By writing that note he left a piece of himself behind. Now we have his scent."

His gaze passed over the trusted faces of his team, who were more like family.

"Let's go hunting."

The pounding in the man's head had abated, just for a moment, when he felt her body go limp and die in his arms. She had been a gift, an opportunity to save another soul, and he could not ignore God's work. For surely that was what it had been. Placing the redheaded woman in front of him had not been a matter of chance but a question of divinity.

He looked down at his hands and was amazed at how little they trembled. He hadn't *wanted* to kill her, of course he hadn't, but how could he ignore her plight? God had thrown her into his path so that he could help her. He had been *chosen*. This work and the salvation he could bring was the reason he had been born.

He was God's holy vessel.

He slept peacefully afterwards, the sleep of the righteous. But the next night, the pain in his skull had returned stronger than before. It throbbed along his nerves, into his ears and across his eyes so that his vision blurred, and he felt sickness roll in his gut. He hadn't known how he would get through the day.

Then he had seen her.

For a moment, it was *her*. The one who filled his dreams. His heart had soared, beating like an eagle's wings in his chest. His loins had surged, like they had years ago, at the thought of finding her.

But it was not her, only a cheap imitation.

Still, he had chosen to save her; it was the only humane thing to do. Now another soul resided in Heaven and he could have sworn he had seen it rising from her body, celestial and ethereal.

As he looked out of his bedroom window into the darkening night, the city lights spread out before him in a blanket of yellow and white. On higher ground above the city, he knew, an iron angel stood watch over the people of Newcastle. It was another sign that his work was *meant*. It was sacred. The people had erected a towering angel to watch over their city, but they had no idea that God had rewarded them by investing one of their number with His holy spirit.

He wondered if he was worthy of such a task and if he was capable of fulfilling his purpose. He was only one man and there were so many other souls to save. Then he felt her beside him. He could smell the sweet scent of her hair, could hear her voice whisper on the air as the lines of reality and unreality blurred.

They stood side by side for a while looking across the city and he wondered when God would send him the next one.

Ryan bypassed the apartment he owned on Newcastle's Quayside and drove south along the A1 towards the neighbouring city of Durham. Revellers enjoying a Friday night in the 'party city' stumbled through the streets and Ryan decided he must be getting old because he was eyeing the short skirts and gravity-defying heels with the kind of expression he imagined his father would wear.

Glad to make the turn over the bridge, he accelerated and enjoyed the breeze which whistled through the gap in the car window. Something about the investigation was bothering him more than he had expected. Perhaps it was the religious element. Why did these crackpots insist upon attaching some sort of moralistic code to their killing? Why couldn't they be honest and admit that they liked killing people, no strings attached?

He smiled to himself, thinking of what Anna would say to that.

They're unwell, she'd say, her natural compassion leading her to pity the men and women who extinguished lives.

They have a mental illness, she'd say, *it's a disease of the mind.*

He slowed for the inevitable traffic along the main road leading from Newcastle to Durham and considered his own views on the subject. Yes, there was mental illness. He saw it daily in those who walked through the doors of CID and into lockup. There were many kinds of madness, so many syndromes and labels a person could choose from. Some of them might even be real. He had spent hours listening to pen-pushers who expounded the virtues of rehabilitation and remorse, lamenting the evils of retribution and recidivism.

On the other hand, he had also spoken to the victims of crime. He had seen the implosion of lives, the breakdown of confidence and capability. He was one of them, Ryan thought bitterly. One of the unlucky few who lived with only memories to sustain him. His sister lay six feet under, her body little more than ashes and dust because one madman decided it was his prerogative to snatch her life away. Well-meaning people told him that he had brought her killer to justice and that was all that mattered. Keir Edwards—or to give him his more evocative title, *The Hacker*—could not kill any young women while he was behind bars. Other families had been spared the torment that the Ryan family had experienced, and he should take comfort from that.

That may all be true, Ryan thought darkly, but not a day went by without him wishing that it was Edwards' body that lay rotting beneath the ground.

CHAPTER 5

Saturday, 26ᵗʰ March

In the early hours of Saturday morning, Karen Dobbs staggered to the front door of her house in a part of Newcastle known as Daisy Hill. Its name suggested fields of white flowers where one could frolic, but the reality was very different. Rows of council and ex-council houses lined the streets, many with boarded windows and splintered doors. Years ago, proud coal miners and dock workers had lived there, toiling to raise great ships onto the water. When those industries died, some of the community spirit had died with them. There was talk of regeneration, of fancy new houses and a community centre, but progress was slow. In the meantime, the CCTV cameras didn't work and there was no money for dead-bolts to protect the residents against the thieves and vandals who preyed upon what little they had.

Not that Karen would have cared if vandals trashed her house. It couldn't get much worse and she didn't notice the filth unless she was sober and shaking, desperate for her next hit—as she was now. At those times, the last thing she felt like doing was cleaning. The comedown hit her hard, dragging her body and her mind back to life, leaving her nauseous and aching for the pain to go away. She wanted the blissful, mind-numbing serenity that only the dragon could bring, and she knew what she had to do to get it.

She stumbled out of the house, wrapping her thin arms around herself to stave off the chill. A solitary streetlight fizzed its brash orange glare as she stumbled towards her usual corner. A group of teenage boys jeered and she smelled the marijuana, heard the crass insults thrown at her back. She felt the spit hit her bare legs and she closed her eyes against the shame, focusing on her need.

Not far to go now.

She hurried around the corner, shuffling on thin, wasted legs she'd tried to dress up in cheap black heels. She ran shaking fingers through her hair and tugged at the skirt which fell just beneath her hips. As the petrol station came into sight, she smiled beautifully, gazing upon it as if it were the promised land.

Careful to avoid the cameras, she scurried around to the back of the gents' toilets and prepared to wait.

She didn't have to wait long.

She saw him before he saw her. Karen wasn't fussed about what they looked like; any kind of fastidiousness had left her long ago—the drugs had taken that along with her pride and her three-year-old son. Still, this one wasn't bad looking.

"Hiya handsome," she slurred. Long-term drug abuse had taken her faculty for clear speech too.

He looked up from his distracted inspection of the tarmac and seemed to come to a halt, his eyes fixing on her in a kind of wonder.

"Whatsamatter sweetie?" she purred. "No need to be shy."

"Is it you?" he whispered.

Karen didn't understand the reverent tone in his voice, but she did understand that his clothes looked smart and pricey.

Plenty of money.

"Why don't you take me for a ride, feller?"

He remained where he was for a second, then he cast a swift glance in either direction and nodded, leading her quickly back towards his car. She trotted after him and decided she had hit the jackpot when he held the door open for her.

"Ooh, this is nice!" she giggled, reaching across to grab his crotch as he slid into the driver's seat. One strong hand intercepted her wrist with a vice-like grip and her smile slipped, leaving her face slack and prematurely aged. Fear quivered along her spine as she looked at his hard profile. It was a gamble every time, and after so many years in the business she could usually spot the kinks. But every now and then, one slipped through the net.

With a sinking stomach, Karen resigned herself to a few cuts and bruises, and hoped that she could avoid another trip to the Accident and Emergency department. It would still be worth it, she reasoned, feeling the fever slick through her blood. Self-preservation would never win against that kind of euphoria.

He started the engine.

Spring sunshine illuminated the city of Durham in a golden light, touching the towering stone walls of the cathedral with gentle fingers and sweeping over the castle which seemed to rise mystically from the banks of the river. From her position at the window, Anna looked out across the water and watched as a pair of swans made their graceful journey upstream. She sipped at a mug of strong coffee and turned as Ryan padded into the room, ready for work.

"Busy day today?"

He paused in the act of searching for his car keys, baffled as to their disappearance.

"We're tugging the usual threads, following the avenues."

"But?"

Ryan smiled slowly. "You don't miss much, do you?"

"Not usually," she replied, sweetly. "What's troubling you?"

Distractedly, he shoved his hands into the pockets of his jeans and immediately found the keys.

"There was a note left on the woman we found yesterday, giving absolution in Latin."

Anna nodded her understanding. If there were two things that Ryan hated, they were religious dogma and murder, especially put together.

"It's not the same," she murmured.

"Isn't it? Last year, we had a bunch of devil-worshippers killing in the name of an imaginary being with a forked tail and horns. Now we've got another nut-job killing in the name of a beardy bloke in leather sandals, with a castle in the sky. Whatever happened to people killing out of jealousy or hate or sex? Since when was *money* not good enough?"

Anna leaned back against the window sill, trying hard not to laugh.

"I think those *are* still the main reasons people commit crimes," she corrected him gently. "However people choose to dress it up."

Ryan stared at her for a long moment, then his face cleared and he walked across to set an arm on either side of the sill, boxing her in. She tipped her face up and looked into a pair of silver-grey eyes, shining with intent.

"Ever thought of changing profession?"

"What? And give up my mediocre teaching salary and long hours as a university historian?"

"You could have all those perks working for Northumbria CID, and you'd get to spend more time with me," he purred.

"You're really winning me over."

"Am I?" He leaned down and bestowed the barest of kisses beneath her left ear. His eyes closed when he felt the tremor ripple over her skin.

"You've got work," she murmured.

"So have you," he returned, lifting his head again to brush kisses over her jaw.

"Well, now you mention it, I think I heard the sound of the gas boiler breaking down."

"That's funny, because my car won't start," he replied.

"What can you do with half an hour?"

"Is that a question, or a challenge?"

Ryan arrived at work just before nine, humming along to something he'd heard on the car radio. Naturally, his buoyant mood had absolutely nothing to do with spending an hour playing truant at home, nothing whatsoever. He slung his jacket over the back of his desk chair and surveyed the mountain of paperwork awaiting him with resignation. There was a skeleton staff in CID today as many of the PCs and support staff were off work over the holiday weekend and consequently the long corridors were quieter than usual.

From his vantage point, Phillips leaned back in his ugly green desk chair and raised a bushy eyebrow.

"Morning." He narrowed his eyes at Ryan. "Managed to get your car sorted, did you?"

"Hmm? Oh yeah, all sorted."

"The mechanic must've come pretty quickly."

Ryan kept his eyes averted and decided not to make any obvious jokes about servicing of parts.

"Mm hmm."

"There! I saw that!" Phillips pointed an accusing finger at Ryan's face and squeaked out of his chair. "I know that face."

"What face?" Ryan schooled his features into a neutral expression, but Phillips wasn't fooled.

"Listen to your elders, son," Phillip confided. "Never, *ever*, say you have car trouble, because it only holds water if you can talk about cars and car-related things."

"I can talk about cars," Ryan said, defensively.

Phillips crossed his arms over his broad chest.

"Lad, what you know about cars could be written on the back of a postage stamp."

"I'll remind you, *sergeant*, that could be classed as insubordination."

Phillips sensed victory was near.

"And I'll remind you, *chief inspector*, to always use the boiler as an excuse. Gas leaks are a classic ploy to get time off work."

Ryan smirked at Phillips' retreating back, then called out belatedly, "Hey! You rang in four times last month to say you were having boiler trouble!"

"Aye, lad, and it's far from being fixed yet."

Ryan snorted but, before he could offer a witty riposte, his phone began to rumble. He answered without checking the screen and all amusement left his face when he realised who was speaking at the other end of the line.

Ending the call quickly, he shouldered back into his jacket and turned to Phillips with a face like thunder.

"We've got another one, Frank. Damn it, the bastard has done it again."

"I should start charging for entry."

Pinter chuckled at his own weak joke as MacKenzie and Lowerson buzzed through the secure doors of the hospital mortuary on the dot of nine.

"Morning, Jeff," MacKenzie said, drawing on a visitor's coat. "Thanks for getting around to this so quickly, we appreciate you taking the time out of your weekend."

Pinter flushed from the neck upwards, a reaction he often experienced in the presence of DI MacKenzie. It wasn't worth mentioning that he only had a fridge full of microwave meals and *The X Factor* to look forward to at home and so he'd rather be at work. Instead, he mumbled something unintelligible and then turned towards Lowerson in an effort to deflect attention from himself.

"Looking a bit worse for wear, Jack," he said, as he waggled a finger at Lowerson, who was breathing hard at the sight and smell of death.

"He'll be grand," MacKenzie said shortly. "Talk to me about Barbara Hewitt."

Pinter led them over to one of the metal gurneys.

"Got a ripe one, here," he began, in his usual tasteless fashion. Whipping off the paper sheet, they were faced with the decomposing body of what had once been a woman.

"I can tell you straight away that this lady did not die as Mother Nature intended."

MacKenzie looked up from the waste with a gleam in her eye.

"Don't tease me, Jeff."

The man flushed again. "Ah, um. Well. As you can see, she's decaying rapidly which can make it difficult to pick up on nuances, but there is one *little* thing," he said, gesturing for them to move closer to the body. "Just here, on her neck."

MacKenzie pulled a mask over her nose and mouth and bent down, telling herself not to react, though her stomach muscles quivered dangerously. Lowerson remained exactly where he was, at a safe distance. Surely, it wasn't necessary for both of them to look? He would take their word for it.

"What am I looking for?"

"Here," Pinter said, lowering his steel-grey head and pointing towards an area of advanced decomposition around Barbara's neck, indicating the presence of severe injury. The skin was raw and mottled, so MacKenzie would never have been able to distinguish it from the other lurid colours of the woman's decomposing skin.

MacKenzie stood up again and crossed her arms.

"Jeff, you've got eyes like a hawk," she said, appreciatively.

"I've got extra strength magnifying glasses, but I'll accept the compliment."

"You're thinking strangulation?"

Pinter nodded.

"Even if she hadn't been found for another week, or even weeks, we would still have been able to detect the fracture to her larynx. A clear indicator that a person has been asphyxiated."

"How?"

"Oh, almost certainly manual. There are compression marks which indicate a forward direction, as opposed to the 'u-shape' mark of a garrotte or ligature of some kind that we would usually expect to find."

"Any idea about the hand span?" Lowerson threw out the question from his position by the door.

"Fairly large, judging from the markings. Almost certainly male but don't hold me to that."

Lowerson flexed his own fingers, wondering what counted as 'large'.

"How about defensive wounds?"

"I've swabbed her nails and skin, so we'll see what turns up. I'm hopeful that something useful will come back, considering the direction of attack. It's common for a victim to lash out at their aggressor, isn't it?"

MacKenzie nodded silently, thinking of possible motives.

"No evidence of forced entry," she mused. "Either somebody let themselves in or Barbara opened the door and trusted them enough to walk back through to her living room. The CSIs think she died where she fell in her living room, rather than being moved from the doorway or the hall.

"Any indications of sexual assault?"

Pinter pulled an expressive face.

"No, and it was no pleasant task to find that out, I can tell you."

"For God's sake," Lowerson muttered from the corner of the room.

"It's funny," Pinter continued blandly. "That makes two victims of asphyxiation in as many days. I've never seen that before."

MacKenzie looked down at the body and then cast her eyes around the clinical space; over the trays of sharp implements and the electric saw gleaming on the countertop.

"Yeah," she said eventually. "*Funny* is one word for it."

The basic white phone attached to the wall beside the main doors began to shrill, its sound reverberating around the four walls of the mortuary. When none of his other staff answered it, Pinter made an apologetic face and hurried across to pick it up.

"Pinter." *A brief pause.* "Alright, give me fifteen—no, twenty minutes and I'll be there. Don't move her."

He rang off and stood there for a moment, lost in thought.

"Jeff?"

His body jerked in surprise and he seemed to focus again.

"That was Phillips," he explained. "They've found another redhead."

There in the chilly room, surrounded by death, MacKenzie felt a tremor pass through her whole body.

CHAPTER 6

The journey across town from CID Headquarters to Heaton Cemetery should have taken a lot longer than it did; the cemetery lay towards the east of the city, along the road from the city centre to the coast and the expansive North Sea. However, thanks to a powerful German engine and Ryan's blatant disregard for the traffic laws, they arrived outside the large iron gates scarcely twenty minutes after receiving word from the Control Room that a second body had been found.

Ryan slammed out of the car and made directly for the jittery police constables who were standing guard at the entrance, while Phillips exited at a more sedate pace to allow his heart rate to return to normal.

Ryan caught Phillips' eye and motioned towards a large blue and white forensics tent which was being erected in one of the far corners of the cemetery. They fell into step and began to make their way across the lumpy ground, their feet crunching over a long, plastic-covered walkway that the CSIs had laid, running all the way from the chapel to the crime scene.

"What's the word?" Phillips asked, puffing slightly to keep pace with Ryan's long strides.

"Our killer tried to be sneaky, this time," Ryan smiled, without mirth. "He dumped a body inside a grave which had already been dug out in preparation for a funeral at ten o'clock this morning. The groundskeeper found her while he was doing a quick check of the site at around nine-fifteen, ahead of the funeral party arriving."

Phillips glanced back towards the chapel building and noticed a few mourners gathered in a huddle outside, craning their necks to see what was happening. He'd also noticed the long black hearse parked on a side street outside the main entrance, waiting to be allowed access.

"What should we do about them?"

Ryan gave an irritable shrug.

"We can't let anybody inside—this is a crime scene. Tell them to make alternative arrangements."

Phillips folded his lips and contemplated the merits and demerits of entering into a heated debate about the pitfalls of such an undiplomatic approach to public relations.

"I'll speak to the funeral director," he said.

As they neared the tent, they spotted Tom Faulkner speaking to one of his junior staff. He was covered from head to toe in a white paper suit, nitrile gloves, hair cap and face mask. The only distinguishing marker was his glasses, which were a jazzy blue rather than his usual thick-rimmed brass. Phillips wondered if the man had met somebody he wanted to impress but decided to save the small talk for a more salubrious occasion.

"Faulkner, you got here quickly."

"Same goes," came the muffled reply, followed by a sympathetic glance in Phillips' direction. Faulkner had ridden shotgun with Ryan several times before and could testify to the loosening effect upon one's bowels.

"I have to admit I was intrigued when I got the call. Two graveyard bodies in as many days? It's too strange to be coincidence."

"Precisely what we thought," Ryan said, gesturing towards the tent. "Are we right?"

Faulkner sighed.

"Take a look for yourself."

Ryan donned his protective gear and squared his shoulders before opening the flap.

Inside, two large freestanding film lights shone a beam down into the grave which, at first sight, appeared to be unfilled given the mound of soil piled neatly to the side of it. Two CSIs knelt beside it and didn't bother to look up as Ryan walked in. The air was thick and hot like a greenhouse, with the unwanted addition of a faint but unmistakeable earthy scent of death which circulated inside the confined space.

Ryan took a careful step towards the edge of the grave and peered inside.

His first thought was that their perp had made some effort to bury his victim by shovelling a few armfuls of soil over her body, perhaps in the hope that she would not be discovered, ensuring that today's funeral would go ahead and forever disguise the fact that somebody lay beneath.

Whether that was the killer's motivation or not, it was a futile one in Ryan's view because even after a cursory glance it was impossible to miss the presence of the woman's thin, cadaverous body lying at the bottom of the murky pit.

"Let's see, then." Phillips shuffled over to stand beside him and took a quick glance before stepping back again, fearful of falling inside face-first. You could never be too careful.

"Aye, that's two."

Ryan's jaw clenched.

"He's on a roll," he said in a voice entirely devoid of emotion. "The placement of this woman's body is slightly different because it looks like he didn't have to dig the grave himself, which could mean one of two things. First, that he was lazy or short of time, so he decided to take the opportunity and use an existing gravesite rather than creating a fresh one. Second, that we were wrong in thinking that he wants the bodies to be found and, in fact, he's just getting better at trying to hide them."

There was a slight pause before Ryan tagged on,

"Or the wildcard option, which is that none of the above applies and we're simply dealing with a deranged, homicidal maniac incapable of planning and executing the perfect murder."

"He's getting away with it so far," Phillips had to say.

They stepped back outside to wait while the CSIs continued their work, enjoying the feel of the cool, fresh air as they stripped off their sticky overalls.

Ryan ran a hand through his black hair and let it fall again.

"Somebody has made an effort to ensure that the woman's arms were left drawn above her head, bent at the elbows and that her legs were drawn together. Just like Krista. This time, there was no blouse to tear, only a camisole top by the looks of it. Given the depth of the grave, it couldn't have been an easy task to arrange her body."

Phillips grunted.

"Do you think he jumped into the grave, arranged her body, then scrambled back out again? He didn't cover her very well, so he might have been interrupted."

"I've no idea," Ryan said. "Faulkner should be able to tell us."

He turned to take another wide, sweeping look at the cemetery and its surrounds.

"Again, there's the problem of access to the cemetery grounds. The place would have been closed after four forty-five since it's a bank holiday, same as the West Road Cemetery. No signs of forced entry, so how did he get in?"

Phillips butted his chin towards the hedgerow bordering the cemetery.

"Could have come through a gap," he suggested. "Behind that hedge, there's a side street. He could've parked and transported the body from there."

"Still highly risky," Ryan said.

"He might have had a key," Phillips tried again, and this time Ryan turned with a light in his eyes.

"Good thinking, Frank. Try to find out who has keys to both cemeteries, who has copies, and if any have gone missing lately."

Ryan ran a hand over his chin and realised he'd forgotten to shave—a sure sign that the case was starting to interfere with his ordinary routine. He would worry about that later.

"Another thing. We don't know whether either woman was killed *in situ,* or killed elsewhere and then transported afterwards."

"Faulkner has a job on his hands to coordinate two separate teams of CSIs, covering acres of ground," Phillips said, fairly. "Two major crime scenes in two days isn't easy."

"That's the job." Ryan wouldn't budge. He expected the highest standards from his team and although the CSIs weren't technically a part of CID, Ryan counted them in anyway. They all knew that the best evidence was found immediately after an incident and the clock was ticking.

"Check out the CCTV cameras in the area and within half a mile of the cemetery. We'll probably find the same problem as before but check it out anyway."

"Will do." Phillips nodded. "I've got a couple of PCs doing the door-to-doors, so we'll see what turns up."

Ryan's eyes narrowed as he gazed across the field of headstones.

"Something has just turned up," he said. Phillips followed his line of sight and watched a news van pull up directly outside the main gates to the cemetery.

"Vultures," Ryan muttered.

"This is turning into a farce," Chief Constable Morrison declared, a few hours later.

"Ma'am—"

She shot Ryan a steely glare.

"I told you to prepare a press release as soon as your victim's next of kin was informed. I understand that happened yesterday afternoon, which means you wilfully disregarded my instruction. Furthermore, a second victim has now been found in almost identical circumstances. Is that correct?"

Phillips pursed his lips and rocked back on his heels, wishing he were anywhere else. In contrast, Ryan stood with his feet planted and looked supremely confident.

"Yes, ma'am."

Morrison narrowed her eyes at Ryan's uncompromising response.

"*Yes*, those timescales are correct, or, *yes*, you were wilfully insubordinate?"

"Both, ma'am, but with all due respect my reasoning was sound."

"By all means," she said, waving a gracious hand. "Enlighten me."

Ryan didn't break eye contact. In times like these, he found that it was best to brazen it out and accept the consequences.

"I felt it best not to advertise the killer's exploits, particularly given the events of last year. Unfavourable comparisons might be drawn, leading to a degree of panic which would be unhelpful at this point in our investigation. Similarly, given the religious connotations, I am conscious that the last thing any of us needs is to incite a witch hunt for anybody who looks vaguely Catholic."

Morrison drummed irritated fingers against the side of her chair.

"That's all very well and good, Ryan. But in case it has escaped your attention, we are now having to deal with the very thing you wished to avoid." She tapped an angry finger on the mousepad beside her, bringing her computer screen to life displaying the front page of an online news outlet. "Thanks to your little foray into the world of broadcast media this morning, every local news channel, including BBC Newcastle, has run the story."

She clicked a button to replay a video of Ryan standing outside the gates of Heaton Cemetery with a menacing expression marring his handsome face as he dished out some choice insults to the local press hounds.

"We have a hard enough job trying to keep these people onside," she gritted out, "without you being captured on film calling a newscaster—what was it?—a *snotty little weasel?*"

Phillips sniggered and Morrison sucked in an angry breath.

"Social media is going haywire with warnings to redheaded women that they should stay inside and lock their doors, whilst simultaneously eschewing church, just in case. Oh, and some helpful person has created a hashtag on Twitter. *#GraveyardKiller*, in case you're interested." She slammed her hand onto the desk.

Ryan raised a single black eyebrow at her tone.

"The press were already aware of the details," he pointed out. "Somebody must have tipped them off, which is how they got up to Heaton Cemetery so quickly."

"It doesn't matter *how* they knew; the fact is we now have a circus to deal with, not to mention hordes of redheaded women stampeding to the nearest supermarket for brown hair dye."

The ghost of a smile played over Ryan's lips.

"Perhaps they're right to be wary," he said, earning himself another venomous look.

"Needless to say, the Deputy Commissioner has been on the phone to give me an earful. I hardly need to tell you he's reconsidering his idea of promoting you to Superintendent," Morrison stated.

"That doesn't concern me, ma'am, considering I have already decided not to apply for the position." Ryan lifted a negligent shoulder and tried to ignore Phillips' eyes boring into the side of his face. "I prefer legwork to paperwork any day of the week."

"You're made for the job and you know it," Morrison argued.

"I could do it, but I wouldn't enjoy it," Ryan said, in a tone which suggested that was the end of the matter. "However, on the subject of promotion, I've been meaning to ask you why DS Phillips hasn't been considered. He's overdue his promotion to Detective Inspector and I'd like to see that remedied as soon as possible."

Phillips' jaw fell and Morrison looked blindsided, completely diverted from the course of their original discussion.

"Yes, yes, of course. Frank, you've been an asset to Northumbria CID for many years. I'd be happy to consider your application for promotion."

As the door to Morrison's office closed behind them, Phillips turned to Ryan with a knowing smile.

"Good tactics in there, lad. You know, going on about me needing a promotion so that she wouldn't keep on about the press—"

Ryan didn't break his stride as they made for the conference room at the end of the hall, but he spared Phillips a sideways glance.

"Don't be a bloody idiot, Frank. I brought it up because you're overdue a promotion. That's the beginning and end of it."

Phillips found himself lost for words and looked around the dingy corridor as if it would inspire him.

"You're welcome," Ryan grinned.

The man had been covered in a film of clammy sweat all day long.

Of course, when people started to notice, he'd told them that he was coming down with the flu and that he hadn't been sleeping well, which happened to be true. They'd offered him well-meaning advice about not working too hard, taking time to himself and all that rubbish.

They didn't understand that he *couldn't* stop. If he did, he would fail her all over again and he would fail in the eyes of God. He didn't know which would be worse.

"Did you hear about the police finding the bodies of those women? Terrible, isn't it?"

He cast an agitated, unfocused glance in the direction of the old woman who had spoken to him and seemed to be expecting a response.

"Yes, awful," he agreed, with apparent sincerity. "I hope they catch whoever did it sooner rather than later."

"You can say that again." She nodded enthusiastically. "It gives me the creeps just thinking about it. I read online that both victims were redheads. What do you make of that?"

He said nothing, but the pain in his head intensified until it was almost a roar. His vision began to cloud, and black spots danced in front of his eyes.

"Anyway," she babbled, "I'll be telling my daughter to stay at home until they catch him. She's got a mane of beautiful red hair and I don't want this maniac getting any ideas."

She laughed, a bit nervously.

"How old is your daughter?" he asked quietly.

"She turned twenty-three last week," the woman said, with maternal pride.

He nodded, thinking that she was too young to interest him.

"At least they've got that detective handling the case," she said, after a moment. "You know, the one who was injured last year after he uncovered all that corruption. He always seems to get his man. *So* good-looking, as well," she giggled. "If I were only twenty years younger!"

He smiled, thinking that he would like to choke the breath from her stupid, chattering body. The throb at the base of his skull pierced along his optic nerve so that he could barely see past the waves of pain.

"Do you think they have any idea who did it?" Amazingly, his voice sounded normal.

"I've no idea. There was no mention of any suspects on the lunchtime news, that's for sure," she replied. He relaxed a fraction, only to tense up again when she added, "That doesn't mean that they don't have their eye on somebody already. I'm sure this Graveyard Killer made some sort of slip-up, as they always do," she said, wisely.

Images of that very morning flashed into his mind and he replayed his movements, worrying suddenly that he had made some sort of minute error. He wasn't wholly in charge of himself when he was performing God's work and he worried that he had put himself—and therefore his work—in danger.

He needed to be careful.

"...do you?"

He blinked, trying to focus on what the old woman had said, but he couldn't remember. He tried smiling and made some sort of non-committal sound of agreement, which seemed to satisfy her.

"Anyway, dear, I'd better get on. Take care of yourself—you're working too hard."

He stared at her retreating form and the pain in his head slowly receded. He knew that ordinary people wouldn't understand his mission and they would try to stop him. People like DCI Ryan, a godless man who obviously had no respect for a Higher Power and no regard for the sanctity of his own soul. Yes, Ryan would try to stop him, so it was important that he kept up appearances until he found her.

She.

The one he had been searching for, all his life.

CHAPTER 7

The Tyneside Cinema was a local treasure on Pilgrim Street in the centre of Newcastle. It had been refurbished to polish up the old-world charm of its art deco interiors and now boasted three screens, a bar and a café. In the absence of any solid leads in Rothbury and to piece together Barbara Hewitt's last movements, MacKenzie and Lowerson decided to retrace her steps on the day she was likely to have died: Friday 18th March. An avalanche of ticket stubs discovered inside one of the drawers at her bungalow in Rothbury told them that Barbara hadn't missed an afternoon showing at the Tyneside Cinema for at least six months.

The silver screen awaited them.

"I love this place," Lowerson declared, looking around at the cosy décor and vintage posters advertising *It's a Wonderful Life* and *To Catch a Thief.* "We used to come here all the time when we were kids. We used to sneak in through the back and hide under the seats, so we could stay for a double feature."

"You're such a rebel, Jack."

"Ah, the days of my youth," Lowerson said, wistfully.

They breathed in the comforting smell of popcorn mingled with hot dogs and MacKenzie lowered her voice.

"The Automatic Number Plate Recognition cameras on the A1 picked up Barbara's Citroen heading south from Rothbury towards Newcastle at 10:27 at the first checkpoint, then again at 10:37 entering the city from the west. I've requested the footage from city centre CCTV but there'll be a wait on that, since it's the long weekend. For now, we know she was in the city by ten-thirty on Friday 18th. The receipts we found inside her purse tell us that she paid for parking at the New Bridge Street car park, which is just around the corner from here. The time stamp on that is 16:48, which must be when she left. You pay for the parking on the way out," she added, just to be clear. "The ANPR cameras confirm that she drove out of the city, apparently alone, at 17:03."

"What did she do between ten-thirty and four-fifty? That's quite a chunk of time," Lowerson said.

"Let's say she was parked up by ten forty-five, we can check the details with security at the car park later," MacKenzie replied. "From there, we know that she bought some lingerie from Marks and Spencer on Northumberland Street, time-stamped 11:09. She must have gone for a wander around the shops," MacKenzie suggested. "She headed down Grey Street to The Lobster Pot for lunch and paid up at 13:38. The only other receipt we found was for the cinema here, showing that she paid for a single entry to see *Batman vs Superman* at 14:00."

Lowerson grinned.

"Interesting choice for a lady like Barbara."

MacKenzie gave him a superior smile. "Why? Muscle-bound superheroes appeal to women of all ages, Jack."

"I'm sure they do," he winked.

"Not that I would know," she added swiftly.

"Your secret is safe with me."

They emerged back onto Pilgrim Street half an hour later sucking boiled sweets from pink-and-white striped paper bags. A discussion with the duty manageress of the *Tyneside Cinema* confirmed that Barbara Hewitt was well known to the staff there, partly because she was a regular and partly because she liked to make petty complaints. Despite that, the staff expressed sadness at her death and assured MacKenzie and Lowerson that they would do all they could to help the investigation.

"What do you reckon?"

MacKenzie sighed. "The staff were honest about the fact that Barbara was a cantankerous old git, but I didn't get the impression any of them wanted to strangle the life out of her," she replied.

"Some people take their cinema trips very seriously," Lowerson said, but agreed with her assessment.

"I'm not getting any kind of buzz from this place." MacKenzie turned to look back inside the foyer for a moment, at the streams of people tumbling down the stairs at the end of a showing. "Let's try the car park and see what we find there."

Michael 'Mick' Jobes was a sullen man in his mid-fifties who bore the marks of one well-accustomed to casual fighting and hard drinking. In MacKenzie's estimation, he had enjoyed both of those pursuits the previous evening. By the time they found Mick in his tiny security office at the multi-storey car park on New Bridge Street, the hangover had well and truly set in. His beady eyes were bloodshot and the left one was puffy with purpling bruises. His upper lip displayed a fresh cut and the knuckles on both of his hands were still raw.

"Hello?" MacKenzie entered the office without bothering to knock. She recognised the man sitting behind the grimy Perspex safety window instantly from her time spent working in Tyneside Area Command, before she transferred to Northumbria CID.

The security guard turned in his chair but didn't bother to turn off the pornographic movie playing on a tiny portable television set wedged between the six other CCTV screens.

"Sorry to interrupt you," MacKenzie added, with disdain.

He scowled at both of them, from his good eye.

"Now, don't bloody start on me today n'all," he said belligerently, heaving his wide bulk out of the chair. Lowerson regarded him with a flinty stare, shifting his feet so that they were shoulder-width apart and ready to square off, if necessary. "You buggers already dragged me inside last night—"

"Been brawling again, Mick?"

The big man turned from his suspicious inspection of the young poser wearing a shiny suit towards the attractive, conservatively-dressed redhead with bright green eyes.

"Non' a' your business," he said, gruffly.

"Howay, Mick," MacKenzie said amiably. "You'd think after thirty years of picking fights, you'd be bored of it by now."

"Aye, well we can't all ponce about like you," the other returned, once again sliding his eyes over Lowerson's suit and tie. He would have given his right arm for a suit like that, instead of the scratchy black two-piece which came as part of his uniform.

"You've had your chances." MacKenzie's tone didn't change, but Lowerson detected the note of warning.

"After the Falklands—" Jobes tried another tack.

"There were a lot of lads who struggled," she snapped. "Nobody's saying it wasn't hard, Mick."

Jobes started to say something else but thought better of it. He recognised the redheaded copper now and remembered that she'd always been decent, as far as pigs went.

"If you're not here to bang on about being drunk and disorderly, then what do you want?"

"Actually, we're here in connection with the death of a woman. We're trying to piece together her last movements," Lowerson supplied, flashing his warrant card.

"Haven't found any dead women around here." Mick shrugged his enormous shoulders. The dingy yellow light from the single bulb shone directly overhead, illuminating the shiny bald patch on top of his shaven head.

"You should check over the cemeteries," he tagged on, and wheezed out a laugh at his own joke.

Behind him, the volume suddenly increased on the television set and Lowerson stabbed the 'off' button to silence the offensive sound.

"She didn't die here." MacKenzie took out the picture of Barbara Hewitt and showed it to Jobes. "Do you recognise her?"

The man screwed up his bulldog face and then let out a raspberry sound.

"I see hundreds o' women passing through here every day, looking just like her," he said, a bit unkindly. "You'd have more luck asking me if I'd seen her car."

"Alright." MacKenzie shrugged a shoulder. "She drove an electric-blue Citroen C1, with a 2014 registration plate."

"When am I s'posed to have seen her?"

"Try last Friday."

Mick scratched inside his ear with a thick finger.

"Nah, not a car like that. If you'd said she drove an Aston or a Jag…"

"She liked a bit of a moan," Lowerson interjected. "You could say she was a woman who liked to make complaints. Ring any bells?"

Mick's eyes lit up briefly.

"Hang on," he said, as he reached onto a shelf for a tatty cardboard file marked 'COMPLAINTS'. After thumbing through the paperwork for a minute or two, he retrieved three sheets of paper.

"Aye, here we are," he said. "Some woman called Barbara Hewitt made two complaints in two months and she drove a Citroen C1, registration LH14 SNJ. Is that her?"

"Maybe." MacKenzie held out a patient hand for the documents.

"Ah, wait a minute, aren't you supposed to have a warrant or something?"

"Balls to that, man," Lowerson flicked the papers out of Jobes' hand and scanned through them. "She says she found scratches on her car."

"Aye, and the reason for that is because she always parked closest to the pillar on the second level, right in the corner. Same bloody parking space every time. She jammed her car between the outer wall and the pillar and that made it hard for her to get out of the driver's side, so she always scratched the car door. Then she tried to say it was kids who did it."

"Did she come and make a complaint to the office, here?"

Jobes looked cagily between them.

"Must've done, I can't remember."

MacKenzie nodded towards the CCTV screens, which were all blank.

"Is there a fault?"

Mick didn't bother to turn around. The cameras hadn't worked properly for nearly two years, but the management didn't want that getting about and they had issued strict instructions about what to say, if anybody should ask.

"Aye, a fault was registered just this morning," he said, affably. "They're sending a technician out later on."

MacKenzie searched his face.

"We'll need a copy of the footage for last Friday and the Friday before that. I presume that won't be a problem?"

He blinked a few times and looked into the space over MacKenzie's right shoulder.

"Course," he said eventually. "I'll—ah—I'll get in touch when the system's back up and running."

"Mick, I have to ask. What times were you on duty last Friday and Saturday?"

The big man slowly turned a shade of red.

'You better not be trying to pin owt on me!"

"Calm down. It's standard procedure—you should know that by now. We will ask the same question of any other security guards working in the building, if you'd be kind enough to let us have their names."

"There's two of us," the other replied, anger subsiding. Quick to flare up and quick to die down again. "We do two weeks on, two weeks off the night shift. The last week, I've been on the day shift and Jamil was doing the nights."

"So the last couple of weeks you were working between—what? Eight a.m. and six p.m.?"

"Eight and eight."

Lowerson made a note.

"What happens when somebody makes multiple complaints, Mick?"

"Management sticks their oar in."

"Did they give you some grief about this?" She held out the pages listing Barbara's complaints and gave Jobes a level, uncompromising look.

After some sort of internal struggle, Jobes bobbed his head.

"Aye, you could say as much," he muttered, then jabbed a blunt finger at Lowerson's chest. MacKenzie noted idly that it bore an old tattoo in the shape of a tiny crucifix, repeated on each of the four fingers of his right hand. "But I wouldn't kill some old bitch for that. As if I give two shits about this place!" He gestured at the office, which carried an odour of petrol fumes and leftover kebab.

He might not care about it, they thought, *but it was the only job he had.*

They left him to enjoy the rest of his film in peace and, after a brief visit to the second level to see where Barbara had preferred to park, the two detectives headed slowly back towards the city centre.

"What's your feeling on Jobes?" Lowerson asked. "Is something like killing Barbara Hewitt his style?"

MacKenzie sighed. "He's a scrapper, there's no denying that. He spends more of his time in trouble than out of it. But strangling Barbara Hewitt?" MacKenzie shook her head disbelievingly. "I can't see him going all the way up there to kill some old woman simply for making a complaint. I might have stretched to a botched burglary because he's got form for that, but there's no evidence that anything was stolen from her house."

"No, that doesn't seem to have been the motivation," Lowerson said. "Mick seems hard as nails, though. You're sure he wouldn't get the idea in his head and drive up to Rothbury, anyway?"

MacKenzie turned her face up to the spring sunshine and took her time before answering.

"When I was working down here, I booked him for all kinds of assault and battery, drunk and disorderly, possession, that sort of thing. I know a bit about Jobes' background: he grew up in the care system and then went into the army, where he was medically discharged for post-traumatic stress. Apparently, he used to hallucinate that the people he'd killed whilst fighting had come back from the dead," she explained, with a trace of sympathy. "So, yeah, he's troubled, but I still don't think he'd kill in cold blood. Not without a good reason, anyway."

Lowerson nodded but cast another searching look back over his shoulder at the towering concrete car park and wondered about the man sitting inside.

Lewis Pinks was a poor excuse for a human being. Everybody knew it, including him. Sometimes, after he'd watched one of those true crime documentaries, he'd reflect on his own psyche and consider whether he might have been a better man if he'd been born to different parents or if he'd had a 'normal' childhood.

Then he'd look out of the window at his brand-new white Range Rover with its shiny silver alloys and bespoke leather interior, reminding him that life was too good to mourn his lack of human empathy. Besides, it wasn't as if he didn't keep in touch with the little man. On Saturdays, he did his regular rounds collecting payments, issuing warnings for those in arrears, and generally checking what he considered to be his livestock.

The next stop on his list was Karen Dobbs.

He drove slowly through the streets of Daisy Hill, feeling like a king. Lewis had been born in one of these poky little houses and he'd learned his trade from the dealers who visited his mother. He'd held her head over the manky toilet seat and cleaned up the slop afterwards. He'd stolen bread and milk from the corner shop to feed himself when she'd been too paralytic to notice that he was starving. He supposed that's where he had learned, first hand, the true meaning of supply and demand.

Lewis pulled up outside Karen's narrow house as the digital clock on his space-age dashboard flashed 13:41. He jumped down from his elevated seat onto the pavement and swore as his new high-tops squelched into a fresh pile of dog shit. He wiped his shoe on the tiny patch of dried-out grass outside the house and eyed the street kids who emerged from the shadows to cast hungry eyes over his car.

"Oi! Touch my car and I'll find you, you little pricks!"

They scattered as he walked the rest of the way to Karen's front door, curling his lip at the peeling paint. He raised his fist to bang a few times.

Nothing.

She was probably off her face, he thought.

He banged on the door again and shifted his feet impatiently, flicking a glance at the heavy gold watch which hung from his skinny wrist.

"Karen! Answer the door!"

If she was trying to get off for another week without coughing up what she owed him, then she'd be sorry. He raised his foot to the door and gave it a couple of good kicks until it swung open to reveal the dim hallway beyond.

He tugged at his new jacket and stepped inside, careful to avoid brushing against the doorframe. You never knew what you might catch.

"Karen!"

His nose wrinkled delicately as he entered the hallway. The place was always a stinking mess but today it was especially bad. The walls were scarred and stained, and the ancient carpet stuck to the soles of his shoes as he padded towards what could loosely be called the living room.

"I haven't got time for this..."

Lewis poked his head through the doorways and saw the usual dilapidation but no sign of Karen. He knew that she preferred to jack up in her bedroom, so he traipsed up the narrow staircase to find her. He only hoped she hadn't taken an overdose; he couldn't be bothered with the aggravation.

Lewis emerged onto the street a couple of minutes later feeling worried. Nobody was more surprised than he, but that was undoubtedly the emotion he was experiencing. He warred with himself and tried brushing it off, but the feeling wouldn't be quelled.

He knew what he had to do.

Less than an hour later, Ryan and Phillips received word that an anonymous call had come in to report a missing woman by the name of Karen Dobbs. The caller had given a brief physical description and stated Karen's address in Daisy Hill before ringing off. It hadn't taken much for a bright-eyed telephone operative to connect the dots between a missing redhead and the woman they had found at Heaton Cemetery that very morning.

A simple cross-check against Criminal Records had elicited a match between their second victim and

Karen Marie Dobbs, a thirty-two-year-old woman with a long history of drug abuse and solicitation.

"Sad business," Phillips said gruffly.

"Yes."

There was nothing more that Ryan could say. He didn't need to climb onto a soap box and lecture Frank about the evils and degradations of drug addiction; he didn't need to tell him about the perpetual cycle of despair that led people to use, to forget their responsibilities and their personal safety.

"It's the same man," was all he did say, while they walked through Karen's tiny house. One of Faulkner's CSIs accompanied them as they made their way from room to room—Faulkner himself was fully occupied trying to record the smallest details from both major crime scenes. The forecast for Easter Sunday was 'scattered showers', which for the north of England was an almost certain indicator of monsoon rainfall. That being the case, Faulkner was racing against the weather as well as the mounting fear that another body might be found before his work was done.

They moved upstairs, where Ryan committed the details of Karen's bedroom to memory since it appeared to be where she had spent the majority of her time. Not that there was much in the way of furniture; just a rickety futon which served as a bed, and a cheap pine chair. A pile of dirty clothes had been slung into a corner and the debris of a well-established user was strewn across the floor.

"I'll speak to the neighbours," Phillips said. "They might have seen something."

Ryan had already considered the possibilities.

"She must have had a regular patch. Speak to social services and the vice team, recall her case files and we'll go through them with a fine-toothed comb. I want to know how she was selected."

Phillips made a rumbling sound of agreement.

"He was either known to her or a pick-up. It's the most likely explanation."

Ryan dipped down to his knees and looked under the futon but found nothing except old needles and a lot of dust. Standing upright again, he moved across to the chair and carefully lifted the clothes to check underneath. As he did, a small leaflet fell to the floor, which he bent down to retrieve.

"Narcotics anonymous," he murmured, slipping it inside a plastic evidence wallet. "St Andrew's RC Church on Friday nights at seven o'clock. There's a Catholic connection, Frank. We'll check to see if she went along—could be that our killer followed her from there."

Ryan cast a final look around the room and his eye caught on a cheap wooden photo frame which sat on the window ledge. He moved across to take a closer look and his heart plummeted. Inside the frame was a picture of a small boy of around three with bright red hair and dimples.

"Ah, God," he muttered.

Over in the city centre, the final stop on MacKenzie and Lowerson's whirlwind tour of 'A Day in the Life of Barbara Hewitt' ended at The Lobster Pot, a classy, brasserie-style restaurant located a short walk away from the Tyneside Cinema on Grey Street. All around them, the city was bustling with people taking advantage of the bank holiday weekend. Mothers with young children dragged them into shops and promised milkshakes as a reward for good behaviour. Young couples strolled along the Quayside hand in hand, tracing the path of the river which glimmered steel grey in the midday sun. Teenagers granted a reprieve from school spent their pocket money on fast food, and packs of girls moved between the window displays, swinging their glossy carrier bags as they went. MacKenzie and Lowerson paused beside the towering monument to Earl Grey and watched them pass by in a whirlwind of colour and sound.

"It's a good place, isn't it?" Lowerson blurted out.

He didn't know why the thought had popped into his mind or why he'd said it aloud. He supposed that he had grown accustomed to the area, having spent all of his life in Newcastle. He kept telling himself that one day he'd move down south and join the Met. Ryan had told him a few stories about the time he'd spent working in London and it sounded exciting to someone who had only visited the capital twice before—and one of those times on a school trip.

But standing here amongst the crowds, he found himself looking at his hometown afresh and, to his surprise, he didn't find it lacking. There was a solidarity to the place; a jovial atmosphere which was reflected in its people and it made him feel protective.

"Come on, let's get going," he said suddenly and MacKenzie parodied a salute.

"Yessir!"

They weaved through the throng of shoppers until they reached the top of Grey Street, which was an architectural dream with its Georgian terraces curving gently downhill towards the Quayside. The Theatre Royal stood proudly to their left, with its classic columns and large boards touting performances of *The Marriage of Figaro* and *South Pacific*. They strolled down the pavement until they reached the large glass doors of the restaurant and Lowerson pulled an expressive face at the red-carpeted entranceway flanked by two small conifers. A fancy gold sign hung above the door with a tasteful depiction of a lobster sitting beside it. Inside, they were immediately met by the scent of delicious food and Lowerson's stomach rumbled loudly.

"Hungry?" MacKenzie grinned.

"Just a bit. I don't suppose…?"

"Not a chance," she said firmly. "We'll grab a sandwich after we've spoken with the manager."

The manager turned out to be a tall, fair-haired man wearing an exquisitely tailored navy-blue suit. MacKenzie judged him to be around forty-five, but with bright blue eyes and a light tan, he could pass for younger.

"Good afternoon," he said politely, casting appreciative eyes over MacKenzie. "I'm Paul Cooke, I own and manage the restaurant here." He held out a hand, which they both shook. "I understand that you're with the police. How may I help you?"

His accent was what MacKenzie would have called 'affected'. Although Cooke had clearly made an effort to adopt the kind of Queen's English spoken by upper-crusty southerners like their very own chief inspector, she could still detect the tell-tale lyrical twang of a northerner, born and bred.

"DI MacKenzie and DC Lowerson, Northumbria CID." She held out her warrant card. "We would like to ask you some questions regarding a regular customer of yours."

A shadow passed across the man's face.

"CID? How sad," he murmured. "Of course, I'll be happy to help you however I can. Let's discuss it in my office."

He turned and, with a subtle gesture to one of the serving staff, led the way up a short flight of spiral stairs to a mezzanine level and along a corridor to a door bearing a plaque with 'MANAGER' engraved on it.

"Please, take a seat." Cooke indicated a seating area with a couple of single chairs and a small two-seater sofa. "Can I offer you a drink?"

"Yes—" Lowerson began.

"We're fine, thanks all the same," MacKenzie overrode him. This wasn't a social call.

"Well, then." Cooke crossed a leg and settled back in his chair. "How can I help?"

MacKenzie handed him a photograph of Barbara Hewitt.

"Do you recognise this woman?"

He didn't flinch.

"Yes, I do. Barbara is a regular customer of ours. She has a standing reservation for lunch on Fridays at one of our window tables on the main floor."

"I see." MacKenzie added it to the growing list of 'habits'.

"Has something happened to her? It must have done, otherwise you wouldn't be here," he answered his own question.

"Miss Hewitt died in suspicious circumstances, we believe sometime late last Friday 18th or early Saturday 19th."

Cooke laid the photograph on the glass coffee table in front of them and leaned back again.

"I'm very sorry to hear that, and it would certainly explain why she didn't turn up for lunch yesterday. We were all very surprised, as it's the first time." He spread his hands. "But I'm not sure how I can assist."

"You could start by telling us what you remember of Barbara's last visit here. What time did she arrive?"

Cooke blew out a breath.

"Ah, well. I couldn't say for certain because it would have been one of our hostesses who greeted her at the door before accompanying her to her usual table. It's worth checking with them but it would likely have been one o'clock or thereabouts. Barbara was rarely late, and she had a standing reservation for that time on Fridays, as I say."

Lowerson scribbled a note.

"Do you know if she was alone?"

"I've never seen her with a guest and last Friday was no different. She was alone throughout her meal, to the best of my knowledge." His eyes brightened. "Why don't I pull out the security tape for you?"

MacKenzie smiled politely.

"That would be very helpful, thank you."

"Don't mention it." His eyes lingered on her face and roamed over her hair. She noticed the action and shuffled uncomfortably in her seat, feeling hot and bothered.

"Ah, next question." She made a show of looking down at her notes. "Did you speak to Barbara personally?"

"Yes, every week I made sure to exchange a brief word with her. It's good business," he explained.

"What did you think of her?"

He let the question sink in and gave himself a moment to formulate an appropriate response.

"Barbara was a very independent lady," he said, politely. "She was also a creature of habit. She ordered the battered cod and chips with a side of mushy peas every time."

"Really?" Lowerson piped up, thinking of all the mouth-watering delicacies he'd seen on the extensive menu.

Cooke chuckled.

"Yes, she told me once that it was traditional to eat fish and chips on Fridays and that was what she would do."

"What do you remember, specifically, about your discussion with her on Friday 18th?"

He frowned.

"Well, I believe she was just about to start her dessert—treacle pudding and custard—when I stopped by to say 'hello.' I asked how she was keeping, she told me she was well. I asked if she had enjoyed her lunch, all those usual things. I'm sorry, detectives, I don't remember anything that stands out."

"You never know what might be important," Lowerson said. "Let us worry about that." MacKenzie threw him a look of approval.

"How did she seem to you?"

Cooke rubbed his chin and grimaced as he forced his mind back to over a week ago.

"I suppose, now that you mention it, she seemed grumpier than usual," he muttered, then looked horrified at the minor indiscretion. "That is—"

MacKenzie held up a hand.

"Please, speak freely."

"In that case, yes, I'd say she seemed to be quite agitated. The waitress who was serving her—Maia," he told Lowerson, for the benefit of his note, "also mentioned that Barbara had been dissatisfied with her meal and the standard of service, right from the start."

"Did she confide in you? Had something happened to her that day?"

"No." He shook his head. "Really, we hardly knew one another except to exchange pleasantries. She seemed to be a lonely woman who liked to treat herself to lunch every Friday. Perhaps she was feeling particularly lonely last Friday, which made her waspish. Who knows?"

"You can say that again." Lowerson snapped his notebook shut and prayed to whichever god was listening for a breakthrough.

As they emerged onto the pavement, Lowerson lamented the fact that he would not be enjoying lobster bisque any time in the near future. He tried, unconvincingly, to tell himself that a ham and cheese toastie from the nearest café was equally good, but his stomach knew better.

"So, Barbara liked to make an excursion into town to do her favourite things," he said, with one last longing look behind them. "Not that you'd have known it, considering she liked to make complaints wherever she went. It sounds like she was a real peach."

MacKenzie began to walk back along Grey Street in the direction of her car.

"She's a dead peach, Jack—just remember that. However rude or obnoxious she was in life, she didn't deserve to die the way she did. Nobody does."

Suitably chastened, Lowerson waited a moment before delivering his next observation.

"Speaking of peaches, that restaurant manager looked as if he wouldn't mind taking a bite out of you."

He grinned at her and wiggled his eyebrows.

"I don't know what you mean," she said, in dignified tones.

"Uh huh." He laughed.

MacKenzie struggled for a full minute to find a suitably cutting retort, but failed.

"Shut up, constable," she muttered instead, and the sound of his delighted laughter followed them all the way up the winding street.

CHAPTER 8

The Powers That Be agreed that the deaths of Krista Ogilvy-Matthews and Karen Dobbs were linked and approved Ryan's request to set up a task force, which he did at lightning speed. By the time MacKenzie and Lowerson returned to CID Headquarters, the largest conference room had been converted into a 'Major Incident Room' and now bore a sign spelling out 'OPERATION ANGEL' in capital letters on the wall outside.

Inside, the room was a hive of activity. Printers and photocopiers hummed in a line along the back wall, as constables huddled over a bank of telephones and spoke in a constant drone of hushed voices while others scurried between the desks with a palpable sense of urgency. Spearheading the operation was Ryan, who stood in front of the long whiteboard at the front of the room arranging images and notes ahead of a briefing scheduled for five o'clock. Phillips sat at one of the desks and barked out a command that some poor minion should "pull the finger out of their arse and get on with it," before slamming the phone down and returning to his inspection of a growing pile of statements.

Ryan caught sight of the new arrivals and raised a distracted hand to greet them.

"Mac, Lowerson, pull up a chair—you're just in time."

"Ah, sir, that case we caught yesterday, about the old woman—" MacKenzie began, but Ryan interrupted her.

"If you need more time to make a determination, I can't give it to you."

"We've already made the determination," she said firmly. "Thanks to a fast post-mortem, we've been able to confirm that the victim, Barbara Hewitt, was murdered. Strangled, in fact. We're investigating."

Ryan's eyes narrowed at the cause of death. That made three deaths by strangulation and the weekend wasn't over yet.

"Strangled—how?"

"The circumstances and methodology are very different to these women." She glanced behind him at the images of the two redheads and then snatched her eyes away again. "Barbara was strangled manually and left in her own home, without any ritualistic features."

Ryan accepted her word without question and moved on to practicalities.

"Understood. The fact is, things are heating up and the press are like bloodhounds. Half of the phone calls we're getting are from women claiming to have seen men dressed up as priests following them home or hiding in the bushes," he said, with a trace of irritation. "We're going to be working around the clock on this and I can't promise not to pull Lowerson—maybe you, too—over to this investigation. I'm sorry, but we need the man hours."

MacKenzie was a practical woman herself.

"I appreciate you're against the wall. Let's hope I can tie up these loose ends quickly, then we can put our combined energies into finding the Graveyard Killer instead."

"The name is certainly catching on," Ryan said caustically, then turned back to the murder board he had created.

Blown-up images of both redheaded victims had been tacked up in a prominent position to capture the attention of every officer in the room. Ryan knew that by creating an emotional connection between the victims and his team, he would be assured of their hard work and dedication over the coming days. He only hoped that the investigation wouldn't run into weeks.

"Can you spare half an hour? You might as well stay for the briefing and keep abreast of how things are progressing."

MacKenzie looked across to where Lowerson was already nosing into the stack of papers on Ryan's desk. She didn't need a psychic to tell her that the young detective would much rather be part of the task force assigned to the Graveyard Killer.

Half an hour couldn't hurt, she supposed.

They settled themselves in the row of chairs that had been placed in a semicircle facing the board. Phillips ended his latest threatening phone call and moved across to join them, followed by the rest of the support staff. As the clock struck five, the double doors swung open and Faulkner hurried in with one of his junior CSIs in tow, carrying a large bundle of files and steaming cups of coffee which Ryan's superior nose detected from across the room.

When everybody was assembled, Ryan moved to the front and thrust his hands into the pockets of his dark jeans.

"Alright, settle down," he called out, and waited for the chatter to dim.

When he had their full attention, he pointed to the images on the wall.

"The woman on the left is Krista Ogilvy-Matthews, a thirty-eight-year-old secondary school teacher whose body was discovered by a council grave digger on Friday morning at the West Road Cemetery. Thanks to the quick work of our pathologist and the forensic team, we've made good progress excavating the crime scene and we now know that she was strangled using a ligature of some kind. As some of you will have heard, Krista's body was arranged into an unusual formation and a Latin note, apparently granting Catholic absolution, was buried beside it. Given the religious overtones, our current thinking is that Krista's body was staged to parody an angel or something similar."

There were a few expected murmurs whilst the team looked through their information packs and surveyed the 'after' photographs detailing the manner in which Krista had been found. Ryan gave them a couple of minutes to digest the information before moving on.

"The woman on the right is Karen Dobbs, a thirty-two-year-old prostitute and mother of one, whose body was discovered by a member of the ground staff at Heaton Cemetery this morning. Again, preliminary observations from our pathologist confirm the same MO. As you will see from the images, her body was staged and a note was once again left beside her. You'll find copies of each note in your packs—they're almost identical in style and the wording is the same. Although we're waiting to hear back from the handwriting expert about the note found this morning, she has already confirmed that the card used in both cases is of the same type. It's a heavyweight cream card stock—around 200 grams—and is widely available from any stationery shop nationwide. Likewise, the ink comes from your average black Sharpie marker pen."

"The handwriting expert did raise one interesting point," Phillips spoke up. "About the handwriting style. According to her, the rigid neatness indicates a highly ordered mind and focused concentration, rather than somebody who was off their chump."

"Highly technical term, there," Ryan said, dryly. "Graphology is hardly an exact science, so I don't want anybody running away with the idea, but it's something to bear in mind. Our killer was organised and focused when it came to planning the act itself, if his handwriting is any indication of his mindset."

"What about the message in the notes?" Lowerson piped up.

"It's the traditional passage recited by a Catholic priest when granting absolution to a sinner. Obviously, we can imagine several scenarios, in terms of motivation. As far as our victims are concerned, Krista's only 'sin' in the eyes of her killer could lie in the fact that she was gay. Likewise, Karen was a member of the oldest profession. That's all we've been able to come up with so far."

"They're both redheads in their thirties." MacKenzie stated the obvious.

Ryan met her eyes across the room.

"That's true enough and we have to consider the possibility that there is, or was, a significant person in our killer's life who was possessed of red hair, around the same age as both victims. Otherwise, it's simply a coincidence."

"You don't believe in coincidences," MacKenzie parried.

Ryan was silent for a moment, then sighed deeply. He believed in a policy of honesty at all times.

"No, I don't. Which is why I haven't downplayed its significance to the press. I want the women of this city to be cautious because there's reason to be."

MacKenzie swallowed and felt Phillips shift towards her. They both knew that Ryan was issuing a warning to guard her own safety, as much as the other women in the North East.

She nodded and looked back down at the papers in her lap.

"At the moment, we have enough to think about." Ryan leaned back against his desk and picked up the thread of his briefing.

"We identified our second victim, Karen Dobbs, after receiving an anonymous call through the local Crimestoppers helpline. We don't know whether the call came from the killer himself or from another concerned party, but the telephone company is working hard to trace the origin of that call. So far, we know it came from an unregistered mobile, but we'll triangulate to narrow down the field. I can't see that happening before Monday at the earliest."

The rumbles around the room intensified as his team listened and looked up at the image of Karen Dobbs taken from her old high school yearbook and compared it with the image of her in death. Though their perpetrator had taken her life, it was clear to see that drug addiction had taken her spirit long before then.

"She looks so different in that early photograph," Lowerson said, voicing what they were all thinking.

"She still had hope back then," Ryan said simply.

Lowerson continued to study the image of a woman who was only a couple of years older than himself, yet, when she died, her face had borne the marks of a woman at least ten years his senior.

"Karen looks older than thirty-two," he said. "If the killer has a 'type' he's looking for, it could be that he thought she was closer to forty, like Krista."

Ryan turned to look at the images and nodded his agreement.

"That's good thinking, Jack. Redheads in their late thirties might be closer to his target victim. But while they might look similar, these two women couldn't be more different in terms of background," Ryan continued. "Krista was educated to postgraduate level and she came from a secure family background. She was happily married and enjoyed her work—and the esteem of her peers. As far as we can tell, she was abducted or lured into a car sometime after nine-fifteen on Thursday night, after she left the *All-American Diner.*" He sucked in a breath. "On the other hand, Karen Dobbs left school at sixteen and fell in with the wrong crowd. She had a long record of drug abuse, shoplifting and solicitation; she went into the Drug Interventions Programme after the first arrest but the story I'm getting is that she just couldn't hack it. Social services did their best to help her stay clean, for the sake of her little boy, but he was taken in by the grandmother two years ago by order of the court. I spoke with Karen's mother, who seems a decent woman, but she hadn't been in contact with her daughter in months."

Ryan thought back to the difficult house call they had made earlier in the day, to the little retirement flat where a tired old woman had answered the door. He remembered the look in her eyes—eyes that were the same shade as those of her daughter and grandson. The look had been one of devastation and expectation in equal measure. It wasn't the first time the police had visited her home to discuss Karen and over the years she had prepared herself for that final visit, when they would tell her that her daughter was dead. Karen had chosen to lead a hard life and her mother had resigned herself to the fact that her little girl was long gone, although in the end 'choice' had played no part at all.

"What about the little boy?" MacKenzie asked.

"The grandmother seems to love him," Ryan said quietly. "He was at pre-school when we paid our visit, but I had a word with the social worker who dealt with the case and by all accounts he's doing well."

"That's something," she murmured. "How about the father?"

"That would be a man called Lewis Pinks."

"Where have I heard that name before?" Lowerson queried.

"Notorious dealer," Phillips said. "He works the area down by Walker, not far from Karen's house. He's a slippery bastard, as far as I remember."

"I strongly suspect that Pinks supplied Karen Dobbs not only with a son, but also with the drugs that eventually took him from her." Ryan paused, looking down at the carpet tiles before he added, "We'll be speaking with him before close of play this evening."

The details of Karen's miserable life left a nasty taste in his mouth, one he wished he could spit out.

"We'll be looking into Karen's movements late last night and early this morning," Ryan continued. "We're working on the basis that she died only hours before her body was discovered. We have to assume that she was picked up by her killer while soliciting, although we can't rule out other possibilities."

Ryan stood up again and gestured towards Faulkner.

"Tom? Give us the latest news on forensics, would you?"

Faulkner shuffled towards the front of the room and tried not to panic in front of the sea of expectant faces.

"Um, yes. Okay. Beginning with Krista Ogilvy-Matthews."

His voice was practically a squeak, so Faulkner cleared his throat and tried again in what he hoped was a deeper, more macho tone.

"The ground was wet on Thursday night and we've been able to find tracks leading from the car park area all the way across to the site where Krista's body was found. The imprints suggest that our perpetrator was carrying a load—we assume her body—because the tracks leading back for the return journey are considerably lighter in comparison."

"How did he enter?"

Faulkner gave a shake of his head.

"There are no signs of the lock having been forced on either of the entrance gates and the footprints clearly lead to and from the main parking area, so we have to assume that he used a key."

Ryan raised an eyebrow and turned to Phillips.

"Who has the keys?"

Phillips licked the tip of his thumb and flicked through the pages of his notebook until he found what he was looking for.

"The short answer is that quite a few people have a key, or access to a set of keys to the cemetery grounds. You've got the ground staff, who are contracted by the Council to come in and tend the lawns and maintain the gravesites; crematorium staff, also employed by the Council; admin staff working within the Bereavement Services team and, potentially, members of the church across all denominations."

Ryan rubbed his left temple as a low-grade headache started to develop.

"The Council are in charge of running ten cemeteries across the city including both of the ones we've seen this weekend, so everything is supposed to go through them." Phillips paused for a second before adding, "In reality we all know how protocols, best practices and whatnot can slip. The Council say they hold two sets of keys to each gate, for each cemetery within their remit, and that their contractors also hold sets of keys for easy access. After a chat with some of the people involved, I can already tell you that there are probably many more keys in circulation than that, not counting families and extended families who might be in a position to access keys if any one of these people failed to keep them in a secure place."

Ryan gave himself a few seconds to stare at the ceiling and let the frustration drain from his system.

"Right. So, anybody in Newcastle City Council who knows the right place to check; anybody affiliated with the church—any denomination—who knows the right place to look; and anybody who works as or knows somebody working as ground staff, crematorium staff or council staff. In other words, half the population of Newcastle, by the sounds of it. Correct?"

"Pretty much, yep."

"I never thought I would hear myself say these words, but it's a pity there isn't more bureaucracy in the City Council."

Phillips boomed out a laugh and then sobered up again.

"Fact is, guv, at this rate we're going to have to go through the whole list of people who we definitely know have access and cross them off the list as we go. I've made a start on their statements and I'll do the follow ups."

Ryan nodded. It was a good, methodical approach.

"Is there a sort of 'universal' key that would give access to all the cemeteries in the city?"

Phillips' eyes twinkled and he tapped the side of his bulbous nose.

"I know what you're thinking and, no, there isn't. I made a start by looking into the contractors and Keith Wilson in particular. He says he turned up for work and discovered Krista's body, but he wouldn't be the first person to return to the scene of a crime, or seek out media attention for his crimes."

"True."

"From what I can see, Wilson has a tight alibi. I spoke to the bars and the club he mentioned and they confirmed his movements. I checked out the other contractor who works alongside him as a grave digger. She's away on holiday in Cornwall and has been since last Saturday."

"Alright, it's still good progress," Ryan said, then turned back to Faulkner who was standing at the front looking awkward.

"What can you deduce from the imprints? Can you give us anything in terms of the physical type?"

"I can give you broad estimations." Faulkner pushed his glasses further back on his nose. "The footprints we found at both sites are of a similar size, although a different shoe was worn each time. I emphasise *shoe*, rather than boot, because it was a smooth sole rather than the heavy-duty tread I would expect to see otherwise."

Ryan filed that nugget away.

"How about sizing?"

"Shoe size around a ten, or ten and a half," Faulkner supplied. "Which would strongly suggest male."

"Which would also tie in with the MO," Phillips threw in.

"Exactly," Faulkner nodded. "We took the depth of the prints found at each site and factored in the weight of each victim to come up with an approximate weight for our killer. In both cases our estimation was the same—somewhere in the region of 180 to 200 pounds—which would support the theory that we're looking for the same man in each case."

"Height?" Ryan asked.

Faulkner blew out a long breath.

"Here, we're getting into the realms of statistical probability. Looking at the stride length, shoe size and approximate weight, the charts tell me that we are likely to find a man within the range of five feet eight to six feet one inches tall."

"Alright, he's edging towards the taller end of the spectrum. That gives us something to think about. What else?"

"Both victims were killed elsewhere. Neither grave corresponded with a kill site and we have been unable to locate anywhere in the immediate vicinity either. The evidence suggests that our perp killed them beforehand, then carried his victims from the cemetery car park to the allotted gravesite, which means that he had transportation of some kind. The tracks were single file—purposeful and direct, you might say—which would also suggest a certain familiarity with the cemeteries."

"In other words, he knew exactly where he was going," Ryan surmised. "He knew there was no functioning CCTV at either of these cemeteries, he had the means to access them out of hours, and he knew that he would be able to take a car and park relatively nearby in the car parks at either site."

"Yes, I would say so."

"Phillips? We need that footage from the street cameras."

"On it like a car bonnet," the other replied.

Ryan moved around his desk and came to stand in front of the murder board. He took a couple of pins and stuck them onto a large map of each cemetery to indicate the killer's approach, then ran a thoughtful hand over his chin.

"He knew the cemetery grid and he knew about forthcoming burials. Phillips? Who has access to that kind of data?"

Phillips tugged at his earlobe and made a face.

"Anyone working in the Bereavement Services team at the Council...any of their contractors hired to dig the graves, church staff booked to do the service, even the admin staff who take care of all that, not to mention the funeral directors. That's just off the top of my head."

Ryan walked slowly back to his desk and leaned against it, crossing his ankles.

"Make a shortlist of everybody who was on shift to book, dig, take care of or give a service for the burials due to take place at both cemeteries on the days we found Krista and Karen. That should narrow it down."

Phillips nodded and made a scribbled note.

"Apparently, it's policy to dig a grave at least twenty-four hours in advance of a burial," he commented, with a sharp-eyed look that was interpreted correctly by his SIO.

"You're saying that, if our killer had access to the listings, he would have had a twenty-four-hour window to dump a body before it was filled over by a legitimate burial the next day?"

It took Ryan less than three seconds to follow the trail of breadcrumbs.

"There was no pre-existing hole dug out for Krista's body but there was for Karen's body. Why the discrepancy?"

Phillips had already looked into it.

"Aye, I wondered the same thing," he said. "I had a word with the lass at Bereavement Services, who tells me that the funeral for some old codger was put back by a day, at the last minute. The grave digger, Keith, was meant to go up to the West Road Cemetery to dig a hole on Thursday morning, but he was put back to Friday morning instead."

Ryan nodded—the picture was getting clearer.

"Which means that our killer had a bit of a nasty surprise. There was no cushty hole already dug out and waiting for him on Thursday night, so he was forced to do it himself." Ryan turned back to Faulkner. "What did you find? He must have left something behind."

"We found evidence of grass stains and turf on the underside of Krista's clothing, which would be consistent with her being placed above ground while her killer dug his hole," Faulkner said. "As far as we can tell, he used a piece of chipped granite to dig out a shallow grave by hand. We found the corner of a headstone discarded near the site bearing the same soil samples."

"I wonder if he panicked," Ryan thought of a man clawing at the soil under cover of darkness. "He must have been shocked to find the ground intact when he arrived."

Faulkner pulled a face.

"He had already carried Krista's body across the breadth of the cemetery grounds, which would be taxing enough. Add on the added requirement of digging a grave...yes, it would have been labour-intensive, especially if there was time pressure."

"What about skin samples?" MacKenzie asked, but Faulkner shook his head.

"Gloves were used, leather ones. We found minute samples of leather fibres embedded on the jagged edge of stone. We're still sifting through the soil, but it's been less than forty-eight hours since we excavated the site. It's possible that we'll find more; we're moving as quickly as we can."

"Don't worry about the resources, Tom." Ryan fixed him with a direct stare. "Leave the money-talk to me, I'll square it with the Chief."

Faulkner nodded gratefully.

"As for Karen Dobbs, the killer had a much easier time of it," he said, moving onto the next victim. "The winch they use to lower a coffin was already set up and covered over with tarpaulin, in preparation for the funeral planned for ten o'clock this morning. Our killer used the winch to lower Karen's body inside, brought it back up and then used the canvas to lever himself in and out. We found hair and skin fibres on the winch canvas belonging to the victim, as well as the same leather fibres we found at the first crime scene and several partial footprints inside the grave."

"If the rest of the evidence wasn't enough to convince us, that adds weight to our working theory that it's the same killer in both instances."

"Exactly." Faulkner nodded.

"He would need a good level of physical strength to carry these women and lift himself in and out of the grave—good upper body strength, in particular," Lowerson chipped in.

With a more vivid picture in their minds, the room took a collective breath. Ryan cast his silver-grey stare over each of them, silently commanding their attention.

"Phillips, I want a list of burials scheduled for the next week, along with all the CCTV footage we can get our hands on. Faulkner, I want to know the minute you find any other samples, if you find a match to any existing profile... damn it, just contact me if anything remotely useful turns up." He pinched the bridge of his nose and then pointed a finger at one of the unsuspecting constables hovering at the back of the room. "Yates?"

PC Melanie Yates almost jumped in surprise.

"Y-yes?"

"You've worked hard for this division—I remember your dedication from last year. Let's see some more of it now," he added. "I want you to assist Phillips. Work through the list of known affiliates and of all the people who might have access to these cemeteries, particularly the funeral directors and Council contractors. Interview and re-interview them all until we find our weak link. Understand?"

Bursting at the prospect of real responsibility, PC Yates simply nodded.

Ryan waited a beat and then clapped his hands.

"Let's go."

CHAPTER 9

The men and women assigned to Operation Angel were galvanised into action and went about the business of tracking the Graveyard Killer with gusto. As the man in charge, Ryan was acutely aware that time was slipping through their fingers. The killer had taken two lives in two days, so he didn't need a postgraduate degree in Criminology to tell him that their perpetrator was escalating; experience and common sense was sufficient. The question uppermost in Ryan's mind was therefore not 'if' there would be another murder, but where and when the killer would choose to strike again.

"Phillips!"

His sergeant loped across the room to join him in poring over a list of cemeteries falling inside the catchment area of Newcastle City Council.

"There are ten cemeteries on this list." He tapped a finger on the innocuous line of printed text. "The killer has visited two of them so far but it's Easter Sunday tomorrow."

Phillips tugged at his bottom lip with thumb and forefinger.

"That could be the end of it," he said, hopefully. "There's been a lot of splash on the news, in the papers and whatnot. It might put him off killing again."

Ryan shook his head.

"Not if he thinks God will protect him."

"Aye, there is that. You can't reason with a fruitcake. What are we going to do about it?"

Ryan placed both hands on the desktop and leaned forward while he thought.

"You told me there are four funerals planned for tomorrow, two at Elswick, one at All Saints and one at Heaton which has now been put back until tomorrow. Of those, All Saints has the easiest vehicular access facilities whereas Elswick would be harder to get into with a car, but it's also the largest at over twenty-six acres so there's a chance he could find an access point. All the same, I'd put my money on him trying for All Saints."

"Why not cover all of the cemeteries, to be on the safe side?" Phillips asked.

"It comes down to resources, Frank. I can order surveillance of each of the seven remaining cemeteries in the city, including those officers already assigned to sentry duty over the existing crime scenes, but it's not going to wash with Morrison."

"It's prevention—" Phillips argued.

"Not quite," Ryan disagreed. "It might help us to catch him but if he sticks to his usual MO the victim will already be dead by the time he reaches the gravesite."

Ryan stood back up again and rolled up his shirtsleeves.

"I'm telling you how it will play out, Frank. I'll sign off the resources and hope that we can keep the surveillance going for longer than just tonight. Morrison will find out and haul me in to justify the expenditure. She's a fair woman," he conceded, "but she has her own chain of command. We're all living with austerity cuts and this is the blunt edge of it. I'll bet you fifty quid that the officers I send out to guard the cemeteries this evening will be recalled by Monday at the latest."

Phillips let out a *harrumph*.

"Wish I could argue with you, lad, but the fact is you're probably right."

"It's hard being right all the time."

"Let's not start getting into the realms of fantasy." Phillips patted Ryan's arm and ambled back towards his own desk, leaving Ryan to flash a grin at his retreating backside.

In their quieter office down the hall, MacKenzie and Lowerson pored over the latest reports which had come through from the CSIs. Predictably, they confirmed that Barbara Hewitt probably died where she fell at her home in Rothbury. No alien substances or DNA samples were found mingled with the fermented residue of her bodily fluids; nor had there been any suspicious samples found inside the house or on any of the doors or windows not belonging to the old woman herself, or to her cleaner, Carole Dudley.

"Carole is five feet three and doesn't strike me as a killer," Lowerson remarked, to which MacKenzie found no argument.

"She wouldn't be first on my list, either."

"We're almost certain that Barbara let whoever it was into the house of her own accord?" Lowerson asked, although he already knew the answer.

"Yup," MacKenzie nodded, without looking up. "All of the windows and doors were locked, including the front door, which means that our killer took Barbara's house keys and locked up behind them. The keys aren't listed on the inventory, which means that they're still missing."

"And Carole is the only other person with a set of keys?"

"Yup, which we now have in our possession," MacKenzie said again, this time looking up to meet his weary eyes with older, wiser ones of her own. The sound of intense activity drifted from the incident room down the hall and she had noticed Lowerson looking up like a curious meerkat every few minutes.

"Focus, Jack," she snapped. "The rest of the boys and girls are working on what looks to be the Next Big Thing, whereas you're trawling through the house inventory of an old woman nobody seemed to care about."

"It doesn't matter to me," he said quietly but couldn't quite hide the sulk.

MacKenzie considered the potential cost-benefits of dishing out a good bollocking, but the hour was growing late and it had been an early start for both of them. Perhaps a good night's rest would help.

"It's not all about high profile cases, Jack," she said, before standing up to stretch out her aching muscles. She waited for her words to register but when no response was forthcoming, she waved her hand.

"Go and get some shuteye. I'll see you first thing tomorrow."

Lowerson scrubbed a hand over his stinging eyes and stood up, preparing to leave with his tail firmly between his legs.

At the doorway, he turned back.

"Mac, it isn't that I don't care. I just don't know where else to look. Nobody saw anything, forensics haven't found anything, and we stomped all around the centre of Newcastle today trying to find a lead, but we've come up blank. Nobody in Rothbury knows anything about it. We're waiting for Barbara's bank and telephone records and for the CCTV footage to come through but, until they do, we seem to be chasing our tails."

The sky was pitch black outside and MacKenzie's reflection was mirrored in the long windows of the room while her face remained shadowed.

"They always leave a trace, Jack," she said. "It's just a question of finding it. We're in the business of playing a long, disciplined game where no time is ever wasted. We're not glory-hunters but, take my word for it, the people of this region are grateful for every one we catch, even if they don't know it yet."

Before turning in for the night, Ryan and Phillips decided to pay a visit to Karen Dobbs' former drug dealer. After a short drive through the city centre towards the run-down edges of Walker and Daisy Hill, they pulled up outside two former council houses which had been knocked together and lavishly redesigned to include large faux-Grecian columns and a video-entry security gate that was almost as big as the house itself. Phillips jerked a thumb towards a fountain in the shape of Michelangelo's *David*, which dominated the tiny garden.

"Looks like Mr Pinks is a man of taste," he joked.

Ryan slammed out of his car. He strolled towards the ridiculous curved gates and stared at them for a moment. Then, without further ado, he stepped to the side and hopped over the boundary wall, which was less than two feet high.

Behind him, Phillips barked out a laugh.

"He'll have you for trespassing."

"A four-year-old could get over that wall," Ryan muttered, scowling at the ostentatious car parked outside, the fancy new windows and the shiny black door with its gigantic knocker that was so drastically out of place on this street, in an area where people struggled to make ends meet. Lewis Pinks profited from his neighbours' misery and he didn't have the basic decency to take his ill-gotten gains elsewhere. Instead, he lived amongst them, rubbing their noses in it daily.

Ryan ignored the knocker and raised his fist to bang on the front door.

A few moments later, a girl—you could hardly call her a woman—answered with a baby cradled on her hip. She was pretty, her fine hair dyed a brassy blonde and bundled atop her head. Her young face was heavily made up in a manner that reminded him of a kid playing dressy-up.

"What do you want?"

"Hello." Ryan ignored the sharp tone. "I'm DCI Ryan, this is DS Phillips. We'd like to have a word with Lewis Pinks, if he's at home."

"Why?"

"That's something that we need to discuss with him," he said gently, mindful of the fact that she couldn't be more than eighteen. "Is he in the sitting room?"

"Well…" She glanced behind her and jiggled the baby as it began to fuss.

"Don't worry, pet," Phillips gave her a fatherly smile and let the baby tug on his thumb. "We're not here for any trouble."

"Okay." She seemed relieved. "Let me see where he is."

She bit her lip and glanced around the street. At least they hadn't brought a squad car this time.

"D'you want to come in?"

"That's very kind."

They watched her move off down the narrow hallway and found their eyes drawn to the garish wallpaper: black, with shiny silver fleur-de-lis. The floor had been carpeted in bright white thick-pile.

Presently, their hostess returned and indicated that they should follow her into an open doorway.

They found Lewis Pinks sprawled on a black leather sofa with a can of lager in one hand and a television remote in the other. He wore a football shirt over jeans and he had the skinny look of someone who had suffered a malnourished childhood.

"Lewis Pinks?"

"Aye," he said, casually. *Too casually*, Ryan thought. "Who's asking?"

"DCI Ryan and DS Phillips, Northumbria CID," he answered, flashing his warrant card.

"You're a way from home," Pinks replied, referring to the fact that Tyne and Wear Area Command were usually the ones to pay him a visit. In fact, they were almost on first-name terms.

Ryan surveyed the man with mounting dislike and the girl hovered beside him while the baby sucked loudly on its hand.

"My throat is parched, pet. Do you think I could have a glass of water?" Phillips appealed to her.

The girl waited for any word from the Man of the House but when none was forthcoming, she moved off in the direction of the kitchen and Ryan took his chance. He recited the standard caution, which received a grunt of understanding.

"I'll cut to the chase. Karen Dobbs was found dead this morning. Do you know anything about that?"

"Naht."

No grief, no remorse, no surprise. Just a flat denial.

"Aren't you sorry to hear that the mother of your child is dead?"

"She says that her kid was mine, but it could have been anybody's. So what?"

"A DNA test proved that the boy is yours," Ryan said, mildly, "but we won't argue about that now."

Lewis slurped some of his lager and shuffled on the sofa.

"What can you tell us about Karen?"

"She was a junkie, man." He shrugged. "What did she think was going to happen?"

"Some people say you supplied the drugs," Phillips threw in.

Pinks set his can on a glossy side table and jabbed at the remote until the screen was muted. Then he stood up and planted his feet.

From his superior height, Ryan looked down his nose.

"If you've come round here to throw accusations and harass me, I'll get straight on the phone to my solicitor."

Ryan folded his arms and angled his head.

"Did you hear that, Phillips? Apparently, Mr Pinks feels harassed."

"Dear, oh, dear," Phillips tutted.

"Look, Lewis," Ryan said, tiredly. "We'll forget for a moment that you're a flea on the arse of society. Right now, all I care about is finding out who killed Karen Dobbs. When was the last time you saw her?"

"Haven't seen her in months."

Ryan told himself to be patient.

"Lewis, don't play games. We can both pretend that you're not a scheming little drug dealer until the cows come home but you're still the man who reported her missing this morning."

"I don't know what you're talking about."

"Look, we're not accusing you of her murder. Yet," Ryan added, silkily, and watched the man's face turn a shade paler. "All we want to know is how she led her life, whether you saw anything, or if you can help us to find who *did* kill her."

They could almost see the cogs turning in his head.

"We're tracing the call, Lewis, and if we find it came from you, we'll be back here to *harass* you again," Phillips added.

It seemed to do the trick, because Pinks licked his upper lip and swiped the back of his hand across his mouth in a nervous gesture.

"OK, look, I *might* have gone by her house now and then, just to see if she needed anything," he said eventually.

"Like the Good Samaritan," Phillips agreed.

"Exactly!" Pinks nodded vigorously and clearly had no appetite for sarcasm.

"Did you happen to make one of these charitable visits earlier today?"

"Maybe, I can't remember."

Ryan raised his eyes to the ceiling.

"Give me strength," he muttered. "Just tell us what you know about Karen and when you last saw her."

The capitalist living inside Lewis Pinks reared its ugly head.

"Aye, and what do I get in return?"

Ryan took a step forward, until they were almost touching.

"You get to keep both legs," he said, with a tigerish smile.

Pinks might have had some bravado, but he didn't have a death wish.

"Hey! I was only asking. Um, yeah, I saw her last Saturday. I usually go around on Saturdays." He stopped himself from saying 'to collect'.

"And?"

"Karen was into smack and she wouldn't turn down a bit of MD and all that," he said, as if describing her favourite packet of crisps. "She would usually run through her dole money by the end of the first couple of days. She'd try and tap up her old lady after that. If that didn't work, I—ah—I hear that she supplemented her income in other ways."

Standing in such close proximity, Ryan could almost feel this man's filth crawling over his skin.

"You *heard* that she supplemented her income. Let's just say it, shall we? Karen prostituted herself to get money for the drugs you supplied to her."

Pinks was about to flare up, when Phillips stepped smoothly into the breach.

"Allegedly," he said, then motioned for the man to continue his story.

"I never gave her nothing," Pinks spat out, but when both men continued to regard him with empty, unwavering stares, he licked his lips again and thought about how much he should say.

"Alright, yeah, alright. I knew she was in trouble with the law for putting it about." He held his hands up, as if the admission were a great concession on his part. "But what could I do?"

Ryan's eyes flashed, but his voice remained calm.

"Did the johns come around to her house? Where did she go, Lewis? Where was her corner?"

Some danger must have transmitted itself, because Pinks made another one of his wide-armed gestures.

"I heard, you know, on the grapevine, that she used to go down to the petrol station—the one at the bottom of Shields Road—and hang around the back so that the shop assistant wouldn't see her."

"You never happened to accompany Karen on any of these visits? Not even to buy a pint of milk?" Phillips asked.

"Nah, man, not my scene," Pinks said, derisively.

"Alright. What else did you happen to hear? Did Karen mention anybody who was giving her trouble, anybody who worried her?"

Pinks had the grace to look away. Karen had been in and out of hospital more times than he cared to remember. He'd heard the horror stories and seen the scars left on her body afterwards. It made him defensive.

"How the hell should I know? She was filthy, man, she asked for it—"

In a flash, Ryan had him up against the wall, one muscular forearm resting heavily against the other man's windpipe while he sputtered and gasped for air.

"How does that feel?" Ryan ground out. "Because that's how Karen felt while some bloke choked the life out of her, you piece of *shit*."

Phillips didn't bother to intervene because he recognised controlled violence when he saw it. Besides, in this instance he agreed with it.

Less than ten seconds later, Ryan released Pinks and the man bent over at the waist to draw gulps of air deeply into his chest. Ryan stepped back and waited until he looked up again.

"I'll report you!"

"Go ahead. In the meantime, I want to know anything else you remember. Otherwise, so help me, I'll come back and finish the job. Rely on it."

As they turned to leave, the blonde girl reappeared with two tall glasses of water she had garnished with little slices of lemon and ice. The baby had disappeared, presumably to bed, and Ryan looked at the water she held in her hands then back into her eyes. Sadness swept over him at the sweetness of this woman-child and the life she led with the man who had resumed his former position slouched on the sofa. He wondered what the future would hold for her.

"Thanks, love, but we'd best be heading off," Phillips said, then led the way out of the house.

Outside, he turned to Ryan with knowing eyes.

"Breaks your heart, doesn't it?"

"She probably thinks he's Prince Charming," Ryan answered, looking away.

"We can't save them all."

Ryan nodded briskly, then strode back towards his car.

CHAPTER 10

It was pitch black by the time MacKenzie let herself into her smart little house in Ponteland, a short drive from CID Headquarters. She wondered whether it was healthy to live so close to the office, to be on hand for any emergency that might arise, but work had always been her solace. The lack of companionship or wider social life hadn't bothered her; she was reliable and punctual and, if she said it herself, she was a damn good murder detective.

Then Frank Phillips had stomped into her life, shaking everything up.

Of course, she had known Phillips for years in a professional capacity. She had admired his calm, easy demeanour and ready sense of humour from afar. They had an amicable working relationship while his wife was alive, which had turned prickly in the years following her death as they acknowledged the unspoken attraction simmering between them. She didn't fully understand what had led her to take the plunge but something about Frank made it inevitable. It was there, in his eyes: endless patience, endless kindness. She never imagined that life could be so easy living with him, as she mostly did these days, and the panic she expected to feel had never come.

MacKenzie searched inside her satchel for her front door key.

There had been another concerning shift in her mindset recently. She had never regretted the lack of children in her life because she had never found any man she wished to procreate with. That was the way it had always been, and it made life simple. While other female friends rushed down the aisle or to the maternity ward, MacKenzie had remained content to be 'Auntie Denise' to their children. It had always been a relief to return to her tidy, stress-free home without the clutter of toys, the squeal of babies or the added responsibility. Life as a murder detective carried enough of a heavy burden and she didn't need any further complications. Besides, she wasn't sure that her professional life would be compatible with a family anyway.

But, just recently, she had caught herself wondering about it. As a woman in her forties, it was no small source of anxiety to find that she had fallen in love and, worse still, that the prospect of creating miniature versions of herself wasn't nearly as terrifying as it should have been.

Was she too late?

With these sobering thoughts crowding her mind, MacKenzie pushed away the day's mail with the toe of her boot and closed the front door behind her, then bent down to collect the small pile, taking it with her into the kitchen.

She dropped the mail onto the countertop alongside her bag and began to shoulder out of her coat. She slung it over the back of one of the wooden bar stools, then reached across to fill the kettle. Her eye came to rest on one envelope that stood out from the others. Setting the kettle to boil, she reached for it and frowned down at the neat black lettering. She didn't recognise the handwriting, nor did she know anybody who would normally use stationery like the expensive, weighty-looking cream envelope she held in her hand. There was no postmark, which meant that somebody had slipped it through her letterbox themselves.

With a shrug, she slid a finger under the flap and broke the seal.

Inside, there was a single sheet of paper that read:

Et ego te absolvo a peccatis tuis in nomine Patris, et Filii, et Spiritus Sancti.

Her fingers trembled against the paper and it fell from her hands, floating to the floor with a soft rustle in the silent house.

Plain-clothed police officers assigned to Operation Angel gave up their Saturday night take-aways and spent their evening sitting in unmarked vehicles around the city. To his surprise, Ryan won his argument with Morrison and dispatched a small army of officers to watch over the seven remaining cemeteries falling under the remit of Newcastle City Council, with extra surveillance assigned to Elswick and All Saints since they were due to host funerals the next morning. As day turned into night and the hours slipped slowly by, they sat stiffly in their cars, eyes aching under dim street-lighting while they completed an exercise equivalent to watching paint dry. Pairs of officers walked the perimeter of Elswick, valiantly covering an area larger than several football pitches.

Nothing moved, nothing stirred.

Under the same skies, men and women set aside their reservations about the Graveyard Killer and threw themselves into all that the city's nightlife had to offer. They ate and drank, danced and flirted, forgetting their fear as they surrounded themselves with laughter.

Amongst them was Tanya Robertson.

She filed out of the Tyneside Cinema with two of her friends after an evening showing of *North by Northwest*. Around her, the restaurants and bars opened their doors to swollen numbers of patrons over the long Easter weekend. A few years ago, she might have been part of their number. However, being a mother to two children did not allow her the freedom to relive her younger days very often. With a surreptitious glance at her watch, she noted guiltily that she would already be later than expected getting home and her husband would have struggled through bath and bedtime alone with the kids.

When her friends suggested a drink, she was tempted. How nice it would be to let her hair down and go out on the town. Then she thought of two cherub faces, scrubbed and dressed in teddy bear pyjamas and the decision was easy. Shaking her head, she wound her scarf around her neck and prepared for a chilly walk back to her car.

"Night, Tanya!" Arms linked, her friends smiled and waved her off.

"See you!"

Tanya turned away and looked forward to the comforts of home, humming the unmistakeable music of Bernard Herrmann and thinking fondly of Cary Grant as her heels clicked against the pavement. The remainder of her evening would likely be spent clearing up the debris of toys and food crumbs from the sofa, but it would be worth it if she and her husband could spend the rest of the night snuggled up together. Smiling at the thought, she walked a little faster.

The streets were crowded with couples and gangs of teenagers prowled around, hoping to sneak into one of the pubs. She chuckled as she watched one group swagger towards a burly-looking bouncer dressed all in black, who promptly turned them away.

There was nothing to compare with the optimism of youth.

She veered right along a side street and suddenly the pavements were empty. The shops had closed their doors for the evening and the sounds of merriment from the city centre grew distant. The temperature had dropped and she rubbed her hands together to counteract the cold, picking up her pace as the grey outline of the multi-storey car park came into view.

Not far to go now.

Tanya watched two cars exit the car park. The yellow-and-white striped barriers lifted and fell like mechanical jaws and her eyes followed their progress until the red glow of tail lights vanished around the corner. The street fell back into gloomy shadow and she paused, suddenly unsure.

Should she turn back?

Chewing the inside of her mouth, she stared into the gaping entranceway and shivered involuntarily. She had used the multi-storey car park more times than she could remember, so there was no reason to feel frightened. Besides, there was a security guard on duty twenty-four hours a day and CCTV cameras all over the place.

She clutched her bag and dashed inside the cavernous entranceway. To her right, the security office glowed a yellowish-green and a figure huddled inside. They didn't look up as she passed the thick Perspex window and made her way towards the stairwell.

Inside, the stairs smelled of stale urine and her nose wrinkled, but it was still preferable to the confined space inside the lift where the stench would be magnified. She plodded upwards to the fourth level and strip-lighting flickered overhead, lending her skin an unnatural white glow. She gripped the metal banister and swore briefly as the rusty metal nicked her palm, drawing blood. Sucking at the wound, she heard the clunk of the ancient lift as it swung into action somewhere behind the concrete walls and she clattered up the stairs, hearing her own breath as her heart rate quickened.

She approached the fourth level and began to root around for her car keys in the large black bag which hung from her shoulder. She smiled at the crumpled tissues and small bags of sweets she had bought for the children, pulling a face as her fingers met with something sticky.

As she reached the top step, the lift doors creaked open. Tanya didn't look twice at the man who stepped out, except to note that he was dressed smartly. She mumbled a polite word of thanks as he held open the door to the parking level and she started to step through it. Sounds of drunken laughter echoed up the stairwell from the ground floor and, ahead of her, Tanya could see her car, waiting to take her home.

She never made it through the doorway.

Her bag fell to the floor, sweets spilling onto the dirty concrete as her hands flew to her throat. Her fingers clawed at the material of her scarf as it pulled tightly across her windpipe, cutting off the air supply to her bursting lungs. Her mouth formed a horrified 'o' as she fought for oxygen and her nails scratched at her own flesh to ease the constriction, missing the man who held himself apart and dragged her back into the stairwell, mumbling words in a language she didn't understand.

The air in her chest exploded and the fine blood vessels beside her eyes burst into a lacy network of dark red. Her hands fell away and, after a moment, the man let out a long, shaking breath.

"There, now," he murmured.

Ryan considered the selection of CDs sitting beside the discreet sound system in the living room and decided that, even if he was in the mood for Miles Davis, succumbing to moody jazz would be altogether too predictable in his line of work. Instead, he swallowed his pride and selected *Simply Red's Greatest Hits*, telling himself that it must be for the love of a good woman.

The lady in question poked her dark head around the door as the music began to flow and flashed him a smile.

"Now there's an unexpected choice," Anna said, handing him a glass of Pinot Noir. "Are you hungry?"

"No, thanks—I grabbed something greasy with Phillips on the way back," he confessed.

"I always knew Frank was a bad influence."

He watched as she settled herself on the sofa and tucked her long legs up beside her, cradling the wine in both hands to warm it while she watched him over the rim. Love washed over him followed swiftly by thoughts of Nina Ogilvy-Matthews, whose love had been taken from her.

"You look troubled," Anna said quietly.

Ryan shed his jacket and hoped that the action would help him to shed the weight of the day. He set his mobile phone in the centre of the coffee table within easy reach and then sank onto the sofa beside her. Warmth spread across his cold skin when Anna folded herself against him.

"I think he's going to kill again tonight."

Worry flickered across the hard planes of his face and Anna wished she could soothe it away, or tell him that he was wrong. But his instincts had never been wrong so far. Ryan's concern for the dead and his constant quest to avenge them was an integral part of his nature. For as long as the investigation lasted, they became a part of his life, a part of *him*. Even more worrying was his ability to step into the mind of a killer; a peculiar skill almost like method acting that allowed him to see the world through their distorted vision.

No doubt about it, Anna thought—she had fallen for a man with many layers. But she was coming to understand him more each day.

"You can't stop it happening?"

Ryan took a sip of wine, then set it back on the coffee table.

"No, I can't. We don't have enough information. But we might get lucky if he shows up at one of the cemeteries."

"They're calling him the Graveyard Killer," Anna said. "I heard on the news that he goes for redheads."

Ryan took one of her hands and simply held it.

"They've got it right, for once. Yes, this one likes the redheads." He looked across at her and felt stupidly grateful that she didn't fall into that category. "But we can't impose a curfew on every woman with red hair. I need a lead, something that narrows down the field…"

"And the only way you get that is with a combination of time, effort and another victim," Anna realised.

Ryan nodded silently.

"It makes me sick to think of it but, yes, that's the truth. We need him to kill again so that we have a better chance of finding him."

"You will," she said, with absolute certainty.

He looked across and into her eyes. There were deep emotions swirling there and a heart big enough to drown himself in.

"I love you, Anna."

"Same goes, detective. Now, let me distract you from your gloomy thoughts with some frivolous wedding nonsense."

Ryan didn't know how she managed it, but he found himself laughing, long and loud.

"You're unstoppable. Come on then, let's hear it."

She gave him a mischievous look.

"I was thinking about our first dance while I was watching *Saturday Night Fever* the other day—"

"I don't like where this conversation is headed."

"I know it would take practice but why don't we do some sort of choreographed routine?"

It took him a full ten seconds to realise that she was joking, then he grabbed her.

"You had me going for a moment, there."

"There was genuine fear in your eyes."

"Any self-respecting man would have felt the same," he said, then thought of how Phillips would no doubt have thrown himself behind the idea of a retro dance routine, white suit and all.

Anna lay sprawled against his chest.

"We could still go along for a couple of practice sessions," she said. "Just so we know what to do with our feet."

Ryan lifted her up for a brief kiss.

"Wait right here," he said.

She watched with frank curiosity as he rose from the sofa across to the main light switch and flicked it off, then wandered around the room turning on the smaller side lamps. Then, he moved back to the CD collection gathering dust on the shelves. Ryan knew exactly what he was looking for, and a moment later the velvety strains of a Louis Armstrong ballad filled the room.

He turned to her and held out a hand.

"Shall we?"

She found herself moulded against his long body as they moved slowly around the room in time to the music. She laughed when he spun her away from him and then curled her back against him, where she tucked her head snugly underneath his chin. She felt the strong beat of his heart through the cotton shirt he wore and knew that she was home.

"Still want to do a more jazzy routine?" he murmured.

She smiled against the warmth of his neck.

"This'll do just fine."

A soporific combination of red wine and relaxed company lulled Ryan into the sleep that he craved. His body registered Anna curled beside him, slotted together like two parts of a jigsaw, and it was that which prevented the nightmare from fully taking hold of his unconscious mind.

Despite the detachment, his body jerked as he relived the pain of a knife being driven into his flesh; his skin felt the cold *slap* of water as he fell backwards into the murky depths of the river, and his heart rate quickened at the remembered fear. But a small voice told him that he was alive and that he had survived.

Only a dream. Only a dream, he repeated.

His mind transported him across space and time to his childhood on the Devonshire coast where he and his sister had played by the sea. This time, he felt a rush of warm water as he sank beneath the waves and emerged again triumphant, shaking the water from his eyes. In his sleep, he frowned against the glare of the summer sun.

Then the sky turned dark. Clouds raced across to blot out the sun, leaving him shivering and cold. There was no longer sand beneath his feet but wet soil oozing between his toes. He looked down at his hands and they were filthy, his nails crusted with dirt. The sky was almost black now.

Not even the moon shone its glimmering light over the cemetery and suddenly he was falling again; down and down into the grave.

He was breathing hard and his mind told him: *stay calm, it isn't real.*

But his body fought against the limbs that entangled him, trying desperately to shrug off the pale arms that clawed at his throat and kept him from rising up again. Soil fell like raindrops and began to cover his eyes and mouth, so that he could hardly breathe.

"*Ryan!*"

He woke with a start and was instantly alert.

"What?"

Anna scowled at him through the early morning light.

"Nothing, unless you count nearly giving me a black eye."

Ryan took in the tangled bedclothes and his racing heart, then remembered the dream he had been fighting to escape.

"I—sorry. Are you alright?"

"I'm fine." *Her shoulder was aching.* "Was it a nightmare?"

"Yeah." He sat up bare-chested and rested his forearms on his knees. "Not as bad as they used to be, but it's been a while since I had one."

"Forget it." She ran a hand over his back and rested her head on his shoulder. She waited a beat, then added, "I know some other distraction techniques besides wedding planning, you know."

Ryan's eyes glowed silver in the morning light.

"You seem to be a multitalented lady."

"You're not wrong."

Overnight, a layer of thick fog settled heavily over the neighbouring cities of Newcastle and Durham. Rain pattered against the windows and turned soil into mud, washing away all manner of sins. Miles away in the depths of the quiet countryside, one man stood with his face upturned and his arms outstretched. The water washed over him like a baptism, cleansing his soul and clearing his mind of shame and fear, so that he could continue.

When he opened his eyes, there was no throbbing headache. There was no self-doubt.

He knew what he had to do, and God had granted him the strength to do it.

He turned and walked back through the rain.

CHAPTER 11

Sunday, 27ᵗʰ March

Easter Sunday

There was an air of expectancy when Ryan arrived at CID Headquarters well before eight o'clock the following morning. The incident room was full despite the early hour and at any other time Ryan would have been encouraged by his team's conscientious attitude.

But not today.

"What the hell is going on?"

Several pairs of tired eyes faced him.

"Nothing, sir," one of the plain-clothed surveillance officers answered. "We were at Elswick Cemetery all night and there was no movement."

"Same story at Jesmond and All Saints," another chimed in, followed by a chorus of other frustrated voices until Ryan held up an imperious hand. He already knew there had been no suspicious activity overnight because he would have been the first to hear about it.

"Hold on a minute. If nothing suspicious happened in any of the cemeteries, that should give us some hope because it's less likely that another woman lost her life." He paused to let the words find their mark, then bellowed out, "Now, who do I have to kill to get a coffee around here?"

A bit of dark humour never hurt anybody, he thought, singling out one of the constables who was sitting twiddling his thumbs. Ryan waved him over, planted a wad of tenners in his hand and told him to come back laden with caffeine and baked goods for the whole team. From the corner of his eye he spied Phillips arriving with MacKenzie beside him, looking pale.

"Alright, whoever was on shift last night, take a break and come back after a few hours' kip. The rest of you, get to work."

He made a beeline across the room.

"What's wrong?"

Neither MacKenzie nor Phillips was surprised that it had taken less than a minute for Ryan to realise that something was amiss.

"I received a note yesterday, posted by hand through my letterbox sometime while I was at work."

MacKenzie retrieved the cream notecard which was now encased in a plastic evidence bag and handed it to Ryan.

His gaze swept over the note.

"It's the same man," Phillips gritted out, in a voice that was shaky with rage. "This is a warning."

Ryan turned to MacKenzie. He judged her to be unnerved but not so much that she couldn't do her job.

"I'm not sure that it is the same person," she said slowly, then reached out for the note again to feel its weight. "Frank, you said that the handwriting expert thought both of the previous notes used cream card, about 200 grams? This feels slightly heavier than the others." She transferred the note between her hands. "And although the writing is neat and tidy, it looks different."

Ryan nodded his agreement.

"The previous two notes used a permanent black marker pen whereas this one looks like black biro," he put in. "I seem to remember the letter 's' being more elaborate in the previous two."

Phillips listened to their analysis and tried to bank down his anger so that he could think clearly.

"So he used a different pen this time. That doesn't change the fact that some bastard put a note through her door!"

"*Her*? Is that the cat's mother?" MacKenzie asked in a deceptively mild tone.

"Howay, lass, I'm worried for your safety!"

Ryan took a subtle step backwards while they worked it out, amused to note that Phillips' accent became more pronounced when he was angry or upset. It was oddly endearing.

"I appreciate that, Frank, but I'm perfectly capable of taking care of myself. I'd like to work together on this, rather than having you treat me like the frightened little woman."

Phillips stuck his chin out, but he could never hold onto an argument when faced with irrefutable logic.

"You know I never meant to do that. But even if it isn't him, it's still some copycat who's fixed his sights on you, and if he so much as comes within twenty yards—"

"You'll plant a fist in his face," Ryan finished for him, judging it safe to return to the conversation. "That's fair enough. In the meantime, let's get this note across to the CSIs for print-testing and then on to the handwriting expert, who should be able to confirm if our assumptions are correct."

"I spoke to my neighbours this morning," MacKenzie added. "Nobody saw anything because they were out for most of the day and some are away for the weekend. No CCTV on my street, either."

Ryan nodded, thinking quickly.

"Although I don't think it's the same man, we can't be certain. I want you to exercise extreme caution, Denise. Keep Lowerson beside you at all times—that's an order."

A short while later, Ryan and Phillips stepped to one side and spoke in hushed tones.

"I want you to move me across to the Hewitt investigation," Phillips demanded. "I need to be with her."

Ryan sighed.

"I understand how you're feeling, Frank, but I can't do that. Not right now."

Phillips stuck a finger in Ryan's chest, which was met with a single raised eyebrow.

"You better transfer me *now*, lad."

"Phillips, get a grip on yourself. MacKenzie is a big girl and she has a mean left hook. Besides, she has Lowerson with her and you know as well as I do that he'd sooner throw himself in front of moving traffic than let anybody harm her."

Phillips retracted his finger and Ryan carried on in the same comforting voice.

"Look at the facts. I admit it isn't pleasant but the Graveyard Killer doesn't issue warnings before he takes a victim, he just takes them. He leaves a note with their bodies after he's finished, that's his signature."

Phillips grudgingly conceded that point.

"I'm not downplaying the threat, Frank. Killers sometimes change their MO to avoid detection. MacKenzie matters to all of us and we won't allow anything to happen to her. I'm going to order surveillance of her home for the next forty-eight hours, day and night. You and I both know she won't thank me for going behind her back, not after the little chat you two just had."

"Aye, she won't thank you, but I will."

Ryan gave Phillips a bolstering slap on the back.

"Thought that would put the smile back on your face."

"Just so we're clear, if she asks me about it, I'll deny all knowledge and say that you acted alone."

"Perfectly reasonable," Ryan said. "I'd do the same thing myself."

To distract herself from the alarming possibility that she had become a target, MacKenzie did what she did best and knuckled down to the serious business of finding whoever had murdered Barbara Hewitt. She supposed one of the few positive aspects of the Hewitt case was that no ritual or religion seemed to be involved. She remembered the good old days when people killed other people to inherit their money or to see off an unwanted spouse.

With no family to inherit her comfortable nest egg and no husband to covet, MacKenzie was forced to acknowledge that neither of those old-fashioned motivations seemed to apply to the murder of Barbara Hewitt.

More's the pity.

With that in mind, MacKenzie spent the best part of her morning piecing together disjointed CCTV footage that had come through from the various cameras positioned around Newcastle and Rothbury. Although there were none around the cul-de-sac where Barbara Hewitt had lived, the Automatic Number Plate Recognition cameras and city centre cameras had come up trumps. She put Lowerson to work and they ran through the grainy footage covering the hours between ten-thirty and five p.m. on Friday 18th, which was the last day anybody had seen Barbara Hewitt alive.

"This is sapping my will to live," Lowerson complained.

"I've spent better mornings," she agreed, then clicked the *pause* button to take another look at an image which had popped up.

Lowerson peeked around the side of his screen.

"Hey, Mac? I, ah, heard about the note and I just wanted to say I've got your back. It was probably sent by some sad case who lives with his mother and spends too much time playing video games—" He started to laugh and then broke off, abruptly realising that he had just described his own present life circumstances.

"But anyway," he continued hastily, "you don't ever have to worry that some crank is going to hurt you."

MacKenzie looked into his earnest brown eyes and felt warmed from the inside out. She was about to tell him that she was really more than capable of looking out for herself and had done so, very successfully, for forty-three years. Instead, she let her heart lead her head.

"I appreciate that, Jack. I really do."

He gave her a ludicrous wink and returned to his screen. She turned back to the slow-moving images rolling across her own desktop computer and propped her head in her hands. Then, she caught an image of Barbara.

"I think I've got her, over here."

Lowerson paused his own reel and moved around to look over MacKenzie's shoulder. She zoomed into a blurred image of Barbara Hewitt walking past the Tyneside Cinema on Pilgrim Street.

"I agree, that looks like her. She's carrying her Marks and Spencer bag and the timing says 11:28 which fits her movements. She bought her knickers at M&S at 11:09 and took twenty minutes to wander down Northumberland Street, popping in and out of a few shops, and then wandered past Grey's Monument. Now, the cameras have her here on Pilgrim Street on her way to the cinema."

"That doesn't fit," MacKenzie disagreed. "She was due to be at The Lobster Pot on Grey Street for lunch at one o'clock and she wasn't at the Tyneside Cinema until nearer two o'clock, in time for the afternoon showing. This footage shows her strolling past the cinema much earlier, at 11:28. That's over two hours before she was due to be there. Where was she going?"

"She had time to spare," Lowerson thought aloud. "Maybe she fancied a walk."

MacKenzie swung back and forth in her chair for a few seconds and then tapped a fingernail against her computer screen.

"Do you see that, Jack? It was raining on Friday 18th."

"So?"

"Why would she want to take a leisurely stroll in the rain without an umbrella? Especially since she'd had her hair done and we already know she was a pernickety sort of woman."

Lowerson pursed his lips and had to admit it didn't fit their existing profile.

"Yeah, I can't see her as the sort of woman who liked drinking pina coladas and getting caught in the rain."

MacKenzie grinned.

"You know what this tells me, Jack? It tells me that Barbara was heading to her next destination, which could be of great interest to us. Carry on going through the footage covering this quadrant—"

She marked out a radius surrounding the Tyneside Cinema.

"All of the other places we know she visited are within a five-minute walk of the cinema, the New Bridge Street car park, and The Lobster Pot. She must have made another stop which hasn't shown up in our search so far."

"I'll chase the bank for Barbara's transaction history," Lowerson offered. "But it's Easter Sunday so I won't get my hopes up."

MacKenzie nodded.

"You do that. I'm going to look at the map again and see what's in the immediate area. Who knows? She might have been on her way to meet somebody and that somebody might have been the person who killed her."

To alleviate the distinct sense of cabin fever which was working its way through their central nervous systems, Ryan and Phillips made a break for it and headed out into the field. Riding high on adrenaline and righteous indignation at the prospect of another serial killer running amok in their city, they decided to put their energy to good use at the All-American Diner.

Phillips remembered the garish, fifties-themed bar-cum-restaurant from his last visit, when they had been investigating the murder of a young waitress who had worked there. But it wasn't the employees that concerned him now, it was the man in charge. Jimmy 'the Manc' Moffa was the youngest of three brothers who had migrated to Newcastle seeking to establish their own empire when life in Manchester had become too heated, even for them. The Moffa brothers had fingers in every pie, from drugs and money laundering to prostitution. There were several ongoing investigations into Jimmy Moffa's 'legitimate' businesses, but witnesses had a strange tendency to disappear or to change their stories.

But it was Jimmy's personal dealings with their former Detective Chief Superintendent, Arthur Gregson, which offended them the most. It was generally believed that he had aided and abetted the murder of Gregson's wife and had carried out countless illegal business transactions. No trace of Cathy Gregson had ever been found and, unfortunately, no trace of Jimmy Moffa had been found at the crime scene either.

As Ryan and Phillips entered the Diner through the brushed-aluminium double doors, they were met by a team of burly security staff dressed in black.

"Can we help you boys?"

Ryan rocked back on his heels.

"Maybe you can. I quite fancy a milkshake, now you mention it. How about you, Phillips?"

"I could murder an Irn Bru," the other smiled toothily.

The bouncers looked uncertainly amongst themselves and one spoke hastily into a tiny microphone attached to the lapel of his suit.

"You need a reservation," he replied.

"Aww, that's a real shame. I guess we'll have to make do with speaking to your boss. Tell him we're here." Ryan stared down the bouncer who seemed to be doing all the talking.

"Mr Moffa isn't available."

Ryan sighed.

"That's a pity. We were looking forward to catching up, weren't we, Phillips?"

"Aye, it's been too long."

"Guess we'll have to go and get ourselves a court order, maybe even arrest warrants for these gentlemen who seem to be obstructing our lawful investigation."

Phillips tutted. "Doesn't look good, that sort of thing, when you're renewing your door supervision licence. Not good for business either, when we put up our neon barriers and close the street outside, slowing up all the traffic. Probably around rush hour, too." Phillips scratched his chin while he thought aloud. "There'd be a lot of talk. Oh, yes, a *lot* of talk."

"Wait a minute, now, wait a minute," one of the bouncers said nervously. He could do without another pop on his record. "I'll have another word with Mr Moffa."

Less than a minute later, they were ushered through a side door and along a darkened corridor leading to Moffa's plush office at the end. A heavyset man with a pock-marked face and shoulders the size of small planets sat on a chair outside the varnished oak door and seemed to be playing Candy Crush. He looked up as they approached and drew himself up to his full height, which was somewhere in the region of ten feet in Phillips' conservative estimation.

"These are the ones, Ludo," one of the bouncers said, and Ryan guessed that the nickname came from an excessive use of hard drugs at some point in the man's life, judging by the slightly unfocused look in his eyes.

The bodyguard said nothing, but turned and led them inside Moffa's office before closing the door behind them. He settled back against it, barring their exit with his wide bulk.

Moffa's office hadn't changed in the past year, Phillips thought. It was still ultramodern and monochrome with its highly-polished surfaces, black tiled floor, white leather sofas and mirrored desk which looked like it belonged in a Las Vegas hotel.

"Detectives." Moffa gave them what could reasonably pass for a smile, but he didn't bother to get up, nor did he offer them a seat. His pale blue eyes moved between Ryan and Phillips before coming to rest permanently on the taller of the two.

Ryan preferred to stand and, in any case, it didn't take Moffa long to realise that by remaining seated he gave Ryan the feeling of having the upper hand.

Hastily, he stood up.

"Now that you've threatened your way in here, why don't you tell me what you want?"

"We're investigating the murder of a woman who was last seen exiting the Diner on Thursday night, at around nine-fifteen. We would like you to provide us with the relevant CCTV footage to assist our investigation."

Ryan kept his eyes trained on Moffa and watched him walk slowly around the desk, like a leopard on the prowl.

"And why would I want to do that?"

"Let's call it a sense of civic duty," Phillips put in, with one of his affable smiles.

Moffa let out a sound halfway between a laugh and a snarl.

"I already do a lot for this city," he said, without any sense of irony. "I provide jobs, pensions…why should I stick my neck out again? The last time I helped any of you lot out, I ended up having to close this place down for a month after you accused me of covering up a murder. Do I look like the sort of person who would be stupid enough to get involved with something like that?"

Ryan decided to take the question literally and swept his eyes around the room, taking in the expensive furnishings, then back to the man himself who wore a sharply tailored suit complete with heavy gold cufflinks and a matching watch. A fat diamond stud twinkled in one of his ear lobes.

Finally, he looked into Moffa's eyes, which were like empty pools of glacier water. Deadly and numb from the cold.

"Yes," he replied eventually. "Actually, you do."

A muscle twitched near Moffa's left eye and Ryan had the distinct impression he was about to snap, but suddenly he stepped away and returned to his desk chair.

"I'm afraid I have a very busy day, gentlemen, so I'll ask you to leave."

Behind them, Ludo shifted, ready to propel them out of the door.

"I'm not finished yet." Ryan didn't move an inch. "I meant what I said to your little gang of T-Birds in the foyer. If you refuse to hand over the CCTV voluntarily, I will get a court order."

He paused and flashed a self-deprecating smile.

"I don't mind telling you that the magistrate has a soft spot for me, so I doubt there'll be a problem. Then, before you know it, Phillips and I will be back here to pay you a visit. It's remarkable what our tech team can do to recover deleted files, isn't it?" He turned briefly to Phillips. "Who knows what *else* they might come across while they're seizing the footage?"

Moffa stared at Ryan for a full minute in complete silence while neither of them moved. Phillips felt a trickle of sweat down the back of his neck as the tension mounted.

"You're bluffing," Jimmy said eventually.

"I guess we'll find out, won't we?" Ryan turned his back and made for the door, with Phillips following closely behind him. Ludo hesitated for an instant and then stepped aside to let them pass.

When the door was firmly closed behind them, Moffa leaned back in his chair and smiled like a cat.

"What do you want me to do, boss?" Ludo asked.

"Give them the footage," he replied. "I couldn't give a shit."

"But I thought—"

Ludo hulked his way across the room when Moffa pulled a small, cream note out of one of the locked drawers in his desk and tapped it against his nose.

"Ryan has more to worry about than some dead ginger bitch. I received a very interesting proposition today, my friend, which means that you're going to be kept busy over the next few days."

He passed the note to Ludo, who squinted down at the writing and then looked up again with comical surprise writ large on his simian face.

CHAPTER 12

Ryan and Phillips emerged from the Diner onto the rain-washed pavement. Instead of heading straight back to his car, Ryan steered them in a southerly direction towards Newcastle Central Station. They walked in a comfortable silence while each man tried to divest himself of the discomfiting, grimy residue left over from their visit. They made a pit stop for coffee but neither had any appetite for food and they passed several cafés and restaurants without interest.

"We need somebody to give us a steer on the religious side of things," Ryan declared, once the caffeine had begun its miraculous work.

"I already did a full background check on the priests who were due to conduct the funerals up at West Road and Heaton. Both of them are fully alibied," Phillips put in.

"That doesn't rule out any of the others. If the killer has some affiliation with the Roman Catholic faith, then we need to speak to somebody inside its fold and try to get a handle on it. Besides, I'd rather we were seen to be working together."

Phillips nodded and stirred a couple of sachets of sugar into his coffee.

"My memory of the brief time I spent as a Catholic schoolboy is limited to freezing cold Sunday mornings chasing Amy Gallacher around the pews," he recalled with fondness.

Ryan smiled and downed the remnants of his espresso before scrunching the paper cup in his hand and lobbing it into a nearby recycling bin.

"Well, all of my information comes from the internet so I'm no better off. I've got Morrison nagging at me to 'build bridges'—whatever the hell that means—and I haven't got a clue where to start."

Ryan threw him a baffled look and Phillips had to smile.

"There's been a lot of daft talk on the news. The press are running all the old stories about abuse within the church and trying to make connections. No doubt Morrison's had the Bishop on the phone mouthing off about it."

"I know. People are clutching at straws wherever they can find them. The sooner we put this to bed, the better."

Phillips stopped and looked around to get his bearings.

"If you want to start building those bridges, we're just around the corner from somewhere you could start," he said. "St Mary's. That's the Catholic cathedral and the seat of the Bishop of Hexham and Newcastle."

"Talk about throwing me in at the deep end," Ryan grumbled. "You know the holy water starts to fizz whenever I come near it."

With a bark of laughter, Phillips prodded him forward.

The Cathedral Church of Saint Mary occupied an imposing position overlooking the mainline station into Newcastle. Its grand nineteenth-century architecture was 'Gothic-revival', so the placard told him, but as Ryan stood at the bottom of a short bank of steps leading up to the cathedral's entrance, he saw only a tower of expensive stones paid for by the poorest inhabitants of industrial Newcastle.

"Impressive, isn't it?" Phillips said, coming to stand beside him.

"Depends on your point of view."

"Apparently, the architect who designed it was famous for working on the Houses of Parliament."

Ryan's face grew even more ominous.

"What leads people to hand over their last few quid for this, Frank?" He flicked a wrist in the direction of the cathedral. "Building this great edifice, this architectural *triumph,* came at a cost. I have to wonder whether the poor of inner-city Newcastle would have preferred food in their mouths than a great big show house where they were expected to go and confess their sins."

Phillips looked up at the sky, watching an aeroplane blazing a trail through the thick grey clouds. The rain had slowed to a drizzle, which settled in a moist blanket on his face.

"You don't set much stock by religion," he said. "As it happens, I don't worry much about Heaven or Hell myself. But for some people these stones represent a *community*." Phillips nodded his head towards the cathedral, "God or no God, the people who come here know one another. They watch out for one another, through the generations. It isn't for us to put a price on that."

Religion and politics, Ryan thought and swiftly changed the subject.

"Speaking of watching out for one another, I've set up the surveillance we talked about. I've got eyes on MacKenzie's house right now and throughout the night. If somebody tries to make another poisoned-pen delivery, we'll intercept them."

A flash of violence passed across Phillips' face but was quickly suppressed.

"I appreciate it. Truth is, I don't know what to make of it all. If it isn't the Graveyard Killer, it's some copycat or somebody with a grudge who managed to find her address. It's not good, whichever way you look at it. We're dealing with somebody who's a couple of sandwiches short of a picnic and that gives *me* the heebie-jeebies, so I can only imagine what it's doing to *her*. Where do I start looking to find this creep?"

Ryan gave his shoulder a reassuring squeeze and pointed towards the open cathedral doors.

"Let's start in there."

The atmosphere inside the cathedral was hushed. The strains of a mighty organ reverberated around its vast, vaulted walls and lone individuals were scattered among the rows of wooden pews with their heads bent in prayer. Ryan watched as an old woman stopped and did a funny sort of curtsy before stepping into a pew to join them. Candles flickered along the wall beside a statue of Saint Mary, her gentle face coming to life in the candlelight. Cataloguing the marble and the woodwork, Ryan was reminded of the last church he had visited on a windy hilltop near Hadrian's Wall. It had been tiny and unpretentious, completely lacking in artifice. Now, he looked up at an enormous golden crucifix which hung front and centre beside the altar, demanding his attention.

Deliberately, Ryan turned away and studied the layout. It might represent the seat of the Bishop of Hexham and Newcastle, but day-to-day management fell under the remit of its Dean; a priest by the name of Father Conor O'Byrne. He spotted a side door marked, 'CLERICAL OFFICE'.

"This way," he threw over his shoulder, before striding down the long central aisle, his footsteps clicking against the chequered tiles as he went.

The door to the Clerical Office opened and a middle-aged woman with thick glasses raised her eyebrows at the sight of the tall, good-looking detective and his shorter associate. She led them through to an anteroom, where they found Father O'Byrne seated behind a chic mahogany writing desk. A pretty mullioned window provided some light, and the sound of rainfall pattered melodically against the glass. In the corner of the room, a long cream robe hung neatly from a wooden clothes horse with a silk amice draped beside it.

"Thank you, Jean." The Dean rose fluidly and moved around the desk with a friendly, open-armed gesture. "Good morning, gentlemen, how may I help you?"

His voice betrayed the gentlest Irish burr and he was dressed down in plain black slacks and shirt, the collar at his neck the only indication of his vocation.

"May we speak with the Bishop?"

"I'm sorry, Bishop McNally is attending a conference in Italy. You're welcome to make an appointment for when he returns?"

"We're here on official business." Ryan held open his warrant card for inspection. "DCI Ryan and DS Phillips, Northumbria CID."

"Of course, I should have recognised you straight away." He looked between them. "I'm Father O'Byrne. I act as proxy in the Bishop's absence so perhaps I can assist? I presume this relates to the deaths of those poor women. I've seen their murders reported several times in the press, not to mention the persistent use of *The Priest* or *The Graveyard Killer* as a catchphrase for their killer."

He indicated a couple of visitors' chairs.

"Yes, we are investigating." Ryan chose not to apologise on behalf of the press.

"I am saddened by the news. However, I'm not sure how I can be of any great help, chief inspector. I didn't know either woman personally, nor anything about how they came to die. I've already taken the liberty of asking my colleagues and they concur; neither woman was a regular member of our congregation here at St Mary's and I can't find their names listed on any of our registers. Of course, they are in my prayers." He paused for a moment in a mark of respect for the dead, then clasped his hands together lightly as if he considered the matter closed.

Ryan made himself more comfortable in one of the sagging visitors' chairs and smiled.

"We don't expect you to have any knowledge of the individual circumstances of either victim, but evidence found at the crime scenes indicates that their killer has an affiliation with Roman Catholicism, in one form or another."

O'Byrne leaned forward slightly, linking his long fingers loosely atop his desk. He fixed Ryan with a direct blue stare.

"The news reports mentioned notes found beside each body. I presume their message contained a religious sentiment. Last rites?"

Ryan nodded.

"Absolution, written in Latin."

The priest sighed.

"There have been cases where individuals have taken their own lives and, fearful that they would not be received into God's merciful care, they have written a suicide note with hopes of absolving themselves."

Ryan forgot the reason they were there and asked a question to satisfy his own curiosity.

"And would it? Would it absolve them?"

O'Byrne looked across the desk into Ryan's silver-grey eyes and saw a simmering pot, one that could easily boil over. He chose his words carefully.

"As in other religious denominations, the taking of one's own life is considered a sin in the eyes of God. However," he inclined his head, "God is compassionate and we must try to be as well. It is a question for each priest to determine on an individual basis. He is best placed to understand the members of his congregation."

Ryan looked away and listened briefly to the constant pitter-patter of rain against the glass panes, then his eyes swung back again.

"The fact is, Father, we're not dealing with suicide in either case. Everything points to murder."

"I see. That puts a different complexion on matters, at least from your perspective. From mine, I'm sad to say there is a long and colourful history of disturbed individuals using church doctrine to justify their own ends.

Many books have been written and films have been made on the subject."

"I appreciate that," Ryan said quietly. "We have no intention of fuelling religious antipathy or misplacing blame, if we can help it."

"And yet, our groundskeepers spent this morning scrubbing fresh graffiti from the walls of this house," the priest returned.

"Bricks and mortar," Ryan shot back, "I'm talking about saving lives."

Phillips cleared his throat and decided it was an opportune moment to step in.

"We're trying to get inside the mind of the person we're looking for. We believe it's a man perpetrating these crimes—it's the most likely probability—and these notes of absolution are his signature, you might say."

Father O'Byrne turned his attention to the sergeant.

"You said they were written in Latin? Nowadays, very little is spoken in Latin. The Church recognised that it needed to be more accessible to ordinary people, so that the words of God could be more readily understood and there's been a big shift towards the standard use of English."

"Even the Creed?"

O'Byrne raised an eyebrow.

"Are you one of the ones we lost, sergeant?"

Phillips pursed his lips.

"Never mind…" The priest flashed a grin. "You're by no means the only one. We'll have to do better."

Ryan interjected, determined to keep the conversation firmly on track.

"You're saying that the use of Latin in these notes could reflect an older, more traditional approach? Somebody who knows the old ways?"

"It's just an observation," he replied, but Ryan could see the sense in it and made a mental note regarding the potential age range of their perp.

"What's the procedure on funerals?"

"What do you mean?"

"I mean, say your granny was a Catholic and you need to arrange her burial. What do you do?"

If O'Byrne was surprised at Ryan's lack of knowledge about Catholic practices, he didn't show it.

"The family would need to arrange burial space at their chosen cemetery by instructing a funeral director or by contacting their local council directly, but in the first instance they would probably speak to their priest. If it was already known that a loved one was likely to pass, their priest should have been on hand to administer to the deceased and support the grieving family well ahead of a funeral."

"Is there some sort of list or accessible database within the diocese to show who is going to be where and when?"

O'Byrne seemed surprised.

"You mean like an online calendar? Well, yes, there is." He frowned. "Like any large organisation, we have an intranet system which is accessible across the diocese.

It contains the diaries of each priest and it helps us to organise our activities."

Ryan gave him a level look.

"Do you employ an IT manager?"

"I don't like where this is going, chief inspector."

"I don't like it either, Father, but the families of those dead women take precedence over our own sensibilities, don't you think?"

The Dean inclined his head. "Point taken."

He reached for a scrap of paper and wrote down the details for the remote IT management company with oversight of their intranet system. "Here are the contact details. I feel I must warn you, it's unlikely that the Bishop will sanction the release of internal information without the appropriate paperwork."

"Thank you, Father—I'll take steps to secure it."

"I'm happy to help wherever I can, chief inspector. I believe you will be able to exonerate the priests of this diocese very quickly. In return, perhaps you would have the goodness to exercise caution when dealing with the press? Unfounded gossip can greatly damage the good work we do in this city."

Ryan's eyes flashed.

"We are not in the habit of spouting nonsense to the media. On the contrary, we share information we deem to be pertinent on a case by case basis, always with the hope that it will encourage people to assist our investigations." He paused, leaning forward a fraction in his chair. "Interaction with the press has always been and will continue to be a matter solely at the discretion of CID."

"And you, in particular."

Ryan smiled and rose from his chair.

"Thank you again, Father O'Byrne. You've been very helpful."

———

Outside, Ryan paused beside an iron statue of Cardinal Hume while Phillips took a call from the office. He rolled his shoulders to loosen his muscles and breathed deeply in an effort to clear his mind. By the time Phillips ended the call, he was calm once again.

"That was Control," the older man explained, a shadow of worry flickering in his button-brown eyes. "A Missing Persons report has come through and it's looking high risk. Some bloke called Oliver Robertson rang the emergency line this morning to report his wife missing."

Ryan searched his sergeant's face.

"What are you telling me, Frank?"

"I'm telling you that Tanya Robertson has been missing since around nine-thirty last night. She's thirty-six and a natural redhead."

Ryan felt his stomach roll.

"It could be nothing," Phillips tagged on, but concern was written all over his face.

"And it could be something," Ryan murmured. "Let's go."

CHAPTER 13

They found Oliver Robertson pacing around the family waiting room back at CID Headquarters. A cup of cold tea sat on one of the tables and had obviously been there for some time, judging by the milk skin which floated on top. Robertson didn't seem to have noticed; he continued to pace the floor, running trembling fingers through his dishevelled hair. His eyes were ringed by dark circles and he wore the look of a man who hadn't slept. An older woman perched on one of the chairs beside him, folding and re-folding the material of her blouse in the kind of nervous gesture Ryan had seen a hundred times before.

Both of them turned as he entered the room with Phillips, who came bearing fresh cups of steaming hot tea.

"Have you found her?"

Robertson surged forwards, searching their faces for answers.

"Mr Robertson? I'm DCI Ry—"

"I know who you are!" Robertson almost shouted, before he visibly drew himself in. "I'm sorry, chief inspector. It's just—please, don't give me any pleasantries. I need to know where my wife is."

Ryan stood a couple of feet in front of him and looked him square in the eye.

"We don't know where she is, Oliver. We're going to do all we can to find out."

Robertson's eyes watered.

"She—Tanya has red hair. I read in the papers that... that..."

He couldn't go on. Belatedly, he registered the simple fact that CID would not have become involved if they didn't strongly suspect that Tanya was already dead. The blood drained from his face and he swayed on his feet.

"Let's sit down for a moment." Ryan took Robertson's arm and led him towards the older woman. Robertson all but melted into a chair and she reached across to take one of his limp hands.

"I'm Oliver's mother," she explained softly. "Tanya's parents are looking after the children."

"Thank you for coming." Ryan told himself to remain detached but he already knew the truth, just as he had known that the killer would not miss an opportunity to strike again on Easter Sunday. He had hoped that an uneventful night would pass and they would have more time.

But there was no more time.

"Mr Robertson, I've read the Missing Persons report you gave this morning," he began. "I'm sorry but I need to go over some of the details with you again."

Robertson held a hand over his eyes for long moments, as if to shield himself for a little while longer, then let it drop back into his lap.

"I'll tell you everything I can."

Ryan reached for a chair and turned it around so that his arms rested along the back of it. He faced the man head on, compelling him to focus.

"Talk me through what happened last night."

Robertson took a shaky breath and accepted the cup of tea that Phillips pressed into his hands, heavily laden with sugar.

"Tanya went to the cinema with a couple of her friends. She goes every week, or every other week. It's her way of taking a bit of time out. The kids can be a handful, sometimes." He tried to smile but failed dismally. "The showing was at seven-thirty at the Tyneside Cinema. They were due to come out of the cinema at around nine-thirty."

"But you reported her missing this morning?"

Robertson nodded.

"I know how it sounds. It's just that..."

He looked across at his mother for support and she gave his hand a squeeze.

"Just tell them, it's alright."

"It feels disloyal, but...I should tell you that Tanya suffers from postnatal depression. She's only recently started on a course of medication after she went missing for several hours a few weeks ago. The doctor said it would take a couple of weeks for her hormones to even out. Last night, I thought that it had happened again and that she would come back when she was ready. I worried all night and I rang the hospitals, just in case, but when she still didn't come home by three a.m., I rang the police."

Robertson's lips quivered and he clamped them together so hard that the skin turned white around the edges of his mouth.

"I understand," Ryan said quietly. "Tell me, when was the last time you had contact with her?"

"I kissed her goodbye at about six-thirty last night and she drove into town. I had a text from her just before seven-thirty to say she was about to go into the cinema, and that was the last I heard from her. I tried calling at ten o'clock but her phone had a dead tone."

"What happened then?"

"I thought maybe her battery had died, but then it would still go to voicemail, wouldn't it? It didn't make sense, so I rang her friends." He gave their names again. "They were in a bar, so it was hard to hear, but they said that they'd all left the cinema on time. They went for a cocktail and Tanya headed off to the multi-storey to get her car. That was it."

"Which multi-storey?"

"I don't know for sure but I think she would have used the one nearest the cinema."

"New Bridge Street," Phillips chipped in.

"That's the one. I rang them this morning and they said there was no sign of her car." He shook his head and a tear leaked from the corner of his eye.

"Phillips?" Ryan turned his head for an update.

"We're searching for Mrs Robertson's car and trying to get hold of the CCTV footage now."

Robertson looked between them with wide, frightened eyes.

"If her car is missing, that means she might be alive. Doesn't it? Don't you think?"

They remained silent, letting him ride out his pain.

"And—and she hasn't been found in any of the cemeteries, has she?" he continued, in a voice thick with desperation. "It must mean she's driven somewhere. I've probably wasted your time. Maybe she just needed to get away—"

Robertson ran out of steam and dropped his head onto his mother's shoulder, where the old woman cradled it like a baby, rocking slightly while her eyes shone with grief.

Ryan swallowed the hard lump in his throat and stood up.

"We'll do everything we can."

Ryan was unnaturally quiet when they returned to the incident room, eliciting several wary looks from his staff.

They had seen a wide range of mercurial moods from their chief inspector over the years, which they were learning to predict. He was often short-tempered and intolerant of anything less than a job well done. His voice spoke of privilege but his preferences were unpretentious. He was physically striking, a fact which he rarely used to his advantage and mostly detested as a distraction for the superficial mind.

Ryan could be sharp, cutting even, towards those he considered incompetent or deceitful. He was prone to long silences during which he ruminated on the possibilities surrounding a case and he knew the value of silence in drawing people out. He had a quick humour and appreciated the same in others. He was not a violent man, nor did he seek it out, but there lingered the suggestion of violence simmering beneath the surface.

The mask he wore to look upon the dead gave the impression of indifference, but it hid an emotional well of feeling.

Right now, it looked like that well was about to flood over.

In his hands, Ryan held a freshly-printed photograph of Tanya Robertson. He looked down at her image and thought of her husband and children, whose lives were on the cusp of being shattered forever. Gently, he pinned it to the murder board, a little distance apart from the existing photographs of Krista and Karen, to account for the fact that none of them knew for certain that Tanya was a victim of the Graveyard Killer. Not yet.

"Frank?"

Phillips was never far away.

"She's a goner, isn't she?" the sergeant said, between mouthfuls of Jaffa Cake. Phillips was not a proponent of self-deception any more than Ryan.

"She's not in any of the cemeteries in Newcastle," Ryan replied. "We know that after last night's surveillance."

Phillips thought for a moment.

"It could be that she's still alive and we're all worrying for nothing but my nose says otherwise." With theatrical timing, his nose twitched to emphasize the point. "He might have stashed her somewhere while he waits out the investigation, hoping that the surveillance will stop."

"He doesn't know the cemeteries are under surveillance," Ryan pointed out.

"I don't think this one is stupid," Phillips returned. "He'd have to assume we'd watch the cemeteries, especially after the second victim."

"Karen." Ryan preferred names to numbers. "You're thinking he still has Tanya?"

"It's possible."

"It doesn't quite fit." Ryan rolled his shoulders and turned to stare at the large map on the wall. "He kills them and he dumps them within a few hours. He doesn't like to hold onto them."

Ryan's eyes traced the line he had drawn on the map to mark out the boundaries of Newcastle City Council and the answer became all too clear.

"He's gone outside the city limits." Ryan spun around, eyes glowing. "The bastard knew we'd be watching the city, so he did the most obvious thing in the world and went to one of the cemeteries outside."

Phillips nearly choked on the remainder of his cake.

"But how will we find her? There are"—Phillips did a quick count—"eleven local council authorities in the North East, not counting Newcastle. I mean, there's North and South Tyneside, Gateshead, Northumberland, Durham—take your pick. All of them with oversight of the cemeteries within their district and all of them within driving distance of where Tanya might have been snatched."

"Then we'll use our heads," Ryan snapped. "First, I want to know about funerals which took place today across all of the cemeteries in the remaining eleven council districts, particularly Catholic burials. Second, I want to know which of those cemeteries also fall within the remit of the Diocese of Hexham and Newcastle and would be easily accessible for somebody with their own transport. Third, I want to know who accessed the information, Frank. Give me a sodding *name*."

Phillips opened his mouth to say something, then thought better of it and simply turned on his heel. Ryan watched him hurry across the room to his desk, where he and PC Yates contacted the outside council authorities with all speed. Then Ryan turned and placed a call to Faulkner's team to issue an advance warning that the services of his CSIs might be required in the none too distant future.

***

After another hour of scrupulous work, MacKenzie and Lowerson narrowed down the radius of their search into Barbara Hewitt's last known movements to within a five-minute walk of the Tyneside Cinema, The Lobster Pot and the New Bridge Street car park. Discounting large office buildings, their choice was reduced to a contest between a pilates studio, a small art gallery, a betting shop, several fast food restaurants, and St Andrew's Catholic Church.

The two detectives hit the streets once again. They began by speaking with the manager of the pilates studio but they were informed that it was a 'members only' establishment with no record of a woman by the name of Barbara Hewitt. Next, they braved the stale, disheartening interior of the bookies' shop but there was no suggestion that Barbara had enjoyed gambling or had any money troubles—the two went hand-in-hand so frequently. They made polite noises at the ugly artwork in the gallery and, in exchange, they were treated to a private showing of the CCTV footage from Friday 18th which confirmed a partial sighting of Barbara Hewitt walking straight past the entrance and on to a different destination.

Couldn't blame her, really.

Spurred on by the small victory, MacKenzie and Lowerson continued to ask around the fast food shops, but to no avail. In the end, when all other possibilities were eliminated, the most improbable of destinations became the only one remaining which fit the timings. Despite all they had been told about Barbara Hewitt's staunch atheism, where else could the dead woman have whiled away over an hour of her spare time?

The answer was simple.

Barbara had gone to church.

***

The police had been around again, asking questions and throwing accusations.

Mick Jobes watched the spotty-faced constable and his bum-chum walk slowly back to their squad car and felt sweat pool at the base of his spine. Another woman was missing and they think she was taken from his car park. They had asked for the CCTV footage and he'd told them exactly the same story he'd told MacKenzie and Lowerson yesterday.

The cameras had a fault but the technician was due to come out on Monday. He'd be in touch as soon as the problem was rectified.

He'd even managed a smile.

The truth was, the cameras hadn't worked properly in years. Every now and then, the one beside the main entrance crackled into life, but the ones in the stairwells hadn't worked the entire time Mick had been there. Management liked to keep up appearances—they said that having them there would be a deterrent for any would-be criminals. But the police had come back and he'd been forced to lie to them, again.

Mick wiped a thick hand over his face and reached for a grubby rag to blot away the perspiration running across his forehead and into his eyes.

They said they had spoken to Jamil, the night security guard, who had told them he stopped by to pick something up yesterday afternoon and Mick wasn't at his post when he should have been. Mick had watched them talking, casting suspicious looks in his direction now and then.

Then, they had asked him his whereabouts.

His *whereabouts,* he sneered.

He would've had more respect if they'd just come out and said they thought he killed those women.

He started to sweat again.

Mick had told them to mind their own bloody business, then thought better of it and told them he was probably taking a piss when Jamil thought he was off-post. Wasn't a man entitled to take a piss on a twelve-hour shift?

The coppers had given him one of those empty, bug-eyed stares and told him to cough up the CCTV footage, which would either corroborate his story, or not.

He had given them the finger but the fact was that he was worried. His hands trembled uncontrollably and he needed a drink. The booze had worn off, leaving a foul taste in his mouth and a monstrous headache as a reminder that he must have doused himself in ale the night before.

There were fresh scratches on his neck and along the left side of his face.

He caught sight of his reflection in one of the empty CCTV screens on the countertop beside him and saw the fear in his own eyes. He couldn't tell the police where he was yesterday afternoon, or at any time during the night. He couldn't tell them how he came to have scratches on his face.

He couldn't remember.

The sounds started again, inside his head. The bombs. The cries. The shouts for help.

A woman's voice.

When he looked back at the blank CCTV screen, he saw other faces beside his own.

Dead faces.

He began to cry, fat rolling tears which dribbled down his ruddy face.

CHAPTER 14

When news broke that another redheaded woman had gone missing, the media response was swift and merciless. The press set up a permanent camp outside CID Headquarters and condemned a lack of police presence on the streets, as if that alone would deter a killer with an agenda. The long honeymoon period following the collapse of the Circle cult had given Northumbria CID a brief respite from the usual complaints about lacklustre policing, but the public had a short memory. Fear had that effect; images of Krista Ogilvy-Matthews, Karen Dobbs, and now Tanya Robertson had been plastered across the front pages and their faces were now embedded in the public consciousness. The mood of the city had changed. Last year, Northumbria CID had cleaned up its act and divested itself of corruption, as far as it could. It had been heralded as a shining example to other police constabularies from all corners of the land and its senior officers had enjoyed a celebrity status never seen before.

Now, that was all forgotten as another major threat presented itself. It was back to business as usual and if Ryan's halo had slipped a little, that was no bad thing in his opinion because he had never asked for it in the first place.

More irritating was the wider domino effect which the Graveyard Killer left in his wake: small bands of extremists took the opportunity to hurl paint and eggs at the walls of St. Nicholas' Cathedral, betraying not only a troubling level of intolerance but also a fundamental misunderstanding of the nature of the investigation, for St Nick's was an Anglican church, not a Roman Catholic one.

Chumps, Ryan thought.

As he had predicted, pressure had come to bear on Chief Constable Morrison from the upper echelons of the police hierarchy and, in time-honoured fashion, she had passed this on to Ryan who in turn favoured Phillips with his wrath at the whole sorry situation.

"Bloody buggering hell!"

"Couldn't have put it better myself," Phillips agreed.

"What does Morrison think I am? Psychic?"

"No use getting all het up about it." Phillips was, as ever, the voice of calm amid the chaos, even if he felt jittery himself.

Ryan passed a tired hand over his face and looked up at the clock on the wall. It was only four o'clock.

"I think we're making progress," Phillips said, with unfailing optimism. "We've got a list of thirty-five funerals that were scheduled for today, across all the other council areas, twelve of which were Catholic burials."

"That sounds promising." Ryan perked up a bit. "That number could have been a lot worse."

"Aye, well, don't get too carried away. Do you want the good news or the bad news?"

"Hit me with the bad, first."

"Maybe you should sit down."

Ryan went halfway and leaned back against the side of his desk.

"Well, the Diocese of Hexham and Newcastle covers five 'episcopal' areas, ranging across eight council areas: Newcastle, Gateshead, North Tyneside, South Tyneside, Sunderland, East Durham, South Durham and Northumberland."

Phillips paused briefly for any comment but none was forthcoming, so he carried on.

"Within each episcopal area, there are a number of 'deaneries'. Father O'Byrne has oversight of the Newcastle city centre deanery, for example."

Again, no comment.

"Those twelve Catholic burials range across four council areas: Northumberland, South Durham, North Tyneside and Sunderland. All of the funerals have gone ahead which means that the graves have all been filled over."

Ryan looked at Phillips for a full minute while his brain processed the magnitude of the operation that lay ahead. When he spoke, his voice was unruffled.

"These figures only apply if we presume that the killer stuck to his previous method and used a grave that had already been dug for him," Ryan cautioned. "It's perfectly possible that he decided to dig his own grave, as he did for Krista. Is there any way to narrow the search even further? On the face of it, we're going to have to exhume twelve coffins in four counties to see what lies beneath them."

A grisly prospect.

"Luckily, that's where the good news comes in," Phillips said enthusiastically. "PC Yates has been yapping at the heels of the IT manager at Newcastle City Council and she's really come through. It turns out that the IT systems over there are actually pretty decent—"

"Wonders never cease."

"Aye, you can say that again. It means there's a digital record of every access made to the Bereavement Services database of forthcoming burials in the district. They sent through the data and the bottom line is that everybody is accounted for. Nobody except the three members of the Bereavement team have accessed the database in the last week and all three of them check out."

He licked the tip of his finger and flipped over to the next page in his notebook.

"I also spoke to the remote services team who manage the integrated computer system for Hexham and Newcastle Church Diocese. I think I put the fear of God into him—ha ha—because some bloke sitting at his desk in Glasgow has just forwarded me a six-hundred-page log of all the individual accesses made to their shared calendar in the past week, alongside the corresponding login IDs. The problem is, almost everybody logs into the shared calendar on a daily basis and there are hundreds of church and admin staff in the Diocese. There's no way of being able to tell suspicious activity apart from normal activity from the login data alone."

Ryan pinched the bridge of his nose.

"Remind me again how this is *good* news, Frank? You've just told me that almost everybody connected with Newcastle City Council has an alibi and we already know that the cemetery ground staff check out, as do the grave diggers and the funeral directors. Now you tell me that we'll have to trawl through a list as long as the Yellow Brick Road to try to figure out if it's somebody within the church."

As the words left his mouth, the penny dropped.

"Phillips, did I ever tell you, you're a genius?"

'Not often enough, lad," the other replied with a twinkle.

"Well I'm telling you now," Ryan declared. "The Diocese of Hexham and Newcastle spans several neighbouring council districts."

"Aye."

"Which would explain how our killer might know about burials due to take place in any one of the council districts in the area, making it less likely that he is affiliated with any particular *council* and more likely that he is connected to the *church* in some way or another."

"Aye," Phillips said again.

"Which means that we're closer than we thought we were. That's good work." He began to pace as he thought of the next steps. "What about the priests who conducted the funerals today? Are there any names you recognise? Anybody whose name comes up twice?"

Phillips scratched his chin.

"Not so far, guv. But I have another bit of good news: the visit we paid to Jimmy Moffa seems to have worked, because that ogre he calls a bodyguard dropped off some CDs earlier containing the CCTV footage from Thursday night, when Krista went missing. I've had a look and they show her walking away from the All-American Diner at 21:13, alive and kicking and in the wrong direction for the taxi rank at the station. It's looking like she planned to walk home. At the same time, I had a trawl through the city centre CCTV and I've got her heading north from the Diner, through the centre, in the direction of home. The last working camera is just before the Tyneside Cinema on Pilgrim Street, which has her passing at 21:24. I've got nothing after then."

Ryan marked the final sighting on the map.

"That makes two victims snatched in the same area of town, Frank—coincidentally free of CCTV coverage. I don't like it."

"Aye, it smells off to me."

"You know what else sits in the area?" Ryan tapped a knuckle against the map. "St Andrew's Church."

Ryan compared the locations where their victims were assumed to have gone missing with the nearest Catholic church in the area.

"St Mary's is only a short drive from where Karen Dobbs lived, in the west end of town."

Phillips made a rumbling sound.

"Both of them are within the Hexham and Newcastle Diocese and both fall under the Deanery of Newcastle City Centre."

"And we found a leaflet for Narcotics Anonymous at Karen's house, which is held at St Andrew's on Friday nights. I want you to ring Nina Ogilvy-Matthews and Oliver Robertson. Ask whether their spouses had any known connections with either church."

On Sunday afternoons, St Andrew's Catholic Church hosted a soup kitchen to feed some of the hungry people who lived on the edges of Newcastle society; the homeless, the poor, or those who were simply in need. As MacKenzie and Lowerson stepped through its beautiful arched doorway they were struck by its hospitality and, had he been there, Ryan might have agreed. Community spirit leaked from every orifice. The last vestiges of murky daylight streamed through the pretty stained-glass windows and provided a stunning backdrop for the modest, unprepossessing altar at the head of the church. Everywhere else was crammed with people chatting and laughing in huddled groups, or in a long line waiting patiently with mismatched crockery bowls for their turn at the tables holding four large soup cauldrons. The ladles were wielded by a group of volunteers and, as they moved closer, MacKenzie recognised one of them as Paul Cooke.

"Well, well," she murmured under her breath, fixing a smile on her face.

Lowerson clocked him and made a funny whistling sound between his teeth.

"Wonder what Cooke's doing here," he muttered.

As if sensing their regard, the owner of The Lobster Pot looked up suddenly and the soup ladle he held in his hand froze in mid-air. He sent Lowerson a polite smile across the room but his eyes passed quickly over him and came to rest upon MacKenzie.

Once again, she found herself the uncomfortable subject of his scrutiny and it made her angry because he had not said anything inappropriate, nor had he even acted inappropriately. If he had, she might have had reason to say something, but in the meantime she was left with the muddling sensation of being the object of his unwanted desire.

At that moment, another man appeared at her shoulder.

"Can I help you?"

MacKenzie turned and was greeted by a pair of arresting blue eyes framed inside the handsome, slightly tired-looking face of the priest of St Andrew's. Though she would proclaim to all and sundry that she loved DS Frank

Phillips, she was only mortal and could mourn the loss of this particular man to the rest of womankind, given the vows of chastity he must surely have taken.

"Hello." She held out a hand and found it clasped in a brief but firm handshake. "DI MacKenzie and DC Lowerson, Northumbria CID."

"Father Conor O'Byrne," he replied.

"You're the parish priest?"

"No, Seamus is accompanying the Bishop on a trip to Italy, so I and another of my colleagues are sharing his duties while he is absent." He paused and smiled down at MacKenzie. "Do I detect a fellow native of the Emerald Isle? County Kerry, perhaps?"

MacKenzie could not help but smile back.

"Right enough, Father. You've got a good ear." She turned her mind to business. "We're investigating the death of a woman called Barbara Hewitt."

Lowerson produced a picture and showed it to O'Byrne.

"We're trying to trace this woman's last movements. Do you recognise her?"

"Yes, I do. She never told me her name but I recognise this lady from, perhaps, a week ago?"

MacKenzie and Lowerson only just held off doing the happy dance. Here, finally, was the breakthrough they had been waiting for.

"We'd be grateful if you could tell us everything you remember about your interaction with this woman."

"Of course." He gestured for them to follow him along the aisle towards a more secluded spot inside one of the front row pews, away from the din of diners beside the entrance. When they had settled themselves, he began to recount his story.

"The lady came in seeking to confess her sins last Saturday… no, it would have been Friday." He pulled a face and then cleared it again. "Yes, definitely Friday. I remember because she was really quite insistent that somebody should hear her confession. As I say, I am not the parish priest of St Andrew's and there are set times when confession is heard. Still, she would not take 'no' for an answer, so I agreed to hear it."

MacKenzie already knew the answer to her next question, but she asked it anyway.

"Can you tell us what was discussed?"

He looked at her as if she should have known better.

"A priest is specifically required, on pain of excommunication, not to divulge anything discussed in a confessional. It is part of my vocation and part of the sacrament of confession. I'm sorry, inspector, that I can't help you on this occasion."

Lowerson looked on in disbelief.

"Are you kidding me? The woman has been murdered— surely, that's more important than some church rule?"

The Dean adopted a patient expression, one that he had worn many times before.

"It can be a difficult concept to explain to those who do not follow the faith but let me try. God's law is considered higher than any man-made law and, as such, we should seek to cleanse our souls through His forgiveness. For the many everyday minor or *venial* sins we commit, a direct confession to God through prayer will suffice. However, in the case of grave or *mortal* sins, confession is necessary otherwise those sins will crush the spiritual life out of the person's soul."

Lowerson was about to say something when MacKenzie put a restraining hand on his arm.

"What *kind* of mortal sins would require confession, Father?"

The Dean smiled, pleased that she had caught on.

"In the simplest of terms, a mortal sin is that constituting a grave or serious matter. It must have been committed with the full knowledge of the individual, both of the sin and of the gravity of the offence. A person must have committed the offence whilst in full possession of their free and God-given will."

"When I was a girl, the priest told me to look to the Ten Commandments to understand what constituted a mortal sin."

"It's a good source," the Dean agreed.

Lowerson managed to drag his jaw from the floor to ask another pertinent question.

"Do you remember how long she stayed? Is there anything you can tell us about her movements?"

The Dean relaxed again now that the ethical questions had passed.

"Yes, I can. I seem to think that she arrived sometime late morning, or perhaps around noon, then left an hour later. Her confession was...extensive."

"How can you be sure about the timings?"

The Dean flushed.

"Ah, well, I remember feeling quite desperate for a trip to the gents." He gave them a pained smile. "As I say, her confession was a long one. I glanced at the clock when we finished and then made directly for the amenities. I'm fairly sure it was just before one o'clock."

Lowerson grinned as if they had shared a manly joke.

They asked him a few more questions but they had already learned something important; Barbara Hewitt had returned to her faith for some reason, something she was compelled to confess or run the risk of losing her immortal soul. MacKenzie and Lowerson decided to renew their search into the woman's past, convinced now that it held the key to everything.

CHAPTER 15

MacKenzie drove swiftly along the A1 towards Rothbury. Traffic in the opposite direction was heavy with people returning from a weekend by the sea, but the road north was blessedly clear and she put her foot down hard to beat the setting sun.

Lowerson sat beside her with his smartphone in hand, skimming through the data they had accumulated on Barbara Hewitt. The light from the screen glowed white against his face, lending it a rakish air as he frowned down at the screen and chewed thoughtfully on his lip.

"I'm getting an 'out of office' message from the compliance officer at the bank and no response from anybody at HM Revenue and Customs, but the telephone company is feeding through its data."

MacKenzie signalled to overtake a slow-moving lorry.

"And?"

"There's hardly any activity on her account and nothing since last Wednesday, two days before she died. As for the numbers she called, a few of them are '0800' numbers, call centres and things like that."

"One of them will probably be the company that runs the New Bridge Street car park," MacKenzie commented.

"Yeah, to make her complaint." Lowerson nodded. "As for the rest, I'd need more time, guv."

"Speaking of the car park, did we ever hear back from Mick about that CCTV?"

"Nope," Lowerson said roundly. "I've called the office a bunch of times but nobody is picking up."

"Alright, Jack, we'll stop by on our way home later and try speaking to the other security guard. Mick is a liability at the best of times. Until then, let's use our heads," she murmured, and flipped down the sunshield to protect her eyes from the glare of the sun as it glimmered low on the horizon. "We need to find out what was so bad, what affected Barbara so much that she went back to church. It's there somewhere in the fragments of her life, we just need to find it."

"Everybody has told us she led a boring life," Lowerson said. "She probably ran over a pigeon on the road and decided she was in danger of losing her place in Heaven."

MacKenzie flashed a grin.

"There'll be a skeleton rattling around in Barbara's closet and I bet it'll be a bloody big one. We'll root around her house and see if we missed anything on the first sweep. She was obsessive about routine and order; there's bound to be something in one of her drawers or in one of her old picture albums."

"Can I at least put some music on until we get there?"

"Sure, I think there's a CD in the glove compartment—
The Corrs: Greatest Hits."

Lowerson sent her a pained expression, which was
studiously ignored.

Sister Mary-Frances Creighton was a sprightly woman of
eighty-five. After spending nearly sixty of those years in the
service of God, she believed that she had Him to thank for
her robust constitution. That, and her daily walks along the
river. Those quiet, stolen moments away brought her peace
from the rest of the world and allowed her to commune
with her God.

Not that there had ever been any answer. In any other
sphere of life, talking to yourself for sixty years would be
grounds for committal. But Mary-Frances had always
followed her heart and in weaker moments she had allowed
the majesty of the natural world to remind her of God's
creation.

Now, as she neared the end of her life, she found herself
doubting everything she had ever believed. With each
passing day her body grew weaker. She could hardly sleep
and, when she did, her mind recalled the events of the past
and she wondered if she had done enough to atone for that
single, unforgettable misstep.

She hoped so.

Dear, merciful God, she hoped so.

A spasm of rheumatism shot through her right hip and she stopped at one of the benches scattered at intervals along the river, sheltered by high banks on either side. She eased her weary body onto the weathered pine and heard it creak alongside the metal joints in both of her hips. She could still remember how slender her hands used to be, before arthritis riddled the bones and swelled the knuckles which now rested on her plain black habit.

Vanity, she thought, with a small shake of her head.

Looking out across the water, she didn't mind that the day was overcast and grey, or that night would soon fall. The cold weather didn't help her old bones but the sounds of the river eased her soul while she rubbed absently at the ache in her leg. It was restful sitting there surrounded by God's handiwork. She watched a seagull swoop down to fish for its dinner in the shallows and smiled.

Sister Mary-Frances remained there for a while longer huddled inside her thick coat until she began to feel her legs stiffening up again. She was on the verge of manoeuvring herself off the bench when she spotted the tall figure of a man walking towards her along the pathway.

He walked quickly, glancing behind him and across the riverbank regularly, but this particular stretch of the River Tyne was hardly ever busy, a fact he was relying on for the next few minutes.

Sister Mary-Frances decided to wait on the bench in case he turned out to be one of the local residents who might be able to help her home. She pasted a friendly smile on her face and, to all the world, was the epitome of a kindly old nun.

As he approached, he felt the rage consume him. It rushed through his veins until his hands began to shake and it was an effort to keep himself under control. To make matters worse, she continued to look up at him with that *ridiculous* smile on her face. He wondered what she could possibly have to smile about. Surely, she must know that her time had come.

But when he looked more closely, it became obvious that she hadn't even recognised him.

Of course she hadn't.

She had absolutely no idea why she was about to die but she *should*. She should have spent every day for the last twenty-six years wondering and worrying about when this moment would arrive. Perhaps, after so long, she thought that the truth would never come out. That he wouldn't find out about her mendacity, the lying *bitch* that she was.

"Good afternoon," she said.

Her face crumpled as she spoke. It reminded him of an apple gone bad, its skin collapsing and rotten all the way to the core. He didn't know whether to laugh or cry, but neither emotion dulled the all-consuming fury.

"You know me." His voice sounded ragged, even to his own ears.

Her face remained politely blank and then it cleared again, the skin stretching back across her bones like a paper fan.

"Oh, *hello*! I'm sorry, it sometimes takes me a moment. Help me up, would you?"

He considered his next move. The place was deserted; there were no dog walkers on this lonely section of the riverbank. He decided to make a quick alteration to his plans and then stepped forward to haul her off the bench.

"You have sinned."

She let out a small sound of pain when his hands clamped brutally on her upper arms and he yanked her upwards.

"You're hurting me!"

He began dragging her towards the choppy water, hardly needing any strength at all against her pathetic mewling cries and the featherweight blows she inflicted.

"Help! *Help!*"

He silenced her with a heavy gloved hand which blocked her nose and mouth. He felt the need rise up inside him, the terrible pleasure he found in taking life and was tempted to move his hands to her neck.

Not this time, he thought, regaining control of himself.

He leaned in close to her ear, so that the last thing she would hear was his voice inside her head.

"*For Grace,*" he hissed.

He flung her into the river and afforded himself the luxury of watching as the old woman's arms flailed around her and the heavy material of her habit began to drag her beneath the cold water. The current finished the job and, within thirty seconds, she was fully submerged.

He closed his eyes and gave thanks to God, tugging the rosary from beneath the folds of his shirt and touching it to his lips.

Amen.

When MacKenzie and Lowerson arrived in Rothbury, the place was a ghost town.

They drove through the empty streets, past the shuttered window of Sally's Snips and around the war memorial in the town centre until they reached the cul-de-sac where Barbara had lived. A single street lamp shone its scanty light beside the entrance but the remainder of the street was shadowed. The sound of their car engine elicited a couple of twitched curtains but nobody emerged from the safety and warmth of their homes because most of Barbara's neighbours were pensioners or couples with young families, and neither demographic was inclined to stick their necks out.

Standing outside Barbara's little bungalow in the falling darkness, MacKenzie could easily see how a killer could have come and gone without being observed. All they needed to do was park a couple of streets away and approach on foot to ensure that nobody heard a thing.

MacKenzie pulled back the police barrier tape which still hung across Barbara's front door and slid the key into the lock. As the door swung open, Lowerson flicked the light switches on and off a few times but to no effect; it seemed the power had already been turned off at the mains. Instead, he selected the 'torch' setting on his phone and shone the beam into the hallway.

Inside, the air still reeked of a noxious combination of hydrogen sulphide, methane and other gases which made for the unique scent associated with death, mingled with a fetid odour of spoilt milk and rotten vegetables wafting from the direction of the kitchen. Lowerson coughed and held the cuff of his jacket in front of his nose and mouth, but there was no escaping it. It saturated their clothes and hair.

"Let's try the cupboards, first," MacKenzie said, reaching for a small tub she kept inside the inner pocket of her coat.

One of the advantages of being older than her detective constable was being able to predict unpleasant situations such as this. She dabbed a little of the minty cream underneath her nose to alleviate the smell and then held it out to Lowerson.

"I want to see family records, medical records, and any employment or financial records we haven't been able to recover so far. If you see any albums or mementos, grab those too."

"The CSIs brought in a bunch of stuff on Saturday but I've already looked through it and there's nothing out of the ordinary."

"That's why we need to go further back in time," MacKenzie reiterated. "If it isn't obvious, then we need to dig deeper."

As they moved from room to room, they experienced the odd sensation that they were not alone. Barbara's presence followed them through the house, watching over them as they rifled through her things and picked apart the fabric of her lonely life. Neither detective uttered a word but they both felt it and they worked quickly, eager to return to the land of the living.

At precisely the moment Lowerson discovered a framed photograph stuffed inside a hidden compartment in the wooden panelling of Barbara Hewitt's desk, the nuns of Our Lady of Charity Care Home in Newcastle reported the disappearance of Sister Mary-Frances. A search party was quickly organised and able-bodied volunteers took to the streets to find her, scouring the riverbank where it was widely known that she liked to walk in the afternoons.

Some of them whispered about old-age statistics on depression and others pooh-poohed the idea as they remembered the nun's zest for life, and her lifelong commitment to God and to the needy.

Nobody worried about the Graveyard Killer because Mary-Frances had been old and grey, not young and beautiful. Who would kill an old nun?

It was unthinkable.

They followed the path of the inky-black river, their torches flickering in the darkness while their footsteps trampled over the ground where the heels of Mary-Frances's shoes had dug tracks in a wasted effort to survive.

CHAPTER 16

MacKenzie had spoken of finding the skeleton in Barbara's closet. As it turned out, the skeleton was a faded photograph of a younger Barbara surrounded by around forty children of varying ages inside a cheap wooden frame. But instead of a closet, they found the photograph hidden inside a panel dug into the antique desk in her spare bedroom.

"There's no way this photograph found its way in there by accident," Lowerson said, to murmured agreement from MacKenzie.

"Which tells us that she wanted to hide it away but couldn't quite bring herself to dispose of it. How interesting."

Lowerson used the edge of a pen knife to ease the backing away from the frame, which had almost welded itself to the photograph after years of heat and humidity.

"*Aha!* Here we go." He gently prised the photograph away from the cheap wood and flipped it over. On the reverse side, Barbara's swirling handwriting read:

OUR LADY OF CHARITY ORPHANAGE

ROTHBURY HOUSE

CHRISTMAS 1989

"I know that name," Lowerson said, and started to root around for his smartphone. He spent another minute scrolling through his e-mail inbox until he found what he was looking for.

"Rothbury House?" MacKenzie queried. "Yes, I think it's on the outskirts of town—"

"No, no," he said, frantically. "Here it is. An old nun had been reported missing and it just came through as a general alert—look at the name."

He handed MacKenzie the phone.

"Sister Mary-Frances Creighton, an eighty-five-year-old nun, was reported missing this afternoon from Our Lady of Charity Care Home," she read out. "An informal search is underway and Missing Persons officers are investigating. Her disappearance is being treated as 'low risk.'"

MacKenzie handed the phone back to Lowerson.

"*Our Lady of Charity*," she repeated, gunning her car into life again. "I have a feeling that Missing Persons will be upgrading her risk category very shortly."

Lowerson's fingers flew over the screen while he performed a series of internet searches and MacKenzie executed a smooth U-turn.

"'Our Lady of Charity' is a network of Catholic-run orphanages and old-age care homes—they have them nationwide. The care home in Newcastle is one of them; it's down near the river at Newburn, which is where they're searching for the missing nun."

"Is the orphanage still operating?"

Lowerson hurried to find the answer.

"No, Rothbury House is now owned by the RAF and it's used as a sort of getaway for service personnel and their families. It's a beautiful old building," he thought aloud, as an image popped up on his screen of a stately home with perfectly manicured lawns and picture windows. "I'm searching archived news articles now."

MacKenzie frowned ahead at the road, her mind working quickly as each new piece of the jigsaw began to fall into place.

"The orphanage closed down in the winter of 1990, which isn't long after this photograph was taken," Lowerson declared.

MacKenzie cast her mind back to the late eighties, when she was a young woman living back in Ireland. Her attention would not have been drawn by a local news item concerning an orphanage in the wilds of Northumberland. But she did remember wider reporting of endemic abuse within Catholic-run orphanages around that time.

"Something happened around then, Jack," she said. "Run a search on child abuse in association with that group."

"I'm searching…wait, here's something. It's not child abuse but it's still a scandal."

He paused to read the news article and, pixel by pixel, the image of a teenage girl began to materialise.

"Oh my God," he whispered.

MacKenzie looked away from the road for a second, filled with concern.

"What's the matter?"

"They're connected, Mac." Lowerson spoke quickly, the words tumbling out of his mouth. "Around Easter 1990, a girl committed suicide—she was called Grace Turner. She threw herself off the roof of Rothbury House, according to this report. The orphanage tried to cover it up, apparently, but it got out and the papers had a field day. The church's reputation was already in tatters after recent investigations into sexual abuse, so the orphanage decided to close for good."

"What happened to the children?"

MacKenzie took the slip road from the dual carriageway towards the west of the city.

"I can't find anything about what happened to the children," Lowerson mumbled. "They probably scattered all over the place or were redistributed into other orphanages. I can only see—"

"What? What can you see?"

"There was an inquest into Grace Turner's death in May of 1990. It was reported in *The Evening Chronicle*. I recognise three of the names reported there: Sister Mary-Frances Creighton, Barbara Hewitt—who's listed as the children's nurse—and…it's…it's *him*," Lowerson stammered. "The priest responsible for pastoral care at the orphanage was Father Simon Healy."

Lowerson looked across at MacKenzie's profile, briefly lit up by the headlights of a passing car. It brought to mind thoughts of Italian sculptures: beautiful in its perfection but stony and unyielding. He was pleased that it was too dark for her to see him blush at his own thoughts.

"When we spoke to Father Healy, he told us that he hardly knew Barbara Hewitt. He never mentioned such a specific connection, having worked at the orphanage together."

"He lied," Lowerson said, bluntly.

"It's precisely the kind of omission that causes people like me to draw adverse inferences about his character," she gritted out.

"Grace Turner was a redhead," Lowerson added. "There could be a connection to Operation Angel."

"Why do you think I'm driving like a maniac?" She threw out the question with a feral grin and flipped the internal switch to operate the siren on the roof of her car, just for good measure. After a few more minutes of speedy manoeuvring, CID Headquarters emerged as a beacon in the night, a port in the present storm. Its long, unappealing windows radiated cheap yellow light and its boxy lines were like an old, familiar friend they hadn't seen in too long.

Both detectives ran the distance across the car park and through its scarred front doors.

The Incident Room was full to brimming with staff, including the unwelcome addition of Chief Constable

Morrison, who positioned herself inconspicuously in the corner but nonetheless managed to convey the enormity of her presence to everybody in the room. Ryan knew that her attendance meant only one thing: that his team was about to receive an edict. The fact that Morrison had chosen to deliver it in front of the assembly and not in private also told him that her patience was wearing thin.

Join the club, he thought.

"Alright! Anybody who doesn't have their arse parked on a seat, sort it out!"

Chairs scraped against the mud brown carpet tiles.

"Before I get into it, I want to thank you all for your hard work over this weekend. I know it's the job we all signed up for but some of you were expecting to enjoy a bit of a holiday, so I want to thank you personally for setting aside your disappointment. I know that the families of these three women are thankful, too."

Ryan sent Morrison a swift glare to drive home his point. If the Graveyard Killer hadn't been caught, it was not because of any slipshod policing from his staff.

"Here's the situation, folks." He walked around to the board at the front and pointed at the row of images. "We now have a potential third victim. Her name is Tanya Robertson, aged 36, wife and stay-at-home mother of two children. As you can plainly see, she has red hair and falls within the same age range as his previous two victims."

He swept his eyes around the room.

"Unlike the previous two victims, Tanya has not yet been found—"

"Honestly, guv, there was no movement over at All Saints Cemetery," one of the constables piped up, a bit worriedly.

Ryan held up a hand to ward off any similar interruptions.

"I'm not suggesting that any of the surveillance teams fell asleep on the job. In fact, our current thinking is that we did *too* good of a job because we managed to scare our killer out of the city altogether."

He let that sink in and there were a few mutters from the bright sparks amongst them.

"How can you be so sure?"

Heads swivelled to the back of the room, in the direction of where Morrison had spoken.

"We can't be sure, at least not yet," Ryan said flatly. "But we have a solid line of enquiry."

He moved across to the map and pointed a finger at an area highlighted in yellow.

"This area indicates four of the counties falling under the Diocese of Hexham and Newcastle, which is where Catholic burials took place today. There were twelve of them, in total."

"Why only Catholic?" Again, from Morrison.

"The content of the notes that the Graveyard Killer leaves behind is Catholic and both of the funerals due to take place where we found Krista and Karen's bodies were Catholic ones. These are both strong factors." He paused, then added,

"Of course, if this line of enquiry fails, we can branch out into other religious denominations, if necessary."

Morrison remained quiet, which Ryan took as a signal to continue.

"Phillips and Yates in particular have devoted a lot of time to a process of elimination over the past two days," he caught Frank's eye and nodded his thanks. "The result of that is we now know that relevant individuals in Newcastle City Council, contractors of the Council and both funeral directors employed to manage the funerals taking place on Friday and Saturday at West Road and Heaton cemeteries are not considered suspects in this investigation."

"Are you saying it's somebody in the church?" Morrison asked, a bit sharply. She had just come off the telephone after a long and heated argument with the Media Liaison for the Diocese of Hexham and Newcastle, who had reminded her in no uncertain terms that, if her department so much as slurred one member of the church without proper evidence, they would not hesitate to bring a private court action.

Ryan could read the Chief Constable like a book.

"Tell the church elders to calm down," he snapped. "I'm saying that it is looking most likely to be someone *connected* to the church. That could include anybody with access to their internal systems because that's the key here. Somebody had access to the calendar of forthcoming burials, was familiar with the individual cemetery sites, and was able to enter and leave using a key, which he most likely copied or stole."

"That doesn't sound promising," Morrison countered.

"It's more than we had this morning," Ryan shot back, eyes flashing. He didn't need naysayers at this point in the investigation, when it was imperative that the team kept their spirits high and focused on catching a killer.

"Geography might help us to narrow our search," he continued, moving back to the map to indicate two large blue pins. "We have St Andrew's Church here and St Mary's Cathedral, further south and not far from the station, here."

Then, he tapped some other pins which marked the spot where each victim was last seen alive.

"I don't need to be Inspector Columbo to figure out that, in each instance, the site where these women were taken was within a ten-minute walk, or a five-minute drive, of one or both of these churches. We also found circumstantial evidence at Karen's house to suggest that she might have, at some stage, attended Narcotics Anonymous—held on Friday nights at St Andrew's Cathedral."

Ryan looked across at Phillips and invited him to jump into the briefing. The latter fiddled with his tie as an automatic gesture before speaking—today, it was a relatively tasteful black silk number with a small row of white piano keys embroidered along one side.

"I had a word with Krista's widow, who told me that she sometimes volunteered at the soup kitchen at St Andrew's on Sundays. I also rang Tanya's husband, who told me that his wife used to go along to the playgroup at St Andrew's with their youngest."

"This sounds like a lot of conjecture," Morrison interrupted him. "I want those twelve sites exhumed immediately and Tanya Robertson brought home to her family."

Ryan gave her a look that would have shrivelled a lesser person.

"If we wait another twenty-four hours, we might have a better idea of where to search," he argued. "The public won't be happy anyway, seeing Tanya brought home in a body bag. They want us to find the person responsible and the best way to do that is to continue focusing the investigation around these two churches."

Morrison thought of the negative press accumulated so far and, inevitably, politics won out.

"Get it done, Ryan. First thing tomorrow morning, I want the wheels in motion for exhuming those bodies. That's an order."

He was about to launch into another argument when the double doors to the incident room burst open. Everybody turned to seek out the source of the commotion and, when Phillips saw that it was MacKenzie, he jumped out of his chair with more haste than finesse.

"Denise?"

She paused briefly to lay a reassuring hand on his arm, then headed directly to the front of the room where Ryan was poised for action, anticipating that they were about to impart some game-changing news.

"Sir, evidence has come to light during the course of our investigation that we believe connects with Operation Angel."

Lowerson handed him the photograph and Ryan looked down at the image. A group of children ranging in age from toddlers to sixteen or seventeen-year-olds stood in two rows, with the smallest at the front. Eight nuns stood to either side, one of whom was a middle-aged Sister Mary-Frances Creighton, as well as a much younger Barbara Hewitt with a blonde fluffy perm, courtesy of the fashion at the time.

Ryan flipped it over and read the inscription on the back.

"Our Lady of Charity? Explain, please."

MacKenzie did, articulately and concisely.

"What about the other nuns or staff members of the orphanage? Whatever happened to them?"

"I looked into that briefly already, sir," Lowerson said. "Father Simon Healy seems to be the only surviving member of the original church executive from Our Lady of Charity Orphanage. All the other nuns are deceased, Barbara Hewitt has been murdered, and it's looking increasingly likely that Sister Mary-Frances is going to turn up dead, too."

Ryan frowned off into the distance while he processed this unexpected development. His eyes strayed to the murder board and to a collection of smaller notes that had been pinned there. His eyes narrowed into silver slits and, like a man in a daze, he wandered closer to inspect the handwriting on one of them and then compared it with another scrap of paper tacked nearby.

"Sir?"

He snapped back to the present and frowned.

"How old is Father Simon Healy?"

"Somewhere in his late fifties or early sixties, sir," MacKenzie replied.

"Which would make him a man in his thirties back in 1990," Ryan deduced. "You believe Grace connects to our present investigation—how?"

"Look at the age range, for starters," Lowerson said. "Krista and Tanya were both redheaded women in their late thirties and Karen looked older than thirty-two. They all fall within the same range."

Ryan accepted a copy of the online article Lowerson had printed as they talked, showing an image of a young Grace Turner, her bright hair glimmering with the sun at her back. The report listed her as being fourteen when she died twenty-six years earlier.

"You're saying that these women are of a similar age to Grace Turner, if she were still alive today?"

Lowerson nodded.

Ryan took a moment to read the rest of the paperwork as it was fed into his hands and Morrison hurried across to join their huddle.

"What do you think?" she demanded.

Ryan ran a hand across the back of his neck and then looked up, a curiously guarded expression on his face.

"I think that Father Simon Healy is either a killer or the killer's next target. He would have had access to internal church systems, he was in the area to kill Barbara Hewitt, but the style is very different to the Graveyard Killer. Barbara Hewitt was killed by manual strangulation without any ritual element, whereas the victims of the Graveyard Killer are all much younger, of a physical type, and have all been arranged in a very specific way, with Catholic overtones—"

"Healy was seen arguing with Barbara Hewitt on the day she died and then he lied about it when we asked him directly. Then, he lied by omission by choosing not to tell us that he had worked with Barbara years earlier at the orphanage in Rothbury and he made out that he hardly knew the woman," MacKenzie argued. "It would have been easy enough for him to gain access to the church intranet because his parish falls with the Diocese of Hexham and Newcastle. Sir, Grace Turner could be his twisted motive for killing redheaded women. As for the others, maybe he blamed them for her death? Perhaps the reason why there was no burial or Catholic rites is that he didn't believe that Barbara Hewitt deserved absolution."

Ryan had to admit it was a good working theory.

"All this time, we've been thinking that the Graveyard Killer is creating angels, saving their souls and all that. But 'angel' has another meaning. It means 'messenger of God'," Phillips thought aloud. "It could be that this fruit-and-nut bar thinks he's God's messenger and he's dishing out holy punishment or some twaddle."

"Never mind that. Let's not forget the very real possibility that Healy might be holding Tanya Robertson," Morrison threw in. "She might still be alive."

The room fell silent, sensing that a call to action was imminent.

Four heads turned towards Ryan, awaiting his command. He looked among the faces of his team.

"Alright, let's bring him in," he ordered, with a final glance back at the board.

Anna was absorbed in a stack of student essays. She lounged at the desk in her cosy study in Durham with a long leg slung indolently over one of the arms of an antique captain's chair, tutting as she spotted several errors. She reached for the red biro she kept tucked above her right ear and began to scribble a comment in the margin.

When the telephone shrilled with an old-fashioned *briiiiing briiiiing,* she nearly jumped out of the chair. Her eyes flicked to the clock and she was surprised to note that the time was nearly eight o'clock.

Where was Ryan?

"Hello?"

"Hi, it's me."

Her body relaxed again as his voice came down the wires, smooth and clipped with just enough edge to keep her guessing.

"How's life?"

"Oh, same old. Chasing bad guys, saving the world. You?"

"Hmm. Pretty similar here," she quipped, eyeing the stale remnants of a cheese sandwich languishing on her desk beside an empty coffee mug. "Non-stop action."

She could almost hear Ryan smile.

"Listen, I haven't got long. I just wanted to let you know I won't be back until late. There's been a break in the investigation and I don't know—" He paused, unsure of himself. "It's a surprising twist and I'm not sure how it's going to turn out."

"How intriguing," she murmured, unconsciously leaning forward in her chair. "Tell me about it later?"

Ryan smiled again.

"Doctor Taylor, you are well aware that I am not at liberty to discuss the details of an ongoing investigation."

"Uh huh," she chuckled. "I have ways and means."

"Ain't that the truth," he rumbled, wishing fervently that he was at home with her instead of standing in the draughty corridor outside the incident room about to head out into the night.

"I—ah—I just wanted to tell you…" Ryan was distracted momentarily by the sight of Phillips strolling past making kissy-kissy faces at him. He flipped him the bird.

"Ah, that is, I wanted to say that I love you."

Back in Durham, Anna snuggled further into her seat.

"Phillips is making faces at you right now, isn't he?"

"Yep."

"In which case, I'm even more touched that you braved ridicule to ring and tell me that. I love you too, chief inspector."

"I'd better go."

"Stay safe," she whispered, before he ended the call.

She replaced the receiver and spent a long moment staring at where it rested in its cradle. There had been a time when Ryan would never have thought to call home to set her mind at ease. He would have been so focused on his investigation, so preoccupied with the urgency of his task that there would have been no room for gratuitous affection or unnecessary telephone calls.

But today, he had called.

Progress was a wonderful thing.

CHAPTER 17

Despite any private doubts he might have harboured about whether Father Simon Healy really was the Graveyard Killer, Ryan acquiesced to the wishes of his superiors and approached the task of bringing the man into custody with military precision. Two firearms specialists were on hand to accompany his team, with strict instructions that force should be used only as a last resort. The staff of Operation Angel had been split into smaller divisions: those who would remain at CID Headquarters, those who would provide technical support, and two smaller teams of field operatives led by Ryan and MacKenzie, who would approach their target from all sides.

It was another mission to distract the intrepid reporters who remained camped outside CID Headquarters. They awaited a juicy titbit to give their viewers in time for the evening news and so Morrison fell upon her proverbial sword and arranged an impromptu press briefing, thereby allowing Ryan's team to slip out of the police compound unnoticed. While the reporters surged forward brandishing mics, four unmarked police vehicles exited the car park and made their way north.

Ryan headed the fleet in a sleek, charcoal-grey Mercedes which he excused on the grounds that he had clearly suffered an early mid-life crisis and shouldn't be held responsible for his actions. As it happened, the car perfectly suited its owner. Besides, on cold March evenings in the North East of England, heated seats were not to be sniffed at, Phillips decided, jiggling more comfortably into the passenger seat.

"Team A, respond."

Ryan spoke into his car radio and heard a crackle in response.

He gave the order and then watched in his rearview mirror as two cars peeled away from the convoy of police operatives. They would take an alternative back road into Rothbury which would allow them to approach from the other side of town so as not to arouse suspicion. It would also allow them to blockade the exit route in that direction, should Simon Healy try to make a run for it.

Ryan looked across at Phillips.

"I had to pull the surveillance team off MacKenzie's house," he admitted. "There was no further activity yesterday and nothing this morning, either."

"Aye, that's fair. Besides, Denise spotted the surveillance car a mile off and chewed my ear about it all night."

Ryan flashed a grin.

"Still, she means to thank you for looking out for her. For us," Phillips corrected.

"Don't mention it," Ryan murmured. "There haven't been any further developments but until this investigation is closed, I don't want her left alone. We still have no idea who sent her that note; all we know is it *probably* wasn't the same man who is killing these women."

"You and me both, son. I won't sleep easy until we get to the bottom of it."

The car fell silent again as each man looked out into the passing night, then Phillips spoke out again.

"You were quiet in the incident room, earlier."

Ryan's lips twitched.

"You don't miss much, do you, Frank?"

"Rarely."

"Alright, if you must know, I don't think Healy is our man."

"There's a growing pile of—"

"Supposition."

Phillips pursed his lips. "There could be some truth in it," he observed.

Conversation paused while Ryan responded to another crackle on the radio.

"I admit there could be something in the theory about Grace Turner but I'm not sure we have all the pieces to this puzzle yet."

Phillips studied the road ahead, mesmerised by the flicker of cat's eyes demarcating where the tarmac ended and the undergrowth began.

"If not Healy, then who?"

Ryan shook his head in frustration.

"I'm working on instinct and that doesn't hold up in court. I need evidence or I need him to slip up somewhere. Faulkner hasn't found anything we can use; the fibres embedded in the necks of both women are a bog-standard silk-cotton blend found in a wide range of clothing. He hasn't left a damn thing behind to identify himself and he's deliberately chosen to snatch women within his chosen hunting ground, free from CCTV coverage. His choice of cemetery is very clever, too. He's flitting about the county like an apparition and to get a search warrant we need something solid, particularly with Morrison worrying about the politics of it all. We have to move very, very carefully."

Phillips brow cleared when he realised who Ryan was referring to.

"He's a big fish, lad. You'll need a sturdy rod to reel that one in."

Ryan gave him a wicked smile.

"It's a pity I won't be able to hang him on the wall back at CID but I'll settle for slinging him inside a maximum-security prison."

Phillips burrowed deeper into his chair and reached for his trusty pack of nicotine gum. Times like these, he needed it.

"If this really is connected to that girl—Grace Turner— and he's been killing women who sort of resemble her, then we could just be looking at the tip of the iceberg," Phillips said. "If Lowerson is right and Krista, Karen and Tanya are around the same age that Grace would have been if she lived today, then…"

"Exactly, Frank," Ryan said, so quietly that he could barely be heard. "Then there's no reason why this killer hasn't been murdering women for all the years since the real Grace died, which makes twenty-six. There could be dozens of missing women, lying hidden beneath coffins in other cemeteries."

Phillips was horrified.

"You don't mean…?"

"Before we left, I asked Yates to start the process of matching every missing teenager or woman fitting the physical description of Grace Turner since 1990, bearing in mind that we're looking for missing persons with the same approximate birth year as her. I've asked Yates to concentrate her efforts on redheaded women who went missing around religious holidays, too."

"Surely we would have noticed a pattern like that before now?"

"Not if he moved around the country, or abroad," Ryan replied. "Senior religious personnel are surprisingly well travelled."

Phillips chewed ferociously on his gum.

"Damn cheap airfares to blame, that's what it is."

There was a stillness in the air which reminded Ryan of the calm before a storm. Nothing moved in the centre of Rothbury and there was no breeze within the sheltered valley. Somewhere out of sight a dog barked and it was a welcome reminder that, in the daylight hours, Rothbury lived and breathed; it was no spectre that would disappear into the hill fog at sunrise.

The teams positioned themselves at strategic points around St Agnes' Church and the presbytery next door where Father Simon Healy lived. Residential streets were temporarily cordoned off and police operatives began their approach, kitted out in protective bodywear.

Not for the first time, Phillips mourned the fact that the bulky gear did little to improve his stocky physique. He felt less like an action hero and considerably more like a hobbit who had enjoyed a long and calorific lunch. To add insult to injury, Ryan stood tall and lean beside him, adjusting the straps on his stab vest like he was James Bond's better-looking brother.

The injustice of it all.

"Team B, into position," Ryan murmured into his radio, then gestured for his own team to move towards the front of the church while others covered the rear exit and the presbytery.

As they moved stealthily across the street, Ryan experienced a growing sense of unease. Something was wrong with the picture that presented itself. The presbytery was completely in darkness; not even a porch light glowed. Beside it, the church of St Agnes appeared equally dark and its doors were firmly shut, although they happened to know that there was due to be a late evening Mass.

It seemed that nobody was at home and yet Father Healy's navy-blue Honda Jazz was parked on the street outside, signalling that he was in residence.

"I'm getting a bad feeling about this, Frank," Ryan muttered.

"Me n'all," the other replied.

A brief radio exchange informed them that the other teams were in place as they approached the entrance to St Agnes.

"Ready?"

"I was born ready."

Ryan tried the door handle and winced as the rusty iron wailed loudly into the night.

But the door was locked, as he had anticipated.

He took a quick glance through the long window to the side and saw an empty, darkened church portico through the prism of rippled ornamental glass. Candlelight was just visible through the gloom, so Ryan backed away and crooked a finger towards two young officers wielding a heavy battering ram and stepped aside to allow them to do their work.

The sound of splintering wood spoiled the supernatural quiet of the town centre and, as the door gave way, faces appeared at nearby windows to see what the devil was happening in Rothbury now.

Tongues would wag, Ryan thought.

But he didn't concern himself with that. He crossed the threshold into the cool interior and was struck again by the quiet; nobody scuttled out of an anteroom in priestly garb, demanding to know why they were there. Nothing moved among the rows of plain wooden pews, except the flame of a single votive candle which flickered beneath a marble statue of St Agnes.

Ryan reached for a light switch and a bank of energy-saving wall lights came to life, but they didn't alleviate the glum feel to the place nor the sensation that, despite the empty silence, they were not alone.

"Father Healy! Northumbria CID! We have a warrant to enter the premises—make yourself known!"

Nothing.

Ryan and Phillips exchanged a long look. The support officers waited a few steps behind and were obviously disappointed that they would not be required to exercise their skills in apprehending a difficult suspect.

In fact, so far, they couldn't see any suspect at all.

Ryan led the way along the central aisle while Phillips and the other officers traced the outer walls, circling towards the altar at the back of the church. They scanned each pew as they went, their steps quiet and sure against the paved floor. Long shadows wavered, moving as they moved, creeping stealthily after them until Phillips let out a surprised shout.

Ryan covered the distance with fast strides and joined Phillips near the back corner of the church to look down upon the lifeless body of the parish priest of St Agnes.

Father Simon Healy's face was twisted into a grotesque, surprised expression. It stared up at them from the floor near the entrance to a small boot-room-cum-utility space which had been built to connect the church with the presbytery next door. His neck was lying at an odd, misshapen angle and, as they moved closer, Ryan could see that a cream silk scarf was wrapped tightly around his neck and had dug so deep that it had torn the skin. Blood stained the cream silk a deep, claret red and seeped onto the floor in a growing pool.

There were no obvious markers to show that anybody else had ever been there, but the direction in which Healy's body had fallen told them something very interesting. He had been walking from the presbytery towards the church and was dressed in his finery, presumably ready to deliver the late Mass. The angle of attack and the knotted material which strangled the man showed clearly that he had been taken from behind.

Putting all of that together, Ryan reasoned that Father Healy had been at ease with whoever had been admitted into his house. So much at ease, in fact, that he hadn't thought twice about turning his back on his killer.

"Faulkner's on his way," Phillips remarked. "How long do you think he's been dead?"

Ryan looked down at the mass of flesh and his mouth flattened into an angry line.

"No more than a couple of hours. Damn it, we probably passed him on the road up here."

He stepped away and spoke quickly into his radio, informing the other teams to stand down. A few minutes later, MacKenzie and Lowerson joined them.

"This is much more vicious than last time," was the first thing MacKenzie noted. "He definitely didn't use as much force when he killed Barbara Hewitt."

"Maybe she was weaker, physically?" Lowerson suggested.

"It's common for people in life-threatening situations to experience a superhuman surge in strength, regardless of age or gender," Ryan said, laconically. "But it's possible that Healy was harder to bring down. They would have been of a similar height."

MacKenzie gave him a canny look.

"It's also possible that Healy's death represents a vengeful kill—he was executed with a fair measure of anger, judging by the violence of this attack."

"Whichever it is, you were right," Phillips said, matter-of-factly. "He was the killer's next target."

Ryan turned and walked swiftly back towards the entranceway, not daring to breathe until he was outside in the street, well away from the sudden bout of claustrophobia. He planted his feet and looked up into the night sky, opening his lungs to draw in the clean air. He focused on the constellations of stars which shone brightly above and resisted the strong impulse to shout or scream. How easy it would be, he thought, to imagine his sister up there amongst them. It would make each day more bearable if he could believe that she was loved by a higher power and that a benevolent god was, at that very moment, caring for her eternal soul.

But no matter how hard he tried, he couldn't bring himself to believe the myth. His sister was gone, taken from the world by a psychopath in front of his very eyes in the kind of malevolent display of evil that no god could possibly sanction. And now, one of His own servants lay dead, brutally killed as he was about to perform his clerical duty. How could that be?

And so Ryan looked away from the heavens and back to Earth, where reality came into sharp focus once again. The first thing he saw was Phillips, who had positioned himself a short distance away and was unstrapping his protective gear whilst he kept a fatherly eye on his SIO.

"This thing is like a bloody corset," he grumbled, good-naturedly. "That'll be all the ham and pease pudding stotties."

"Or the fish and chips," Ryan offered.

"I'm contributing to the local economy," Phillips improvised.

Ryan smiled but it didn't quite reach his eyes.

"It doesn't help to know that you were right, does it?"

"No. I hoped that I was wrong. It would have been so much easier if Healy had been our man. It would be over and we might be one step closer to finding Tanya Robertson. Instead, I'm going to have to put the wheels in motion this evening to begin excavation of all twelve burial sites tomorrow. My only consolation is that I'll have my loyal sergeant to help me with the paperwork."

Phillips gave him a beady-eyed glare.

"It'll give the press something to talk about until next Christmas. Are you sure, now, of who it is?"

There was an infinitesimal pause, then Ryan nodded. Phillips blew out the air in his chest.

"Have you got a plan?"

Ryan smiled slowly, and his eyes shone diamond-bright in the moonlight.

"I have an idea, Frank, that's all. It'll take some planning to pull it off and I have an important phone call to make before we can begin."

Phillips stretched out his back and then, to Ryan's everlasting surprise, doubled over to touch his toes in a move to rival that of any professional dancer.

"Tell me what you need me to do."

"A couple of things. First, I need you to scour the ANPR footage of the main roads leading out of Newcastle in the direction of the four counties where we will be excavating tomorrow, from around the time Tanya Robertson went missing last night until sunrise this morning. You're looking for a black Lexus sedan, late model and I'll get the number plate for you when we're back at the office. We already know there's no footage of when these women were taken, thanks to careful planning on the killer's part. But if he was forced to take Tanya to another cemetery outside the city limits, he's been forced to show himself."

"Is the Lexus his car?"

"Nope. If I'm right, I think it's the car he's been 'borrowing.'"

Phillips rubbed his hands together eagerly.

"Consider it done. What was the other thing you needed?"

"Oh, right." Ryan snapped his fingers, as if he had just remembered. "If you're not doing anything better on 28th August, I'd like you to be best man at my wedding."

Phillips' jowly face went lax and quivered a bit while he pulled himself together. Ryan crossed his arms and looked on with considerable affection.

"My father will be there and a few mates from my uni days but…hell, when it comes down to it, Frank, you're the best friend I've ever had."

Phillips puffed out his chest.

"It would be an honour."

Grown men weren't supposed to hug like bears— especially not just outside a crime scene, in the middle of a high-profile murder investigation.

They made an exception, just this once.

"Now, there's one condition," Phillips said, sternly.

"Ye gods! What is it?"

"As far as the stag do is concerned, there'll be no namby-pamby spa weekend in Bath for you, my lad. Same goes for wine-tasting or go-karting. I require a list of invitees and no arguments." He paused, then asked seriously, "Is your health insurance up to date?"

Ryan gave him a cocky smile and waved it away.

"Scare tactics, eh? You forget, I've been stabbed, drugged…I've diced with death more times than you've had hot dinners."

Phillips gave him a pitying look.

"Child's play. You'd best start preparing yourself for the night of your life, son."

The headache had returned.

Even when he closed his eyes, the pain remained strong. He clutched at his head, tugging at the hair above his ears and slamming the heel of his hands against his own skull to relieve the terrible, crushing pressure, moaning like a wounded animal.

Despite everything, the police were getting closer. God was supposed to protect him and shield him from harm in exchange for all his good work, but the police had found Healy's body already. He had barely made it back to the city when the call had come through—the car engine was still warm.

It was too close. Far too close for comfort.

The man wasn't aware that he had risen from the chair in his bedroom, or that he was pacing.

Back and forth, back and forth.

He muttered unintelligibly as he wandered the room in a trance, pausing now and then as if to answer a question, like a man possessed. He had been a dutiful messenger, he thought, all these years. He had saved so many souls— so many, now, that he was beginning to forget what they looked like.

It didn't matter, because there was only one face burned inside his mind. *Her* face. Her beautiful face.

His hands shook as he thought of what the others had done to her. What they had done to his *child*.

Evil sinners, every one of them, and they deserved to die.

God could not perform such vengeance himself but the man understood that he was the tool. He was the sword that would deliver justice.

Minutes turned into hours as he shuffled around the room and his mind would not rest until her hand touched his arm. His body shivered and burned at the same time, rapturous at her return and he followed her to bed, curving himself around her lithe body. There he lay, wrapping himself around the bedclothes as if they were human flesh.

He slept deeply and dreamlessly until morning.

CHAPTER 18

Monday, 28th March 2016

Easter Monday

There was 'late', Anna thought, and then there was *late*.

She found herself checking the time on the little carriage clock in her bedroom every half hour until finally she gave up on sleep entirely and threw back the covers. As the clock struck three a.m., Anna headed out into the night, stopping in at the 24-hour pizza place on her way out of Durham. The lights were all blazing on the second floor of CID Headquarters when she arrived forty minutes later, while the rest of the world slept. Even the press had slunk back to their own homes, but would no doubt return before sunrise so as not to risk missing any of the action. Anna hefted her goods across the car park and entered the foyer where she was met by a frankly jubilant duty sergeant who recognised her immediately and showed her the way to the incident room in the hopes of pilfering a slice of pizza for himself.

"My prayers have finally been answered!" Phillips cried.

Immediately, she was set upon by a pack of hungry police staff who relieved her of the stack of fragrant cardboard boxes she carried. Phillips gave her a tight hug and waggled his thumb towards the main desk, where Ryan was speaking in what sounded like fluent, angry Italian on the phone to an official in the Vatican City State in Rome.

"Non me ne frega niente di che ore sono, vai a buttarlo giù dal letto!"

Ryan caught her eye and flashed one of his lightning-quick smiles before delivering another stream of fast Italian.

"Stupido scribacchino di merda!"

Anna turned to Phillips with a question in her eyes.

"Nope," he said roundly. "I haven't got the foggiest idea what he's saying. Feel sorry for the bloke at the other end, though."

Eventually, Ryan switched back into English and spoke for around five minutes in quick, urgent tones before replacing the receiver with a look of deep satisfaction. He rose nimbly from his chair and strode across the room to greet Anna properly.

"Ciao bella."

There were the customary wolf-whistles when he leaned in to bestow a brief kiss.

"Pipe down, you animals!" he threw back over his shoulder. "Are you still looking for a job here?"

Anna gave him a haughty look.

"Well, I've been involved in your last three big cases so I thought I'd better check in and give you a helping hand."

"With pizza?"

"You're damn right."

"Always was a good 'un," Phillips put in. "She's wasted on you, lad."

"And you can pipe down, too," Ryan replied, with a grin.

Anna looked around the incident room and noted the activity which showed no signs of slowing down just because it happened to be the middle of the night.

"I didn't know you speak Italian," she said.

Ryan's eyes swept over her face and he was loath to acknowledge that life was just better when she was around. That was the simple, basic truth. They weren't joined at the hip—she had her own successful career and he supposed that he had his. But the times when he was beside her, touching her, were when he felt most at home.

"I'm full of surprises," he promised.

The room melted away for a moment, the sounds of tapping keyboards and ringing telephones dimming to a distant buzz in her ears as they stood there, cocooned in the world he had created.

"Don't tell me you're a cunning linguist," she warned, eliciting a shout of laughter from Phillips.

"I take it your lead didn't quite work out." Anna moved things back to business. "But it looks as though you've found another?"

Ryan nodded briskly and stepped back, mentally shifting gears again.

"Yes, you could say that. At first light, we'll begin work excavating four burial sites, then move on to the next four, and the next until we find what we're looking for."

"Tanya Robertson," Anna guessed.

Ryan nodded. "She doesn't deserve to be hidden in the ground, beneath somebody else's coffin as if she had no soul or life of her own".

"As if she didn't matter?"

"The irony is that each woman mattered, very much so. For a brief moment in time, I believe they mattered a great deal to him."

The legality of the emergency exhumation of twelve coffins across four council districts was, to say the least, a grey area. Particularly because the police investigation did not concern the deaths of any of the individuals *within* those coffins but rather concerned what might, just might, lie *beneath* one of them. And if the families of the recently deceased were upset, then the church was even more so. Chief Constable Morrison spent the greater part of her morning fielding irate threats from the Media Liaison for the Diocese of Hexham and Newcastle, who accused

Northumbria Police Constabulary of inciting a witch hunt against members of the faith.

When Ryan entered her office, Morrison was standing beside the window with her back to him. The sun hadn't yet risen fully and the overhead lights were blazing in an effort to brighten the room and her mood. There was a weight on her shoulders, he thought. One that he would have been required to share if he had taken up her offer of promotion. Her world was a step removed from the cut and thrust; from interviewing suspects and running an active investigation. She concerned herself with high-level budgets, with policies and procedures, and the business of being accountable to the people they served. Normally, she was happy to delegate, but in the absence of a superintendent, Morrison was finding herself more and more embroiled in the kind of legwork she hadn't seen in a long while.

In too long, she admitted to herself.

"Take a seat, Ryan," she murmured. Though he preferred to stand, he responded to the fatigue in her voice and took a chair.

She turned around and he could see dark circles beneath her eyes. He imagined that he didn't look much better, since he hadn't been home at all last night and nor had many of his team.

"How the hell do you manage to look so damn normal?"

Well, that answered that question, Ryan thought.

"Caffeine, ma'am."

"I need some of the good stuff," she decided, moving across to a small coffee machine. She dropped two pods in the top and waited for the aromatic liquid to percolate.

Ryan accepted a cup with a touch of surprise. This was turning into a cosy chat, rather than the tense conversation he had anticipated.

Morrison took a long swig from her mug and closed her eyes for one blissful moment.

"It isn't even eight o'clock in the morning and it feels like I've had most of the senior members of the Catholic clergy in the North East on the phone, in addition to half the national press."

Ryan took a drink of his coffee.

"I also heard from an Italian cardinal, who was on the warpath about some sort of heated exchange with one of our officers. Would you know anything about that?"

Ryan's face didn't move a muscle.

"You don't have any smart comments?" She opened her eyes again. "No wisecracks?"

Ryan raised an eyebrow and she held up a finger.

"I retract those comments," she said, wearily. "I know you're doing everything you can, it's just that this thing keeps getting bigger and bigger. We've got two dead redheads and another missing, suspected dead. Last night, we thought there was a connection between these women and the deaths of Barbara Hewitt in Rothbury and an old nun by the name of Sister Mary-Frances Creighton, whose body is still missing, presumed dead. The man we thought

connected all of them is now lying in the mortuary himself."
Morrison reeled it off like a newscaster. "Now, tell me some
good news before I lose my mind."

Ryan set his cup aside.

"Father Simon Healy was connected, just not in the way
we suspected—he was a target, not a killer. As it happens,
I believe we will have the real killer in custody within
twenty-four hours, ma'am."

Morrison's eyes widened.

"Care to tell me who it is, or do you want me to start
guessing?"

Ryan's lips tugged at the corners.

"I believe the man responsible for all of the recent
murders, and possibly a great deal more besides, is Father
Conor O'Byrne."

Morrison stared at him.

"The Dean of Central Newcastle, right-hand man of the
Bishop. A senior cleric with an exemplary track record of
charitable work."

"That's the one."

It was Morrison's turn to smile, slightly hysterically, as
the impact of his bald statement hit home.

"If you're so certain, why isn't he in custody at this very
moment?"

"For the simple reason that we haven't found a shred
of hard evidence against him. Not even enough to
request a DNA sample. But I have an idea how we can
trap him."

Ryan checked his watch and then stood up to look out of the window. It was almost nine o'clock and he was gratified to see a healthy gaggle of reporters outside the main building, ready to capture the sight of Father O'Byrne being led into CID Headquarters. Right on cue, MacKenzie and Lowerson turned into the car park with a squad car in tow and the press began to swarm.

From his position beside the window, Ryan watched Father O'Byrne exit the squad car with dignity; a tall, good-looking man in his early-forties who had admirable poise despite having just emerged into a maelstrom of cameras and noise.

He was unsurprised to see an expensive two-seater sports car pull up shortly afterwards, out of which jumped a sharp-suited lawyer he recognised from one of the city's premier law firms.

"He's just stepped into the building," Ryan explained, turning back to the Chief Constable, who waited with a harried expression on her face.

"He…right, okay. How are you going to—"

Her phone began to ring again and she reached for it.

"Look, I'll keep the bigwigs sweet for now but whatever you've got planned, make it *quick* and make it *tidy*."

"A few hours—that's all I need," he vowed.

She picked up the telephone and he left her to field the latest barrage of questions from the Northumbria Police and Crime Commissioner.

CHAPTER 19

Father Conor O'Byrne looked perfectly at ease within the stifling confines of Room C of the interview suite at CID Headquarters. His long, artistic fingers were linked in his lap while he chatted with his lawyer and he neither slouched nor sat on the edge of his chair. His dark hair was brushed away from a strong face dominated by a pair of deep blue eyes that had, ever so briefly, rested with great interest upon DI Denise MacKenzie. Ryan watched him for over ten minutes through the viewing panel, studying his mannerisms and body language. He watched the way his eyes flickered and noted the slight tapping of his right index finger which moved in time with his right foot against the floor.

"Hard to believe that he could kill," Phillips said, coming to stand beside him.

"Why?" Ryan demanded. "Because he's wearing a collar?"

"No, because he looks like such a *nice guy*."

Ryan huffed out a laugh. "There's no such thing. You know that as well as I do."

"Well if I didn't before, I certainly do after spending so much time around you," came the pithy response.

"How do you want to play it?"

"The usual way," Ryan said. "You can be his best friend and I'll be his worst nightmare."

Phillips shuffled his feet. "I never get to be the bad cop."

"Diddums."

"Keep at it, lad, and I'll keep thinking of new and interesting ways to pay you back on the stag do."

"Promises, promises," Ryan jibed, then collected his file and led the way out of the viewing space to begin the next stage of his plan.

While Ryan and Phillips prepared to interview Father Conor O'Byrne, MacKenzie and Lowerson were given leave to hurry home for a quick shower and change. As Ryan had already observed, DC Lowerson would rather have prostrated himself in front of moving traffic than allow anything to happen to her, so MacKenzie was forced to accept that Lowerson would be with her for a while longer.

"I don't need a bodyguard, Jack," she complained, for the umpteenth time, as they exited her red Fiesta and walked towards her front door.

"Yeah, but I would if anything happened to you and Phillips found out that I'd left you alone."

MacKenzie shoved a hand on her hip but had to admit that was probably true.

"Come in, then."

Her boot caught on the welcome mat outside her front door and she nearly tripped. Lowerson caught her elbow just in time but the action dislodged the mat so that the edge of a small cream note suddenly became visible.

Lowerson reached for it, but MacKenzie stopped him and reached for a fresh pair of gloves from a pouch inside her enormous work bag. Only then did she peel open the envelope to look at the message on the card inside. It consisted of only three words:

SEE YOU SOON

MacKenzie felt her chest contract and she struggled to breathe. She bent over, drawing slow, deep breaths as she fought to quieten her instinctive fear. Lowerson threw protocol aside and drew her in for a quick hug.

"It's alright," he murmured. "You're alright."

The nausea receded and she began to shiver.

"I don't know how long this has been here," she managed. "It could have been left before the last one, which was posted through the letterbox. It could have been left yesterday afternoon, or last night, or this morning—"

She stopped herself and took a few more deep breaths.

"Let's go inside," he suggested, with a sharp-eyed look around the street.

Ryan and Phillips entered Interview Room C after a suitable 'sweating' period and went through the preliminaries for the official recording, noting the names of those present. O'Byrne offered them both a cordial smile, which Phillips returned and Ryan ignored.

The detectives took their seats opposite the Dean and his lawyer, and Ryan looked straight into the other man's eyes. O'Byrne stared boldly back and didn't so much as flinch.

"Father O'Byrne, we're grateful that you agreed to attend voluntarily for an interview and we acknowledge that you have exercised your right to have a solicitor present."

"As I've told you before, chief inspector, I'm happy to assist wherever I can—within reason."

He was a cool one, Ryan thought. He'd give him that.

"Chief inspector, my client would like to make it clear from the outset that he considers this interview to be an intrusion into his private life and a calculated move on the part of Northumbria CID to smear the Catholic church in this area."

The solicitor's nasal voice grated, but Ryan supposed the self-important little man had to be seen to be earning his fee.

"Duly noted," Ryan snapped. "Anything else?"

"On the summary sheet that was provided to us less than thirty minutes ago, it is clear that my client will have very little to say considering he has no knowledge of, nor involvement in, any of the crimes you are investigating."

"Well, it's a small world," Phillips chipped in. "You never know."

"It certainly is a small world," Ryan agreed. "For instance, I understand from my colleagues DI MacKenzie and DC Lowerson that you had a discussion with them yesterday afternoon at St Andrew's Church. Is that correct?"

The priest glanced at his solicitor.

"Yes, that's correct."

"During the course of that discussion, you recalled that a woman by the name of Barbara Hewitt had visited St Andrew's Church to confess her sins on Friday 18th March. Is that correct?"

The solicitor leaned in to whisper something in the priest's ear.

"I was shown an image of a woman I recognised and was later told that her name was Barbara Hewitt. I didn't know that was her name before then."

"I see. Would you mind recounting your experience with this woman, for our benefit?"

The solicitor leaned in again.

"I have no objection, although I have already cooperated fully with the other members of your division," O'Byrne was careful to point out. "I recognised the woman I later learned was Barbara Hewitt because she entered St Andrew's Church around lunchtime on Friday 18th March, when I was attending to certain church duties within the remit of the deanery. I am the Dean of the Central Newcastle district and from time to time I run several charitable services—"

"And I'm sure the people of Newcastle are grateful," Ryan overrode him. "Let's stay focused on Barbara Hewitt and what she had to say to you."

Something flickered behind the Dean's eyes. Ryan caught it and kept pushing.

"You told my colleagues that she came in to confess her sins?"

The solicitor leaned forward to murmur something else but the Dean's eyes remained fixed on Ryan.

"Yes, she came to confess."

"And can you tell us what was said during the course of that confession?"

Here, the Dean fell back on well-worn ground and relaxed into his usual spiel.

"As I made abundantly clear to your colleagues yesterday afternoon, I am bound by my faith. Were I to reveal the content of our discussion, I would likely be excommunicated and rightly so."

"Then you may have an unfortunate choice to make between excommunication and prison," Ryan ground out. "Barbara Hewitt gave confession and was killed later that very same day, yet you refuse to tell us what was said. Why?"

"It can be hard to explain to people outside the faith—"

"*Screw* the faith!" Ryan slammed his hand on the table and watched the other man baulk at the deliberate blasphemy.

"Chief inspector, I'll remind you to remain respectful of my client," the solicitor began, self-righteously.

"And I'll remind your client to respect the memory of an innocent woman who's lying dead at the morgue," Ryan snarled.

The Dean's eyes flickered at the use of the word 'innocent', Ryan noted. He pressed harder, prodding at the wound.

"Barbara Hewitt was an old woman who hadn't harmed a fly in her entire life. She deserves justice and her killer deserves to rot in a prison cell," he continued.

The small, polite smile slipped from the Dean's face.

"Only God can grant the final judgment."

"If you believe that, Father, then you must agree that the taking of life is an abomination. It's a sin and would put you in danger of losing your immortal soul."

The Dean blinked and looked away as his solicitor inched forward.

"Are you accusing my client, chief inspector?"

Ryan smiled grimly.

"If he continues to stonewall, I'll have no choice but to view your client's actions as a deliberate obstruction of justice. I ask him once again: tell us the content of Barbara Hewitt's confession."

The Dean folded his hands.

"I am bound by my faith," he parroted. "No comment."

Ryan flipped open his file and a photograph fluttered onto the table between them, showing a lurid image of Karen Dobbs lying dead at Heaton Cemetery.

"Oops," Ryan drawled.

Slowly, he turned the image around so that O'Byrne would be afforded a better view. "Her name was Karen Dobbs," he said. "She had a little boy."

O'Byrne peeled his eyes away from the photograph and found himself trapped by Ryan's hard stare.

"I pray for her soul."

Ryan drew out another photograph, this time of Krista Ogilvy-Matthews.

"This is Krista. She was a teacher."

The Dean looked at the air above Ryan's head and his mouth moved, as if he were about to say something.

"Pardon?" Ryan leaned forward and cupped a hand to his ear. "I didn't quite catch that."

The Dean clamped his lips shut.

"Chief inspector, these theatrical parlour games are both predictable and pitiful," the solicitor whined.

"Maybe I'm just clumsy," Ryan said, without moving his eyes from the priest's face.

He drew out a different image this time, of Grace Turner. As he turned it over, he watched the Dean's face closely.

His gaze remained fixed somewhere in the distance.

"Look at her," Ryan said softly. "Look at Grace."

The use of her name had the Dean's eyes whipping back round, unable to control his instinctive reaction. He sought her out and came to rest on her face, as it had been all those years ago. Ryan thought he saw a sheen of tears.

"Do you know this girl?"

The Dean swallowed and then shook his head, slowly back and forth.

"Chief inspector, there is no mention of a Grace Turner on the summary sheet. If you choose not to stick to the agreed lines of questioning then I shall be advising my client that he is not required to remain."

"That's your prerogative," Ryan shrugged, then held up the picture of Grace. "This girl's nobody, really."

His casual statement drew a look of pure venom, just as Ryan had intended.

"Can you tell us your whereabouts between the hours of five p.m. on Friday 18th and five a.m. on Saturday 19th March?"

The solicitor tapped something on a piece of paper he held in his hand.

"As I have previously told you, I was at St Andrew's Church until after nine p.m. attending to certain church duties, including the weekly Narcotics Anonymous group."

Ryan smiled to himself.

"Didn't happen to see Karen Dobbs, did you?"

O'Byrne's index finger started to tap.

"I returned to my home on Clayton Street and spent a quiet evening reading."

"Nothing like a good book," Phillips put in. "What did you read?"

The Dean cast him a confused look.

"The—the Bible. I was preparing a reading for the next day."

"How about Thursday 24th?" Ryan demanded.

The solicitor patted his client's arm and drew himself up to his full measly height.

"My client is prepared to cooperate with your investigation because he feels that he has nothing to hide. He will read a statement regarding his activities over the course of the past few days, following which he expects to return to his good work."

Ryan sat back in his chair and waited for it.

"On the evening of Thursday 24th March, I was engaged in an administrative meeting held at St Mary's Cathedral until around six o'clock, following which I returned home for the evening and stayed there until eight o'clock the following morning of Friday 25th, whereupon I drove across to administer the services at St Andrew's Church. I was engaged at St Andrew's until after nine p.m., as I have been for the last two Fridays in a row while the parish priest is temporarily absent. Again, I returned home and spent a quiet evening there. On Saturday 26th, I rose at around seven o'clock and spent much of the day at St Mary's Cathedral attending to my duties there until after eight o'clock when I returned to my home, less than a two-minute walk away from the Cathedral. Finally, I spent Sunday 27th back at St Andrew's Church to supervise the weekly soup kitchen."

Ryan rubbed his palm over his jaw and cut to the heart of the matter.

"In other words, you have no alibi for the hours of darkness on any of those dates?"

"My client does not need an alibi, chief inspector—"

"Oh, I think I'll be the judge of that," Ryan replied.

"No, chief inspector," the Dean surprised them by saying. "God alone will be the judge."

"I'll leave you to worry about that."

"What do you drive?" Phillips asked, throwing a quick curve ball.

"I beg your pardon?"

"Your car, I mean. What do you drive?"

O'Byrne clasped his hands to steady them.

"The church provides a Vauxhall Corsa for my use. I can provide you with the paperwork, if you need it."

On safe ground, Ryan surmised.

"I understand that you act as the Bishop's proxy, in his absence. Is that correct?"

"Yes, I have that great honour."

"Where is the Bishop at the moment?"

"He is currently in Rome but is planning to return ahead of schedule, next week, given all the recent troubles."

Ryan took a surreptitious glance at his watch and then looked over at Phillips.

"I guess that's all for now," he said, trying to sound disappointed.

"Yeah, thanks for coming in." Phillips managed to convey the impression that they had been scraping the barrel. "We know how busy you must be."

"No problem at all, sergeant. I understand that you have a job to do."

"Aye, it's been hard without any real leads—"

Ryan gave him a mock hard look and Phillips looked crestfallen.

"Anyway, thanks again for coming in."

They all shook hands like gentlemen and they waved the Dean off. In silence, Ryan and Phillips moved across to one of the long windows overlooking the car park and watched him exit the main building with a regal air, pausing to thank the small group of pro-Catholic supporters who had materialised at some point during the last hour. They watched him say a few words to the news teams who clamoured for a soundbite before moving off.

Morrison hurried out of the viewing room to find them.

"You let him go? Why?"

"Oh, ye of little faith." Ryan continued to watch the Dean until he and his solicitor had swept out of the car park with a screech of expensive tyres.

"He has no alibi, you heard it for yourself," she said.

"Which is exactly what we expected," Ryan reminded her. "I thought he would have been able to come up with something more original than 'I was writing sermons all night.'"

Phillips chuckled.

"We need hard evidence, something irrefutable that we can use in court. By morning, we'll have it."

Morrison let the air hiss out of her chest in a whoosh. "I hope you know what you're doing. If this goes south—"

"It won't."

Ryan turned to Phillips. "Get in touch with MacKenzie and Lowerson. Tell them break's over."

While Ryan and his team focused their efforts on catching a killer, Jimmy Moffa's stooge exited the city in a nondescript blue van, freshly spray-painted with the logo of a fictional carpet-cleaning company. Ludo hummed along to Elton John's *Greatest Hits* and kept strictly to the speed limit. He had been given clear instructions not to draw any unwanted attention by speeding, and he did not deviate. The success or failure of their current venture depended upon his following Jimmy's instructions to the letter, and Ludo did not question the sanity or sense of it all. He was loyal as a basset hound and had been trained well.

He knew the rewards and he had dealt out enough of the punishments personally to know that he wouldn't ever want to be on the receiving end of Jimmy's wrath.

He turned up the volume and kept the speedometer dead on sixty, all the way to Humberside.

CHAPTER 20

In the space of a few short days, the people of Newcastle upon Tyne had divided themselves into two camps. There were those who believed that the Graveyard Killer was a religious fanatic, and those who believed that any killer lacked true faith, regardless of denomination. Once the line had been drawn, those on either side of it fought bitterly. Pickets sprang up outside St Mary's Cathedral and beside Earl Grey's monument; Union Jacks and English flags began to appear in shop windows—though what they had to do with anything, Ryan couldn't say—and the news was filled with it. The newscasters fairly brimmed with purpose, reading their copy to the masses in serious tones which served only to fuel the fire.

The sight of the Dean of Newcastle being taken in for questioning provided ample fodder for both sides. Conor O'Byrne was a photogenic man with an unblemished track record of public service but, as Ryan knew to his cost, killers didn't need to be low-achieving, sexually-repressed prototypes of Norman Bates to take lives. They could be highly-functioning, intelligent people with a great capacity for control, and that made his job all the harder.

But what was life without a challenge?

Ryan looked down at the sheaf of papers he held in his hands. On the top sheet was a complete list of the names of all the children registered at Our Lady of Charity Orphanage in Rothbury at the same time as Grace Turner. Running a fingertip down the list, he could see nobody by the name of 'O'Byrne'.

But he *could* see a 'Conor Jones'.

Ryan scanned the text relating to Conor Jones which PC Yates had retrieved from the orphanage records. Conor Jones would be the same age as Father Conor O'Byrne and he matched the physical description. But it was the note penned by one of the nuns that was most interesting:

Conor is a quiet boy who has difficulty socialising with the other children. However, when a new child joined us last month (GT), we noticed a sharp change in him. The two have become inseparable and the obsessive quality to his behaviour has given rise to concerns expressed by several members of staff—the matter is tabled for discussion at the next meeting chaired by Father Healy.

No other file notes had been recovered because the Church Records Office had suffered an arson attack in the late nineties, the perpetrator of which had never been identified.

Ryan looked up and into the face of the Dean of Central Newcastle, whose image played across the television in the Incident Room. He watched the man schmooze with the cameras, waxing lyrical about love and forgiveness as if he were a romantic hero rather than a cold-blooded killer.

"Enjoy your sense of freedom," Ryan murmured. "It'll be your last for a good long while."

Father Conor O'Byrne didn't know how much longer he could hold himself together. He could feel his hands shaking and held them tightly together so that it wouldn't show. He felt faint with the sheer effort of remaining in control, and sweat caked the skin on the back of his neck, blessedly hidden beneath the material of his shirt and collar.

Everywhere he turned, there were people. Reporters, activists, church staff and gossip-mongering volunteers who sought him out to appease their own curiosity.

A sea of faces awaited him inside St Mary's Cathedral— at least three times the usual number. They watched him enter the church but didn't move forward to greet him, choosing instead to remain in their huddles, whispering and worrying about the Dean of Central Newcastle.

He knew what they were wondering, too.

They wanted to know if he was a killer, if he was capable of taking a life with his own bare hands. He could see it in their eyes as they spoke to him; wonder mingled with a measure of fear that hadn't been there before. He recognised that look because he saw the same thing each time he looked in a mirror.

Let them look.

Let them wonder.

A golden effigy of Jesus on the cross looked down upon him from where it hung above the altar. He stared into the carved face, searching it for clues, to understand what he should do next.

But no otherworldly voice spoke to him. There was nothing but deafening silence, punctuated by the whispers of the small-minded people around him. They couldn't possibly understand. They had no conception of the great burden, the great *gift* which God had bestowed. They were like vermin, crawling all over the Earth, polluting it, despoiling it.

He felt hatred rise up in him, so strong and powerful that he nearly vomited. Sick and shivering, he retreated to his office and shut the door behind him. He leaned his forehead against it for a long moment while he tried to find his equilibrium.

When he turned around, she was sitting at the desk waiting for him.

"*Grace!*" he cried out, happy as a boy.

O'Byrne's equilibrium did not last for long.

The telephone screamed around the walls of his office and shattered the brief peace he had found with Grace, leaving him alone once again. He sank into his desk chair wearily and picked up the telephone, hoping that it would not be another reporter seeking an interview.

But it was worse than that.

"*Conor?*"

"Bishop." He sat up straighter in the chair. "It's good to hear from you. Are you enjoying Italy?"

"*Now is hardly the time to discuss my trip,*" came the severe response. "*I have just spoken with a Chief Inspector Ryan from Northumbria CID. He seems to think that we are obstructing his investigation.*"

O'Byrne gripped the handset.

"I've been fully co-operative with the police." He fought to keep the panic from his voice. "Just this morning, I attended the police station voluntarily to answer questions."

"*Yes, I heard.*" There was a short pause while the Bishop glanced at the script in front of him. "*The inspector is seeking my authorisation to conduct a search of church property.*"

O'Byrne tried to swallow the constriction in his throat but his mouth was bone dry. He fumbled with the water jug on his desk.

"A—a search? Of what? Where?"

Panic rose again in fresh, nauseating waves. Thousands of miles away, the Bishop heard it and dropped his head into his hands. He had hoped that the police were wrong and that it would all be an awful mistake, something they could chalk up to experience. But he was a consummate professional and a principled man. No matter how much it hurt him, no matter how much it might cost him, he would see this through to the bitter end.

It was the least he could do for all those women.

"It seems there was a discrepancy with one of the victims," the Bishop explained. *"Something about a missing earring... something like that. Anyway, if this man has been using church property to kill these poor women, they think he might have overlooked it when he tried to clear up afterwards. If the police can find the earring, they're more likely to find the killer."*

O'Byrne's mind whirled. An earring? Who had worn earrings?

His pupils flickered as he tried to bring the faces of the dead back to life. It was a great effort, and he struggled to recall the details of each woman, seeing only Grace each time he tried. The prostitute? Had she worn earrings? He could barely remember.

"Where...ah, where do they want to search?"

"They think he might have used St Andrew's after dark," the Bishop was saying, and the relief was so great that O'Byrne could have cried. *"So they would like to conduct a search of the premises this afternoon. Is that going to pose a problem?"*

The Dean drew in a long, satisfying breath and when he spoke again his voice had returned to normal.

"It's no problem at all," he said, honestly. "They can search St Andrew's for as long as they like."

The police would find nothing there.

A couple of hundred miles away in a pretty village near Humberside Airport, Ludo parked his van outside a red-brick detached house with a bottle-green door. He sat for a few minutes hunched over the steering wheel while he assessed the neighbourhood and was delighted to note that the house was not directly overlooked.

Anything for an easy life.

There was a light but persistent drizzle which encouraged pedestrians to stoop and study the pavement rather than anything else that might be happening around them, which was all to the good as well.

Ludo tugged a baseball cap over his wide forehead and checked his look in the wing mirror, admiring the embroidered logo on the rim of the hat—a nice touch to match the van. He kept his head down when he stepped onto the pavement and then unlocked the double doors at the back, leaving one wide open for ease of access. He would need to be quick but he had performed similar feats a dozen times before.

He ambled up to the front door and pressed the doorbell with a bulky, gloved finger. He painted a crooked smile on his face when he heard a woman's voice.

"Just a minute!"

The door swung open and he found himself looking down into the flushed face of a young woman with cropped blonde hair and kind eyes.

"Can I help you?"

Before embracing a life of crime, Ludo had been a highly successful car salesman with a wardrobe full of natty suits and a shiny red convertible on the driveway of his five-bedroomed home. His success had ultimately been the cause of his descent into Quaaludes in the late eighties and the subsequent loss of his home, his job and his reputation. But the fact remained that, when called upon, he could still sell ice to an Inuit.

"Sorry to disturb you, Mrs…?"

"Ah, Hayworth," she provided.

"Mrs Hayworth," he repeated, drawing out a business card. "I won't keep you long. I'm in the area at the moment and my company is running an offer on steam cleans— carpet and upholstery are both fifty percent off the usual price."

He gave her a friendly smile.

"As a parent myself, I understand how dirty sofas and carpets can get with little sticky fingers!"

She laughed along with him and began to think that the place could do with freshening up. "Anyway, here's my card—have a think about it. We're running the offer until the end of next week."

She was happy to take his card and pleasantly surprised by the inoffensive, soft-sell manner coming from such an enormous, weathered man.

"Thanks, I will," she smiled, and he tipped his cap in an old-fashioned gesture, ready to turn away.

Then, he hesitated and gave her an embarrassed look. "Ah, Mrs Hayworth, I wouldn't normally ask but I wonder if I could use your cloakroom? I've been on the road for the past three hours."

He remained a respectful distance away from the front door, so as not to intimidate her. Still, she hesitated.

"Um, well—"

Ludo could see that she was struggling to find a polite reason to refuse and he held both hands up, palms out in a classic, non-threatening gesture.

"Not to worry, I'll see if I can find somewhere…" His voice trailed off and he cast his eyes around the area, across the empty fields and scattered houses on the edge of the village. "Perhaps one of your neighbours will be home."

He turned away and had only taken three steps when she called him back.

"No, please, it's fine. Follow me, this way."

"I'll be very quick, I promise," he said, smiling again.

CHAPTER 21

MacKenzie set aside any niggling concerns for her personal safety and chose to immerse herself in work. She entrusted the latest poisoned-pen note to Faulkner's capable hands and hoped there would be a stray fingerprint that would lead them to a lonely person who wanted to bask in the reflected infamy of the Graveyard Killer. Until then, she was tasked with overseeing the excavation works at each of the twelve burial sites where Tanya Robertson was most likely to be found. There had been one small development that helped them to narrow down the search: Tanya's car had been found abandoned in a supermarket car park near Newburn, an area to the west of the city where the River Tyne wound its way through a quiet stretch of the countryside.

MacKenzie instructed the excavation team to concentrate their efforts on burials that had taken place within the remit of Northumberland County Council, the nearest county in that westerly direction. The search was reduced to three relevant burial sites and, by late afternoon, two excavations had been completed with due pomp and ceremony under her watchful eye without anything sinister being uncovered. The final excavation site within the Northumberland catchment area was Edgewell Cemetery in Prudhoe.

Consequently, MacKenzie and Lowerson found themselves dressed for inclement weather in dark green wellington boots and waterproof jackets while a team of grave diggers extracted a coffin from a freshly covered grave at Edgewell Cemetery. A sour-faced priest looked on with extreme disapproval and murmured prayers for the unfortunate soul who had been laid to rest the previous day. It was a dismal job, one they would not have wished upon any of their colleagues. Nor would they have wished to inflict further trauma upon a grieving family, but needs must.

In silence, they watched the coffin rise up from the ground. With careful handling, it was placed onto a wide sheet of tarpaulin to the side of the re-opened grave and the two detectives stepped forward to peer into the empty hole where the coffin had recently lain. Immediately, they could see the imprint of its weight against the soil beneath and, more importantly, they found what they had been searching for.

Tanya Robertson's body was almost unrecognisable, but the impact of six feet of earth and wood had partially removed the layers of soil that had hidden her from view the previous day. Now, they could see the emerging outline of a woman with her arms stretched above her head.

MacKenzie reached for her phone, intending to call Ryan straight away. But first, she looked across at the shocked, slightly bilious face of the priest who crept forward to stand next to her.

"Say a prayer for this woman and her family," she appealed to him.

Detective Sergeant Frank Phillips prided himself on being an efficient man. He approached his work with subtlety and a smile, which usually brought results. Failing that, a few veiled threats usually hurried things along. It was therefore an unusual departure from his ordinary methods to be overseeing a search of St Andrew's Church with the primary objective that it should be drawn out for as long as possible. Ryan's precise instructions had been to ensure that the search team closely resembled, '*a cross between a Benny Hill sketch and Inspector Clouseau on a bad day*'. Phillips had to say that they were certainly meeting those criteria.

He stifled a chuckle as he watched one of his constables bend to look behind one of the long, draped curtains, whipping it back as if he expected somebody to jump out from behind it.

"You'll not find the killer behind there, lad," he said, shaking his head apologetically towards the tall, stony-faced man standing a few feet away.

"We've been here for two hours already," Father O'Byrne bit out. "How much longer is this going to take?"

Phillips hid a smile. "Oh, could be a while longer yet," he warned. "You know what it's like, trying to find something that small. It's like losing a contact lens."

"Surely there has to be a more coordinated way you can search for this—what did you say you were looking for? An earring?"

Phillips made an expressive face and looked over his shoulder.

"Shh! Better keep our voices down. That's not common knowledge," he said.

O'Byrne rolled his eyes.

"Your constables seem to have covered every inch of this floor," he repeated. "The church is hardly large, either."

"Aye, they're diligent officers," Phillips said proudly.

O'Byrne cast him a disbelieving glance and looked at his watch for the fiftieth time. The day was slipping away and he had other, more important places to be.

And urgent business to take care of.

"Sergeant, I'm certain that the Bishop would be satisfied that your officers are conducting a careful search. There's no further need for me to be in attendance—"

"Ah, now, the Bishop was very clear about wanting you to keep a careful eye on the search from start to finish. I don't want anybody trying to say we planted evidence—"

"I'm sure he would do no such thing."

"You say that"—Phillips scratched his nose and settled down for a long and boring conversation about police procedure—"but it wouldn't be the first time CID has come in for some flak. Now, only last month, a mate of mine down in Teesside..."

O'Byrne snapped his mouth shut and resigned himself to a long wait.

The skies reflected the mood of the city. Thick grey clouds had gathered, blotting out the sunshine so that the transition from day into night went by almost unnoticed. Icy winds blasted through the streets and ushered the river towards the sea in surging waves that crashed against either side of the riverbank. As the water swelled and shifted, Sister Mary-Frances's body moved with it, dragging and battering against the mossy stone walls. Her long skirt became entangled in some rubbish which had collected underneath the high-level railway bridge, where a man and his dog had the misfortune of finding her.

Thirty minutes later, Ryan stood in the shadow of the bridge, bundled inside an all-weather jacket. The wind pummelled him from all sides and his eyes watered, but he remained there until Jeff Pinter rose from his inspection of Sister Mary-Frances's body and made his way back to him.

"Well? Is it another strangulation?"

Pinter blew his nose heartily before speaking.

"No, not with this one. She drowned, although the fish have certainly done their work."

Ryan experienced a moment of doubt.

"You're saying it could be a suicide?"

"I didn't say *that*. I don't know of many suicide victims with deep bruising on their upper arms, do you? It certainly doesn't look as if she could have done that to herself."

Perhaps, Ryan thought, her killer had changed his usual method and had forcibly thrown the old nun into the river.

But why?

Perhaps because Father Conor O'Byrne had hoped that her death would not be connected with that of Barbara Hewitt and Father Simon Healy. He had known that, if the police identified the victims as former staff members of Our Lady of Charity Orphanage in Rothbury, they would search for anybody else who might be connected and who might hold a grudge.

The strategy told Ryan something very interesting indeed. It told him that Father Conor O'Byrne was no frenzy killer; he was not at the mercy of uncontrollable impulses, unable to distinguish fantasy from reality as his ritual murders of redheaded women might suggest.

He was not insane.

Hundreds of miles away in Humberside, Mrs Hayworth left Ludo to use the downstairs cloakroom and stepped quickly into the kitchen to pour him a glass of water. Kind-heartedness was her failing but she couldn't help thinking that if he hadn't stopped in over three hours, he had probably encountered a lot of rude people who weren't interested in steam cleaning. She ran the tap at the kitchen sink and watched the water bubble into the glass as it filled. Besides, he was a family man himself. He was just trying to earn a living.

That's funny, she thought, suddenly. *He assumed that she had children, but how did he know that?*

She kept a tidy house and most of Alfie's toys were kept in the playroom, not left around the hallway, so there were no obvious giveaways.

The thought preyed on her mind and water began to run over the top of the glass onto her hand.

He's been in there a while, she worried. *What if he won't leave? What if he…?*

Thoughts of rape and murder flooded her mind and she dropped the glass, which shattered against the sink. She ran back into the hallway and stopped dead, with a sob.

Ludo stood there, waiting for her.

But he was not alone.

In his arms, he held Alfie, whose chubby fingers clung around his wide neck with the kind of childish trust that brought tears to her eyes. She ran forward, intending to snatch him back, but sobbed again when Ludo drew out a flick knife. The blade glinted, inches away from her child's face.

"Mama!" he gurgled. "Mama!"

He began to reach out his arms and she held them open to take him, her eyes pleading.

"*Please*," she implored Ludo. "Don't hurt him. What do you want? Tell me what you want!"

Ludo hitched the child onto his hip and gestured towards the door with his knife.

"I want you to pack a small bag. Do it now and make it quick. If you come quietly and don't make a fuss, nobody has to get hurt."

"Why? Where…?"

"Stop talking and do it."

He followed her around the house while she grabbed nappies and clothing, shoving them into a holdall. She spied her mobile phone on the bedside table and tried to grab it, but Ludo beat her to it, knocking it onto the floor where he stamped the heel of his foot against the screen until it was obliterated.

She cried, silently, while fear made her stomach cramp.

When it was done, he nodded.

"Good. You're doing the smart thing. Now, we're going to walk from the front door to my van. I want you to get into the back and I'll hand the baby to you. If you try to run, or try anything at all, I'll take him with me and you'll never see him again. Do you understand?"

Tears ran down her face and Alfie began to wail.

"Are you going to kill us?" she whispered.

Ludo's face remained impassive.

"That all depends on your husband. You'd better hope that he does the smart thing, too."

CHAPTER 22

East Denton Hall was the formal residence of the Bishop of Hexham and Newcastle, only a few minutes' drive away from the West Road Cemetery, from Karen Dobb's house in Daisy Hill, and from Newcastle city centre. It was also situated beside the major roundabout where motorists could join the A1 north or southbound, which made it the perfect base for a man needing direct access to his chosen hunting ground.

The large, Jacobean-style house stood empty while the Bishop remained in Italy, but it was not the mansion that was of interest to the two specialist technicians from Ryan's team. While Father O'Byrne was forced to supervise a search of the disabled toilet at St Andrew's Church, they parked a safe distance from the Hall and made their way on foot up the long gravel driveway. The entrance gates stood open and they headed for a separate garage building which had been built away from the main house.

It took less than thirty seconds to unlock one of the garage doors and they slipped inside, tugging the door shut behind them.

A polished black Lexus sedan was the only car parked inside.

Back at St Andrew's, Sergeant Phillips excused himself to take a phone call. Smiling across at Father O'Byrne, he confirmed that the man was safely tied up and would not be leaving any time soon.

With that assurance, the technicians went to work.

Conor O'Byrne paced around the small entrance portico of St Andrew's Church, his simmering frustration almost at boiling point. He had spent four hours watching the band of police officers stumble and trip over their flat feet while they scoured the floor for a missing pearl earring that had belonged to one of the victims, though they wouldn't name her.

They didn't need to.

Since he had nothing better to do than stand around and watch their pitiful display of incompetence, he had spent the last four hours racking his brain to remember which of the women had worn pearl earrings. No matter how he cast his mind back over the past few days, he could not bring their faces to his mind and the details of their clothing were little more than a blur.

Eventually he had fallen back on a process of elimination.

The last one—Tanya, they called her—hadn't been found yet and there was every chance she would never be found, which meant they could not know if she was missing an earring or not. He had been careful, this time, to cover her body with enough soil and the gravesite had been ready and waiting for him as usual so there had been no unexpected surprises at Edgewell as there had been last Thursday night at the West Road Cemetery.

He had been *exhausted* after that experience.

The one from the petrol station—Karen, or Carol? She had barely worn any clothing at all and, even if she had worn jewellery, it would not have been pearls, he was sure of that.

Which left the first one, from Thursday night. Now that he thought of it, she had been smartly dressed in workwear when he'd picked her up and it made her the most likely possibility.

His face fell into hard lines of anger at his own monumental stupidity.

In all these years, he had never left a trace; he had always been so cautious. But in overlooking this tiny detail, he had jeopardised his mission and everything he had accomplished so far.

It could not be tolerated.

The man looked as if he were in a daze, Phillips thought, from his position across the room. O'Byrne's eyes were glazed with a faraway expression but his jaw was clenched and firm, as were the hands which had formed into fists.

"I'm not sure how much longer we can make this look genuine, sir," one of the constables came over to murmur in his ear.

Phillips offered him a stick of gum and gave him a bolstering slap on the shoulder.

"Another half an hour, that'll do the trick."

Just before six o'clock, the Chief Pilot of the new helicopter Search and Rescue base at Humberside Airport headed home to see his wife and son. Andy Hayworth was an experienced man with fifteen years' service in the Royal Air Force before he had taken up his new position working for the SAR. Previously, the RAF had supplied local SAR helicopters but the service was now provided through a private defence company which paid for brand new, state-of-the-art helicopters equipped with more advanced search technologies. The company opened new bases around the country, and Humberside was one of them. Although it was not exactly local, it provided the rescue services for any unfortunate souls who found themselves stranded on the causeway at Holy Island or fell overboard from a fishing boat anywhere along the Northumbrian coastline.

The day had been long but productive, delivering training to some of the new pilots who had recently joined the SAR team, and Andy was more than ready to read his son a bedtime story and settle down for a nice bottle of wine with his wife.

He let himself into their smart, red-bricked house not far from the air base and was surprised to find that the television was blaring but none of the lights were on around the house. It was getting dark outside and he reached across to turn on the hallway light.

"Helen?"

He dipped his head into each of the ground floor rooms but found them empty. The remains of Alfie's snack still sat on a plate in the lounge but there was no sign of either of them.

"Helen? *Alfie!*"

He was starting to panic as he moved from room to room. He took the stairs two at a time and burst into the master bedroom, where he noticed stray clothing on the bed. Moving around the bed, he found Helen's mobile phone crushed against the carpet.

"Oh my God," he whispered.

Running from the room, he began to pull out his own mobile phone to dial 999 but as he looked into Alfie's bedroom his hand fell away again. There, propped against the cot, was a large cream notecard. With shaking hands, he picked it up and read the instructions that had been left for him.

MacKenzie and Lowerson found Ryan back at CID Headquarters, standing at the helm of what had formerly been an Incident Room but now resembled the flight deck of a spaceship. Lights beamed, charts and diagrams covered the available wall space, and telephones rang without pause while the men and women of Operation Angel bustled around. Amidst the organised chaos, Ryan stood kitted out all in black talking to the two specialist technicians who had recently returned from East Denton Hall.

"Sir?"

He turned and greeted them both with his usual direct stare.

"You look done in," he commented.

"Thank you, sir," MacKenzie replied, deadpan.

"What can you tell me about Tanya Robertson?"

"As you know, we located her beneath a gravesite at Edgewell Cemetery, which falls within the catchment area of Northumberland County Council but also within the remit of the Diocese of Hexham and Newcastle."

"As we expected."

"Yes, sir. Faulkner has requested additional forensic resources to help cover that site, because he's overwhelmed with work at the other crime scenes. His preliminary view is that the interior of Tanya Robertson's car has been thoroughly cleaned but he'll need more time to confirm whether there is any remaining trace evidence."

Ryan nodded. He had already approved the request and had it rubber-stamped by Chief Constable Morrison.

"And the staging of the body?"

"Identical to the other two redheads," MacKenzie confirmed. "Her arms were positioned over her head with the elbows bent and her blouse was shredded to resemble a wing, as was the case with Krista Ogilvy-Matthews."

"We found a note, too." Lowerson pulled out an evidence bag and handed it to his SIO. "Looks pretty similar to the others."

MacKenzie looked away while the note passed under her nose and she thought of the other one she had found on the doorstep of her home earlier that day. She had scrutinized them both for clues and come to the same conclusion as before: they were not written by the same person.

Ryan cast his eyes over the note.

"Yes, it's the same wording and the same handwriting as the other two, by the looks of it."

MacKenzie cleared her throat.

"Sir, it isn't a priority at the moment but I should tell you that Lowerson and I found another copycat note hidden beneath my doormat when I returned home to shower and change earlier today. I can't say how long it had been there."

Ryan's brows drew together in a dark, angry line.

"Another one?" He looked away and then back again. "Denise, I won't risk you coming close to O'Byrne, not until we know for sure who sent you these notes. You match the physical type and age range of his victims and he's met you in person. We'll be bringing him in very soon but I don't want you within grabbing distance."

MacKenzie's face flushed with annoyance.

"I can handle myself—"

"This isn't about you being able to take care of yourself. This is about taking sensible precautions about your safety and the integrity of the operation we have in process. I'm sorry, Denise, I can't compromise on this."

She fell silent, which Ryan took as acquiescence.

"Good." He turned to Lowerson. "Jack, I want you to stick with MacKenzie—"

"Oh, but—"

"I don't need—"

Ryan held up an authoritative hand.

"It's not up for discussion. Besides, there's plenty to be doing here." He waved around at the hub of activity surrounding them. "PC Yates has already found a host of potential victims from the last ten years and the number just keeps growing. It's going to keep us busy for months, even after we collar him."

Ryan nodded towards a large picture of Conor O'Byrne sitting beside a blown-up image of the boy he had identified as Conor Jones, taken from the orphanage group photograph found at Barbara Hewitt's home.

"He's been killing for years."

Phillips was true to his word. Half an hour later, he instructed the police search team at St Andrew's Church to pack up for the night. As they collected their gear, he wandered over to the entranceway where Father O'Byrne stood waiting for him.

"All done, Father," Phillips said cheerfully. "Thanks again for being so accommodating."

"I hardly had any choice in the matter," came the terse reply.

It was like water off a duck's back to the sergeant.

"All the same, we're grateful for your cooperation. Obviously, we were all wrong about St Andrew's. Tomorrow, with the Bishop's permission, I think we'd like to look over St Mary's."

O'Byrne nearly laughed. Six hours spent searching every nook and cranny of the church for a phantom earring and they wanted to do it all again tomorrow, which meant they still had no clue at all about where the earring actually was.

Let them chase their tails, if they wanted to. They would find nothing and be forced to issue a grovelling apology at the end of it all; to the Church and to *him*.

He might have to consider a private suit against Northumbria Police Constabulary for—what did they call it?—pain, suffering and loss of amenity. He could certainly attest that he had lost considerable access to his amenities over the past twenty-four hours.

"I will be happy to oversee the search of St Mary's," he said. "Shall we say nine o'clock tomorrow morning?"

"That'll be just fine." Phillips smiled broadly and zipped up his coat. "Have a good evening."

O'Byrne watched the short, barrel of a man and his group of idiot constables as they wandered off into the night. Back to their insignificant, meaningless lives, he thought unkindly.

He waited until the last of their vehicles had left before turning to lock up the church behind him. He jogged across the street to where a former bus station now served as a makeshift car park and hopped behind the wheel of his Vauxhall Corsa, then drove the short distance back to his home near St Mary's Cathedral. He parked the car outside as usual, then sat behind the wheel with the engine off for another fifteen minutes while he watched for any movement on the street.

There was none. He could see no suspicious-looking surveillance vans or cars he didn't recognise as belonging to his immediate neighbours.

Slowly, he unfolded himself from the car but instead of walking the short distance to his front door, he turned and jogged quickly to the nearest bus stop beside Central Station that would take him to the West Road. Dressed in black trousers and shirt, he undid the priest's collar at his throat and stuffed it into his pocket.

With his blazer draped over one arm, Father O'Byrne looked just like any other attractive man, making his way home after work.

CHAPTER 23

The rain that had threatened for most of the day finally broke free from the clouds and fell heavily over the city, engorging the river and pooling on top of the forensic tents so that they sagged against its weight. The darkness was a further cloak of invisibility to the man who walked briskly along the West Road in the direction of East Denton Hall, down the steep hill past the gateway to the West Road Cemetery where he had taken Krista Ogilvy-Matthews only a few days before.

It felt like a lifetime ago now, he thought, passing the cemetery gates without a qualm. He knew that the police had nothing on him. No CCTV, no DNA and no other link between him and the women he had killed, otherwise they would have arrested him by now. He worried that they might have made the connection between the old women and Father Healy, that they would be able to trace him back to the orphanage and to Grace. But a different boy had lived there nearly thirty years ago. A boy called Conor Jones who became the man known as Conor O'Byrne only after he was adopted in Ireland.

The records had all gone up in flames years ago—he'd seen to that.

The only thing that could possibly incriminate him was the missing earring, once they realised that the Bishop had entrusted him with the keys to his home and his car.

He must find that earring.

As O'Byrne approached the gates to the Hall, his steps slowed and he kept his head down, scanning the street for any signs that he was being watched.

They weren't even close, he thought joyously.

Turning into the driveway, he ran across the gravel, feet crunching against the stones underfoot until he reached the garage and drew out the key fob to activate the electric door. Up ahead, East Denton Hall was a dark outline against the night sky, like a sleeping giant he did not wish to awaken.

The doors lifted smoothly and he ducked inside.

"It's a go!"

The moment Phillips rang to tell him they had left O'Byrne to his own devices for the evening, Ryan and two specialist surveillance technicians made their way to the agreed rendezvous point in a suburban street around the corner from East Denton Hall. They sat inside a plain white van whose interior was kitted out with high spec screens which provided a direct link to the tiny surveillance cameras planted in strategic places around the Bishop's Lexus. The cameras had night vision capabilities, if necessary, and the recording devices had good sound quality. The three men sat staring at the dark, grainy screens while they waited for the action to start, their ears covered by large headphones.

Phillips joined them a short while later, clambering into the back of the van. He nodded to the two technicians and scooted across to perch beside Ryan.

"Hot in here, like!" he observed, unzipping his jacket again. "Can't we crack open a window?"

Ryan pointed towards the button for air-con.

"Where's Denise?"

Ryan's eyes didn't move from the screens.

"Back at CID," he replied shortly.

"I thought she would be part of the clean up—"

"She had another note," Ryan interjected, rendering further explanations unnecessary. Phillips told himself not to be annoyed by the fact that MacKenzie hadn't called to tell him about it herself, but approved of Ryan's decision to keep her away from the action, where the walls of CID headquarters could protect her.

"Put it out of your mind now," Ryan instructed him. "Lowerson is with her, back at the fort. If our estimations are correct, O'Byrne will be joining us any moment now and I want your full concentration."

Phillips did his best to focus.

"Is everyone assembled?"

"Gathered and ready," Ryan confirmed. "I've got two firearms specialists on standby around the corner in a separate unit, with another two detective constables. Air support are also on standby if he tries to rabbit his way out."

They watched the fuzzy screens until the picture changed and the cameras positioned at either end of the garage, high up on the wall, showed that the garage doors were now opening. A moment later, the garage lights were turned on and O'Byrne stepped into view.

"*Bingo*," Ryan murmured.

O'Byrne turned on the overhead lights and made directly for the Lexus, deactivating its alarm using the set of keys the Bishop had given him. He spent some time searching all around the front passenger seats, feeling along the felt flooring for a small pearl earring but he had vacuumed it thoroughly the day before and disposed of the contents, so if he had managed to suck up anything incriminating it was now long gone.

Then, he moved on to the car boot.

He could hear his own agitated breath as he searched feverishly, the sound of it reverberating around the empty garage. His fingers traced the edges but despite the garage lighting it was difficult to see. Muttering to himself, he looked around for a torch and found one on a shelf along the back wall where the Bishop kept his work tools.

O'Byrne returned to the boot and shone the torch beam in all four corners, eventually climbing fully into the boot himself to gain a better view. He peeled back the carpeted base with anxious hands to reveal the spare tyre underneath and searched all around it.

He was about to give up, satisfied that the earring had been lost, when he found it.

There was a small, shining pearl winking at him from the very depths of the boot where it must have fallen and become lodged. He was always careful to line the boot with thick plastic sheeting but he supposed it was always possible for something so tiny to work its way underneath.

He emerged from the boot and held up the small earring to the light, as if he had found buried treasure.

That had been a close shave.

He was too relieved to notice that the garage doors had begun to open again, of their own volition.

Back at CID Headquarters, MacKenzie and Lowerson tuned into the radio frequency and munched listlessly on packets of crisps as they lived vicariously through Ryan and Phillips. It was like listening to a radio play and was no real substitute for being in the thick of it all. But if she was completely honest, MacKenzie was more than happy to step down on this occasion. The sense of creeping danger had followed her like a dark cloud for days, preventing her from sleeping properly and filling her with a constant urge to look over her shoulder as she went through the ordinary motions of life. If Conor O'Byrne was responsible for the notes left at her home, then they would bring an end to it when he was brought into custody—something that was very imminent now.

"Did you hear what happened down at the New Bridge Street car park?"

MacKenzie lifted the right ear of her headphones.

"What's that?"

Lowerson reached across and picked up his notepad, flipping over a few pages.

"Things have been moving so quickly, I forgot to mention it. We sent a couple of PCs around to chase up that CCTV footage which never came through. Mick Jobes told them the same story he told us: the cameras were faulty and they were due to be repaired."

Lowerson started to put his feet up on the table but MacKenzie slapped them down again. "Anyway, they smelled a rat. The boys decided to go over Jobes' head and speak to the management. You remember, when *we* spoke to them, they confirmed Jobes' story about there being a technical fault but now they're telling a different tale. Turns out the cameras haven't worked in over two years and they're denying they told their security guards to peddle the story about them being faulty."

MacKenzie grabbed another mouthful of crisps.

"So the company lied to cover themselves. Wouldn't be the first time."

"Well, it gets better. The PCs went back to double-check Jobes' story and he'd abandoned his post. They found him wandering around outside a pub half a mile away, apparently with no idea who he was. Doctors think he had some kind of 'episode.'"

"Episode?"

Lowerson reached across for a handful of ready-salted.

"Yeah. He wasn't even drunk; he was disorientated. The PCs say he was ducking, as if there were snipers trying to get him. Jobes tried to tackle them to the ground, apparently."

MacKenzie thought sadly of what she would have called Post Traumatic Stress Disorder. They probably had some new acronym for it now but that's what it used to be called in her day.

"It doesn't surprise me," she said. "I told you he was medically discharged from the army, years ago. He's had a drink problem and run-ins with the law ever since."

"He's in hospital right now. I guess they'll want to assess him."

MacKenzie nodded.

"I hope they take care of him," she said sincerely. "He's not our man."

"Poor bastard." Lowerson thought of the security guard and tried to imagine him wandering around the centre of Newcastle, terrified that bullets were flying all around.

MacKenzie resumed listening to the radio. The incident room was nearly empty of its former staff, most of them having been assigned to field operations or sent home to their families. There were no support staff to answer the desk telephones, one of which hadn't stopped ringing for the past twenty minutes.

Although he risked missing some of the action, Lowerson took off his headphones and picked it up when it rang yet again.

MacKenzie listened with only half an ear.

"—from where?"

Pause.

"You're sure it was him? Absolutely sure?"

Another pause.

"No, no. That's very helpful. Thank you for calling this in, we'll be in touch."

Lowerson replaced the receiver and when he returned to their miniature camp of snack food and headphones, his face was animated.

"Mac! You'll never believe who I've just spoken to."

She hung the headphones around her neck and gave him her attention.

"Who?"

"That was an investigator from the Solicitors Regulation Authority," he began. "Apparently they've been trying to get through for ages."

MacKenzie pulled a face.

"We've been a little tied up. What was so important?"

"Well, they've been investigating one of the solicitors firms in the city for serious professional misconduct and they were granted an order to seize documents from the firm, which they exercised on Friday. They have their eye on one solicitor in particular and they looked over some of her recent e-mails as soon as they came in."

MacKenzie sighed.

"Where is this going?"

"I'm getting to it," Lowerson said. "They haven't had time to go through everything yet, but they came across some e-mails that were seriously concerning. Turns out this particular solicitor represents Keir Edwards."

"*The Hacker*?" The man who had killed Ryan's sister.

"Yes. The solicitor has allegedly been accepting bribes from Edwards to perform certain errands for him, among other things. One of those errands was to deliver some hand-written notes to your home."

MacKenzie turned pale.

"Written by him?"

"That's unclear. The solicitor might have written them herself before driving over to deliver them. Either way, we have our answer."

MacKenzie searched Lowerson's enthusiastic face and tried to work up some excitement of her own. It was good news, she supposed.

"Where's the solicitor?"

"The Fraud Team arrested her on Saturday night. She has a bail hearing tomorrow."

MacKenzie nodded and stood up to pace around a bit until she found her bearings. It was unsettling to learn that a notorious serial killer had chosen her to be the recipient of his intimidation. It was disgusting to know that Edwards would use the exploits of the Graveyard Killer to copycat his signature so that she would feel threatened, even if only for a few days.

She nibbled the inside of her lip while she tried to understand his motivations. Edwards had always preferred slim brunettes, although if he was given the chance to brutalize, he wasn't too fussy.

All the same, why *her*?

Then, all at once, it came to her. Last June, the team had investigated the deaths of several brunette women who had been killed by the psychiatrist Doctor Paddy Donovan. That man had connections with Keir Edwards and, to draw him out, MacKenzie had gone into HM Prison Frankland disguised as one of the pathetic, lonely women who wrote fan mail to Edwards.

For a few hours, MacKenzie had been 'Ruth'.

He must have found out, she realised. Edwards' ego was monstrous and would not tolerate that kind of deception since he prided himself on being highly intelligent and capable of seeing through police subterfuge. He had a long memory and a long reach, she thought uneasily.

"Are you alright?" Lowerson asked.

"I'm fine." She took a drink of water and painted a bright smile on her face. "In fact, it's definitely good news. We know that Edwards was responsible for those notes and we also know that he's safely behind bars. It wasn't pleasant while it lasted, but there's no real threat after all."

Lowerson nodded his agreement.

"Thank God for that," he said. "You'll be able to move around without me babysitting you all the time."

MacKenzie folded her arms.

"You're the only one with a baby face around here, boyo."

"It gets them every time," he winked.

CHAPTER 24

"What have you got there, Father?"

Conor O'Byrne turned in wide-eyed horror towards the garage doors, which opened slowly to reveal Ryan and his team, dripping wet and silhouetted against the thunderous rain which fell around them. He watched Ryan take a few steps closer until he came underneath the canopy of the garage and they were face to face, with the Lexus between them.

He clutched the pearl earring in his hand and thought about throwing it away, but they would still find it. Looking out into the rain, he saw four, maybe five, other police officers and two of them were armed.

Ryan watched him struggle.

"It's over, Conor."

O'Byrne looked down at the earring and shook his head. "Sheer dumb luck that she lost an earring." He laughed, but the sound held no mirth.

Ryan raised an eyebrow. "She didn't," he said, ever so smoothly.

"What?"

His hands began to shake as a slow, sneaking suspicion crept over him.

"Nobody lost an earring," Ryan repeated.

O'Byrne looked incredulously at the pearl stud clutched in his palm, then back up into Ryan's merciless face.

"Take a look around the garage, Conor," Ryan advised. "It's rigged with cameras which were planted earlier today in anticipation of your visit."

O'Byrne didn't bother to check.

"You don't have any evidence against me. I didn't kill anyone," he argued.

"You're right, we didn't have much in the way of forensics." Ryan began to move closer again and O'Byrne circled around the car away from him. "Although we do now have some footage of this Lexus driving in the direction of Edgewell Cemetery after ten o'clock on Saturday night, returning again just before eleven. That's suggestive, but it was possible that others had access to the Bishop's keys. We needed you to show your hand, and now you have."

The Dean's mind raced, trying to follow the steps.

"You contacted the Bishop and he authorised all this," he realised, waving a hand at the hidden cameras. "Then you asked him to plant the idea of a missing earring and made me believe it was real."

Ryan nodded.

"We knew you wouldn't use church property to kill those women, or at least not the bricks and mortar kind,"

Ryan said. "But we knew that if we gave you enough rope, you would hang yourself by leading us here. You had to be certain that the earring hadn't fallen out somewhere inside the car. Only the killer would think to do that."

O'Byrne smiled nastily. "Clever bastard, aren't you?"

"Time to go." Ryan stepped forward, intending to place him under arrest.

It all happened in an instant. One moment, O'Byrne was leaning on the other side of the car, and the next he had slipped inside the Lexus, slamming the heel of his hand against the internal locking system.

Ryan swore and made a grab for one of the door handles, trying to open it.

"*O'Byrne!* Don't be a bloody fool, man. Open the door!"

He slid the key into the ignition and fired up the engine, while Ryan ran around to the front of the car and put his hands on the bonnet.

They looked at one another through the windscreen.

"Don't do this," Ryan told him.

In answer, O'Byrne slammed his foot down on the accelerator and the car surged forwards, knocking Ryan off his feet. The other members of his team sprang out of the way to avoid being run over, with Phillips finding himself face down on the gravel driveway. The firearms officers were on their feet again within seconds and, at Ryan's signal, aimed at the tyres of the car that was now speeding down the driveway in a cloud of dust and rain.

At the gates, the Lexus rammed through the squad car which blocked the exit with a hard metallic crunch, and the police vehicle spun away and into the path of oncoming traffic on the main road. Despite a massive dent to its front end, the Lexus sped off into the darkness.

The team ran back to their vehicles while Ryan shouted down the radio for immediate air support as they gave chase.

The atrocious weather made for an arduous night flight from Humberside to the North East and Andy Hayworth was not in full possession of his faculties. The chopper dipped and swayed without his usual skill and the high winds and rain made the journey all the more treacherous. He had turned the radio off as per his instructions and was taking his life into his own hands by completing the flight without the support of the control tower. He followed the coastline, keeping a good distance from the shore and flying barely fifty feet above the waves to make his presence harder to detect.

Fear was a living, breathing thing inside him and its power was matched only by his terror at the thought of what would happen to his wife and child if he failed.

Their pictures hung from a small chain in the cockpit of the helicopter.

Another helicopter circled above the western end of Newcastle city centre, shining its powerful searchlight through the dark and the rain until it latched onto a black Lexus hurtling along the A1 southbound at breakneck speed. Closing the distance behind him, Ryan was at the wheel of the white surveillance van and pushed its performance to the limits. Phillips braced himself against the dashboard with one hand while the other clutched a mobile phone to his ear as he spoke with colleagues in the Durham Police Constabulary. O'Byrne was heading in their direction, flying over the River Tyne with no immediate signs of stopping and they would need to head him off at the other end with as little risk to ordinary motorists as possible.

"Shame those roadworks have finished," Ryan joked. "We could have used some traffic right about now."

Phillips was too busy keeping control of his bowels to laugh but he appreciated the thought. Behind them, more sirens joined the chase and blue lights filled the rearview mirror as they whizzed past an enormous shopping mall on the south side of the river.

"Where the hell does he think he's going?"

"He's not thinking straight," Ryan replied, but then he thought of the geography and the meaning behind it all.

Unconsciously, his foot eased off the pedal and Phillips threw him a nervous look.

"What's the matter?"

"I know where he's going," Ryan said. "He's going to the Angel of the North, to see Grace."

"Grace Turner? The girl died years ago."

"Yes, but he remembers her through these women. Every time he kills them, he gives them the proper burial she never had. Didn't you notice, Frank? The paper reported her death as a suicide and there's no burial record for a Grace Turner in the Diocesan registers around that time. I'm guessing that Father Healy and the nuns denied her a proper burial on account of it being a mortal sin to take her own life. O'Byrne never got over it. Maybe he thinks the Angel is a monument just for Grace."

"He's mad as a hatter," Phillips pronounced.

Ryan put his foot down again while his sergeant liaised with Durham Police, telling them to set up a road block around the entrance to the Angel of the North.

The car chase was reported across every major news channel and the residents of the North East gave up their usual nightly soap operas to enjoy the real-life drama playing out before their eyes. TV helicopters were scrambled to get live footage of the Graveyard Killer's desperate flight across the river and in the meantime, newscasters relayed garbled eye-witness accounts from fellow motorists who used their five minutes of fame to discuss their own brief encounter with the country's newest serial killer.

Oblivious to the coverage, Conor O'Byrne drove the Lexus onwards without any particular idea of where he was headed, although he found himself steering the car towards Gateshead. He heard the sirens howling somewhere behind him and the lack of traffic ahead told him that the police must have shut down access to the main road, so he knew he didn't have long before they would close in.

As he followed the A1 south along the edges of Gateshead, an enormous iron angel came into view, stark against the navy-blue sky with its aeroplane wings angled forwards as if to welcome him. How many times he had looked at the Angel of the North and wondered if God had commissioned it himself, as a permanent monument to his messenger?

His angel.

It was *his* monument, O'Byrne realised, feeling the old energy coursing through his veins. God had erected it so that the people might know there was an angel here on Earth, one empowered to punish and to save in equal measure.

Andy Hayworth almost lost his nerve countless times on the journey north from Humberside. He visualised flying the helicopter into the black depths of the sea or careening into the rocks, rather than being forced to go on. But then he thought of his family and what they might be suffering; the unknown was far more terrifying than what he faced right now.

So he mustered the strength to carry on.

The city lights and his own experience told him that he was not far from his destination and he turned on the satellite navigation system once again so that he could locate the pick-up point.

He was running exactly on time.

CHAPTER 25

They found Conor O'Byrne kneeling at the foot of the Angel.

The Lexus had been discarded in the small visitors' car park nearby with the driver's door left wide open to the wind. Its engine oozed smoke from beneath the crumpled hood and one of its back tyres was completely flat, the rubber burned away almost to nothing. Ryan and Phillips led the procession of police vehicles and, after a brief word into his radio, their wailing sirens were turned off so that the only sound that could be heard was the rain drumming against the tarmac.

They stepped into the torrent and found their clothes plastered to their skin within seconds. The wind sang around their ears and Ryan had to shout to be heard.

"Get a medic out here!"

It was not so much that he minded seeing the man hurt or bleeding, certainly not after the hurt he had inflicted upon so many others. But Ryan would not take the chance that he might, at some later stage in his prosecution, accuse the police of failing to provide him with his basic right to medical attention.

They made their way through the driving rain and up the short incline to the foot of the Angel with two firearms officers in tow. Powerful uplighters shone a beam of white light on the monument and the rain glistened like falling stars against it. It was not beautiful so much as masterful, reflecting the industrial heritage of the surrounding landscape. Despite its colossal size, Ryan thought it suited the area perfectly.

O'Byrne knelt in the mud at its feet, shivering in the wind and rain, and clutching a rosary between his trembling fingers. Ryan held out a hand to signal that the others should keep back as he approached the man with slow, careful steps.

"Conor?"

He didn't look up from his prayer.

Ryan took another step closer, until he was within touching distance of O'Byrne's crouched figure.

"Time's up," Ryan shouted through the wind. "Conor O'Byrne, I am arresting you on suspicion of murder. You do not have to say anything, but it may harm your defence if you do not mention when questioned something which you later rely on in court. Anything you do say may be given in evidence."

The man looked up and, just for an instant, he thought he saw two angels—and both of them were made of iron.

"God will protect me!" he shouted back. "I am his servant!"

"You don't really believe that." Ryan reached down and hauled the man to his feet. He was tired of looking down and what he had to say needed to be said eye to eye. "You killed those women because you liked it. You killed the others because you were angry at their decision not to bury Grace on consecrated ground. Why pretend otherwise?"

O'Byrne wrenched his arm free of Ryan's grip.

"You know nothing, absolutely *nothing* about Grace. You have no conception of what she meant to me; what we meant to each other. You're not fit to utter her name."

Ryan swiped a hand over his wet face.

"I've heard it all before, Conor—countless times. You were the loner. That loser kid who nobody wanted to play with, abandoned by your parents and left to grow up in an orphanage. So far, you have my sympathies." He stepped forward again, into O'Byrne's personal space. "Then, a new girl came to the orphanage and she took pity on you—"

"No!" O'Byrne spat. "We loved each other!"

Ryan didn't pause for breath.

"I've read the nun's report, Conor. It said you were obsessive and a cause for concern. Did you know that? Or did you think you'd managed to destroy all the records in the fire?"

O'Byrne's eyes shifted away, which gave Ryan all the answer he needed.

"Grace jumped from the roof of the orphanage because she couldn't stand to be around you—"

"That's a lie!"

"Is it? Tell me why she was so special, Conor. Tell me why you killed all those women in her memory. *Tell me!*"

O'Byrne's face crumpled and, just for a moment, Ryan thought he had gone too far. But then the face morphed again, into something hard and unrecognisable. As the rain fell around them, he laid himself bare.

"Grace was everything to me. *Everything.* You can't understand what it was like in those places—how could you?" He cast derisive, hateful eyes over Ryan's face. "You won the lottery of life. You wouldn't know what it feels like to be utterly and completely alone in the world."

"You were adopted."

"The Church is the only mother and father that I recognise."

Ryan said nothing, while the cold seeped through his jacket and into his bones.

"All these years, I believed that Grace took her own life. I believed that she wanted to be rid of me and that she couldn't go on. I thought that she had abandoned me."

Now the tears started to fall, mingling with the rain which ran down his cheeks and dripped from his chin.

"They told me it was suicide, and that was a grave sin. Father Healy would not allow her a proper burial; he said that the taking of one's own life was to falsely assert dominion over God's property, something that he could not sanction or forgive. So they cremated her. They turned Grace's body into ash, as if she had never existed at all."

Behind him, Ryan sensed that his team were growing impatient but he held out his hand again to signal them back while he allowed O'Byrne to continue. He needed to understand what had led the man to kill so many people.

If he could ever bring himself to understand.

"Grace never left me. Do you understand?" The priest searched Ryan's face with wild eyes, then shook his head as if to answer his own question. "You couldn't understand because you don't have the gift. But God invested me with His spirit and made me his messenger. He let me see her, too. After...after the first time I saved a soul, I started to see Grace again. She stayed with me, everywhere I went. Some days, she would disappear and on others I only saw her for a fleeting moment. But for every soul I saved, God rewarded me with her presence in my life."

Ryan no longer felt the rain, or the cold. He was completely absorbed in his study of the man in front of him, watching for the tiny behavioural signs that would reveal O'Byrne to be a fraud. But the more he watched and listened, the more he realised that he had been wrong about the man. He might not have killed in a frenzy, he might have been fully aware of his actions, but he was no longer sure that the man understood that those actions were *wrong*. He was not what ordinary people would have called 'sane'.

Whether the law agreed with Ryan's assessment remained to be seen.

"You're saying that the women you killed were a kind of sacrifice, for which God rewarded you?"

O'Byrne closed his eyes, screwing them up tightly.

"They *were* Grace. When I took them, I thought they were Grace. I wanted them to be—I wanted them to be her—"

He started to sob, deep and gut-wrenchingly loud.

"But they weren't her. I know they weren't her. I saved them, though." He opened his eyes again. "I gave them peace and a proper burial."

"How kind of you," Ryan said. "I'm sure their families will be delighted to hear it."

O'Byrne switched again from sadness to anger, in the blink of an eye.

"The others deserved no proper burial. I gave them no absolution, no rites. I hope they burn in the fires of Hell for all eternity."

Well, Ryan thought. He couldn't be clearer than that.

"Why? You said that the Church is mother and father to you. As a priest, you understand Catholic theology on the subject of suicide; you told me so yourself, in your office at St Mary's. Therefore you above all people should understand Father Healy's decision not to bury Grace."

O'Byrne began to laugh, long and loud.

"So I did," he agreed. "But Grace didn't commit suicide, as I'd been led to believe."

Ryan frowned and realised that he was missing a piece of the puzzle.

"On Friday 18th, just over a week ago, Barbara Hewitt came into St Andrew's to confess her sins. It was fate that led her to me, or God's divine hand." O'Byrne's voice was so quiet, Ryan strained to hear as he blinked the rainwater from his eyes. "God sent her to me, so that her lies might be revealed after all these years."

He shook himself and smiled bleakly.

"She didn't recognise me at all," he recalled. "She burst into the church demanding that somebody hear her confession and, I admit, I was curious to hear it. Barbara had been the nurse at the orphanage but she was also a midwife. I suppose I forgot about that, because it never occurred to me—"

O'Byrne broke off and looked down at his shaking hands, remembering how good they had felt wrapped around the old woman's throat.

"You see, she confessed that she had told a lie, back in 1990, when she worked at an orphanage in Rothbury. The lie, she said, concerned a girl who had fallen from the orphanage roof as she had tried to run away. The girl had been beautiful, Barbara told me, with long red hair and blue eyes." His voice quivered, but he carried on. "When the girl died, the committee in charge of the orphanage wanted to hush it up altogether but, when they couldn't, they said it was suicide to avoid having to admit something much worse.

"Grace was pregnant, you see." O'Byrne delivered the bombshell in a queer, flat voice. "She went to Barbara to ask for help and Barbara—the bloody hypocrite—tried to pressure her into having an abortion, to commit a mortal sin, just to preserve the *reputation* of the orphanage and its staff. So, to protect the baby, Grace decided to run away."

In the short silence, Ryan asked the burning question.

"Who was the baby's father?"

"The baby was *mine*," O'Byrne snarled. "What we had was pure, it was *special*. There was nobody else."

"Why didn't Grace tell you?"

O'Byrne shook his head. "She was fourteen, chief inspector, and I was only two years older. Perhaps she thought that I would panic and try to pressure her into having an abortion as well. She must have been so desperate at the thought of our baby being taken away from her—all she could do was run."

Ryan's jaw clenched. O'Byrne was guilty of statutory rape, to add to his other crimes.

"Barbara told you that the Church wanted the pregnancy covered up?"

"They painted it as suicide and denied her any proper burial rites. And Barbara had *known*. She was the one responsible for killing Grace and our baby."

"What did you do?"

"I listened to her whining confession, begging for God's forgiveness. She asked me how she could atone for it and I told her that it would take some time and that she needed to dedicate herself to rejoining the faith. I said that I would be happy to pay her a house call, to discuss things in confidence. She seemed so pathetically grateful."

He laughed unkindly. "I took the car and drove up there, the same night. She was surprised but happy to see me."

"And Healy?"

"To save his own reputation, he let Grace's soul be damned. He deserved to die."

Ryan remembered the sight of Father Simon Healy's head hanging limply from the rest of his body.

"The nun—Sister Mary-Frances?"

O'Byrne nodded, tired now that he had purged himself.

"She was the last one. I only wish that I had known about her deception years ago."

The words were spoken with such malice that Ryan almost took a step away, but he held firm.

"Tell me something, Conor. Now that you've killed all those people, do you feel better?"

O'Byrne waged an internal war for long minutes but finally he shook his head.

"Grace has gone now. I can't see her anymore."

Ryan stepped forward again to grasp his arm. This time, O'Byrne allowed himself to be led back down the hill towards the army of police at the bottom.

CHAPTER 26

MacKenzie yawned widely and looked across the empty Incident Room to where Lowerson had fallen asleep at his desk. She smiled and walked across to place an affectionate hand on his mousy brown head.

"Jack?"

He mumbled something incomprehensible and she shook him gently.

"Mmm? What? I'm awake...I'm awake," he repeated, yawning until his jaw clicked.

"Time to go home," she said. "Phillips just rang to tell me they have O'Byrne in custody. They're bringing him in now."

"Do they need us?"

MacKenzie shook her head.

"There'll be plenty of forms to fill out tomorrow, no doubt, but our work is done for today. "Besides"—she broke off to check the time—"it's nearly midnight. It's past your bedtime."

Lowerson scrubbed his hands over his face and had to admit his eyes were drooping. It had been a long weekend, in the worst possible sense.

"Would you like me to take you home, Mac?"

He was adorable, she thought. Even though he looked like he could quite happily fall asleep where he stood, Lowerson was still concerned for her safety.

"No. I appreciate everything you've done over the past few days. I know I don't say it often but it made all the difference to me, knowing that you were there."

Lowerson felt a blush creep up his neck.

"Anyway, the threat to my personal safety has been neutralised. We know who's been sending the notes and the Hacker is behind bars. Sticks and stones..." She shrugged. "While he's writing his sad little notes in his cold cell, I'm going to go back home and have myself a nice long bubble bath."

"I'm going to have myself a nice long beer," Lowerson thought aloud.

They shut down Operation Angel for the night and locked the Incident Room door behind them before making their way down to the ground floor of CID Headquarters. They said 'goodnight' to the duty sergeant at the front desk and walked out into the rainy night.

"Night Jack."

"See you tomorrow, Mac."

She held her blazer over her head and scampered through the rain towards her car.

Lowerson opened his mouth to call her back and then shut it again, feeling foolish. Instead, he waved a hand as she manoeuvred her red Fiesta towards the main gates of the car park and told himself he was a superstitious idiot when she tooted the horn in a cheerful *beepety-beep*.

A moment later, she had gone.

Ryan personally went through the procedure of booking Conor O'Byrne into his cell for the night. If experience had taught him anything, it was that big fish tended to be slippery and surprisingly capable of wriggling off their hooks, particularly with the help of a fancy lawyer.

O'Byrne's solicitor had been right there waiting for his client when they drove into the car park. Swift and personal service came at a cost, but it was one that the Church was willing to pay to ensure that any potential embarrassment was kept to a minimum.

But now, O'Byrne was alone once again inside the uninspiring surroundings of a holding cell with only his memories of Grace Turner to accompany him.

"I want a twenty-four-hour watch," Ryan instructed.

A medic had pronounced the man physically fit and well enough for detention overnight, but it wasn't his skin and bones that Ryan worried about. It wasn't uncommon for men like O'Byrne simply to end it all, suicide being preferable to spending the remainder of their lives in prison or in the maximum-security ward of a hospital.

Phillips made a rumbling sound in his chest and took one last look through the peep hole to where the priest sat on the edge of his iron bed, staring at an empty spot on the wall of his cell.

"Aye, I wouldn't put it past him," he agreed. "What do you want to do about a psychiatrist?"

Ryan blew out a breath. There were a couple of 'go-to' forensic psychiatrists and psychologists that CID used on a routine basis to assess whether their charges were capable of being detained, but the bigger questions surrounding the man's overall sanity or capacity to stand trial would be hotly contested by his legal counsel. The Crown Prosecution Service had their own list of preferred experts they tended to instruct when putting together a case.

"Everything has been done by the book so far. Let's wait to hear from the CPS tomorrow morning and take it from there."

Phillips nodded and rubbed at his eyes, which were bloodshot.

"That's everything tied up here then—"

Ryan's phone drummed out its electronic rendition of the *Indiana Jones* theme tune and he slapped his hands against his pockets in an effort to remember where he had stashed it.

He found it in the back pocket of his dark jeans.

"Ryan."

Phillips watched the chief inspector's eyes turn from a dull grey to a bright silver and his face drained of all colour.

He thought the man might keel over and he reached out immediately to put a supportive hand on Ryan's back while a funny jitter passed through his body, a premonition of bad things to come.

"What's the matter, lad?" he mouthed urgently, but Ryan was rapping out a series of sharp questions followed by a barked order to the mysterious caller.

"I want a squad car over to her house, *now*. He should be considered armed and dangerous." He reeled off the address of Anna's cottage in Durham. "I'm on my way."

Ryan ended the call and then, for the first time in Phillips' memory, fumbled in his haste to bring up Anna's number, which he called next. He held the phone to his ear while he waited for her to pick up and began to run towards the exit.

"Ryan!" Phillips trotted behind him. "Ryan, for God's sake man, what's happened?"

Ryan didn't pause but he turned bleak eyes towards his sergeant.

"Edwards. Edwards is out."

Phillips stopped dead.

"What? What do you mean he's *out*?"

"He's *out*!" Ryan shouted, sprinting towards his car. "He's broken out of prison!"

Phillips stood in the rain while Ryan reversed out of the car park with precise, jerky movements and was gone a few seconds later with a squeal of tyres. Phillips sent up a prayer to anybody listening that he wasn't killed on the roads because he had never seen Ryan like that before, so wild with worry that he was a danger to himself and possibly to others. It was after midnight and the roads were dark and wet.

But Phillips knew he would have behaved in exactly the same way, were the tables reversed. Keir Edwards, otherwise known as the Hacker, was a dangerous psychopath with a preference for slim young brunettes and an all-consuming hatred of Ryan, the man who had lost his sister in exchange for bringing her killer to justice. He thought of Ryan's fiancée Anna, who lived within a short drive of HM Prison Frankland and could hardly bring himself to imagine what would happen if Ryan was too late getting across to her.

Phillips could still remember the sight of Ryan lying injured with his sister's body lying in his lap; how he had cradled her head while blood pumped out of her body through the ragged gash at her neck. He would never forget the desolation on Ryan's face and Phillips knew that he had blamed himself for her death ever since. He hadn't known if the lad would come through it. Now, there was a risk that the Hacker would take the other woman he loved, leaving him with nothing.

Ryan would be destroyed completely.

Heart sore, Phillips hurried back into CID Headquarters and turned on the news, which was just starting to report a 'major incident' at HM Prison Frankland, on the outskirts of Durham:

News is just coming in…we can report that there has been what the police are describing as a major incident at

HM Prison Frankland...breaking news just coming in now of an apparent prison break at HM Prison Frankland...it is believed that Keir Edwards, the man known as 'The Hacker', has broken out of his maximum security, category A prison... people are advised to remain inside their homes as a manhunt is now underway. Edwards is considered highly dangerous and may be armed.

The double doors behind him swung open and Chief Constable Morrison tore into the foyer. Her sandy blonde hair was wet from the rain and she wore baggy sportswear, suggesting that she had recently been to the gym despite the late hour.

Worry pinched her face and she looked ten years older than she had that morning.

"Frank, thank God you're here. I heard from the CC down in Durham. He's worried and so am I. The Commissioner rang me at home and he's liaising with Durham Constabulary to put out a statement. The Warden at Frankland is beside himself—"

"How did Edwards get out?"

"Helicopter," Morrison panted as they rushed along the corridor to her office, where more calls would be made. "He got a helicopter to land right inside the bloody exercise yard."

"How is that possible?" Phillips stammered.

"It's been done before—the last time was in Canada a few years ago. Apparently, the Warden in Durham requested a wire roof covering to prevent exactly this kind of thing from happening, but it was rejected due to lack of funding."

Phillips swore roundly.

"Where's Ryan?" Morrison looked up, suddenly noticing she was a man down.

"Edwards will do everything he can to hurt him," Phillips said. "The best way to do that is to take his fiancée. Ryan is driving across to Durham like the hounds of hell are after him. He needs to get to Anna before Edwards does."

"Oh my God."

Morrison sank into her desk chair and held her head in her hands. Her eyes darted back and forth while she thought of how to help.

"Firearms—" she started.

"Already on their way," Phillips confirmed. "First thing he did was order a squad car to get down there and secure the property. He won't rest until he's seen her for himself."

Morrison sent him a look of utter helplessness. "And if he's too late?"

Phillips just shook his head and left her to answer the ringing phone on her desk.

The first thing that Phillips did next was to key in the number for MacKenzie. After a minute or so, he heard her soft Irish voice at the other end of the line.

"Frank? I was about to call you. I've just stepped out of the bath and seen the news—do you need me to come back in? It's a living nightmare."

He closed his eyes and savoured the sound of her.

"Aye, lass. Best if you do. It's like a nuclear explosion has gone off down here," he said, watching as officers began to filter back into the major incident unit. "Ryan's gone straight down to Durham to find Anna. All we can do is hope and pray that Edwards hasn't beaten him to it because, if I were him, she would be the prime target."

MacKenzie felt tears spring to her eyes. Anna Taylor was a woman she admired and had come to love. Just last month, she had taken her to the bridal shop to pick out the ivory tulle dress Anna planned to wear at her wedding. She had been stunned and moved when the girl had asked if she would come with her to stand in for the mother she no longer had, just for the day.

"Dear God, Frank—I can't think of it."

"Aye, I know."

"I'm on my way," she said firmly.

Lowerson was one of the first to arrive back at CID Headquarters after receiving the alert. He had only made it halfway home when the call came through on his hands-free phone and, besides, he couldn't have missed the breaking news which interrupted every radio channel. That included the late-night dance classics he had been blasting out to keep him awake until he made it home.

A quick U-turn, and he was heading back to the office.

He found Phillips in the open-plan office used by the major crime teams including Ryan's division of staff and clocked all the usual faces.

"Where's Ryan?"

Phillips walked over to him and set a plastic cup of black coffee in his hand.

"He's on his way to Durham," he replied. "Edwards will go for Anna, first chance he gets."

"I can't believe it," Lowerson said, taking a scalding sip of the mud brown liquid. "Mac and I were only talking about the Hacker an hour ago."

Phillips felt that odd frisson snake up his spine again, and he grasped Lowerson's shoulder.

"What do you mean, son?"

Lowerson frowned and the coffee sloshed a bit.

"I thought—I thought she had told you? The Solicitors Regulation Authority called us after hours because it was urgent. They're investigating Edwards' solicitor for serious malpractice and they've already discovered that the solicitor was taking bribes to hand deliver those notes from Edwards to MacKenzie."

Phillips' hand gripped Lowerson's shoulder harder, but not intentionally.

"Denise."

Lowerson scanned the room desperately, but he already knew that she wasn't there.

"Frank, I swear—we thought the threat had passed and that Edwards was still in prison. We thought he was just trying to pay her back for posing as one of his pen-pals last year."

Phillips remembered the hollow, dreadful sense of impotence he had felt when he and his late wife had been told she had terminal cancer. He had argued with the consultant, begged and pleaded, then privately broken down so that Laura would not see his tears and be frightened. That had been one of the worst times of his life, matched only by the final weeks before she died.

But that terrible feeling had returned to haunt him, and as he looked into the terrified face of the young detective constable, he almost doubled over.

"Get a team dispatched to her house," Phillips whispered, before thrusting him aside to run as he had never run before.

Ryan drove like a man possessed, through the darkened streets of Newcastle and across the river along the same route he had chased Conor O'Byrne only a few hours before. The roads were sodden as the rain continued to fall in almost biblical proportions. He knew that his eyes were tired, that his body was exhausted and required refuelling, but there was no question of that now. He opened the windows to feel the wind whip around him, keeping his eyes sharp and focused on his destination.

He barely glanced at the Angel of the North as he sped past.

In an extraordinary display of willpower, Ryan commanded his mind to shut off treacherous images of Anna lying dead in a pool of her own blood. He had seen Edwards' handiwork before and his imagination threatened to go wild with possibilities.

Anna with her fingers hacked off, one by one.

Anna drugged and abused, unable to fight back.

Anna with her head separated from her body, her dead eyes staring at him.

He bit down hard and his jaw clenched painfully. Later, much later, he would be grateful for the lack of any other traffic on the roads because he could not be held responsible for his driving prowess on that long, seemingly endless journey. His fingers clamped the steering wheel like a lifeline and his foot pushed the pedal to the floor, barely lifting until he entered the outer limits of Durham city.

Anna heard the revving of the engine and jumped off the sofa to meet him as he burst into the cottage.

His eyes sought her out and he crossed the room in three long strides.

"Anna."

He held her head in his gentle hands, kissing her face, wrapping her in his arms.

"I didn't know—I thought—"

She heard the shudder in his chest and hugged him harder.

"I'm alright, I'm safe," she murmured. "I heard what happened."

Ryan buried his face in her hair and gave himself another minute to compose himself. Only then did he notice two constables from the Durham Police Constabulary sitting awkwardly on the cosy armchairs Anna had arranged around the inglenook fireplace.

"Sir," they greeted him.

Ryan didn't move an inch, but nodded his thanks to them both.

"We'll be just outside." They drained their coffee mugs and made a tactical retreat back to their squad car.

"I couldn't get through to you," Ryan said eventually, and she sighed.

"I know, I'm sorry about that. I was in a late lecture at the university and then I got caught up with some work and took the phone off the hook while I finished it. I, ah, well your mum has been calling quite a bit lately—"

Ryan smiled against the top of her head.

"Badgering you about wedding plans, no doubt."

"Normally, I love it," she assured him. "But this evening I really had to push on with a paper I've been working on and so I took it off the hook for a little while. I guess the time ran away with me. I'm so sorry you were worried."

Ryan continued to hold her against him and showed no immediate signs of letting go.

"It doesn't matter now. What matters is that you're safe, here with me."

"But Edwards has escaped? How could that happen?"

A shadow crossed his face as he thought of the damage that man would wreak. Untold horrors lay just around the corner, he was sure. He wasn't proud of it, but he was profoundly grateful that, if some poor woman lost their life that night, it was not going to be his future wife.

But his heart broke in the certain knowledge that another soul would suffer in her place.

"He's cunning and he has money," Ryan said dully. "We do everything we can to stop the contraband, to stop the corruption, but you can't fight human nature. A part of me thinks that this was inevitable."

"What did he do—dig a tunnel or something?"

Ryan huffed out an unexpected laugh.

"This isn't *The Great Escape*, but you're not all that far off. As far as I know, a helicopter picked him up."

Anna stared at the wall of his chest and then drew back to quiz him further.

"Just like that?" She snapped her fingers. "He's not a Columbian drug baron, for goodness' sake!"

"It's surprisingly common," he said. "It happened a lot in the 70s and 80s and had a bit of a renaissance in the last decade. It prompted a lot of prisons to erect a sort of see-through wire covering over their outdoor areas to prevent a helicopter landing there, but apparently Frankland Prison didn't have the cash to front it."

Anna realised that his body had started to shake, tiny rippling tremors that transmitted across her skin.

"Ryan? When was the last time you ate?"

He ran a hand through his hair and shrugged.

"I can't remember—but I'm not hungry."

"Sod that," she muttered, and thrust a digestive biscuit into his mouth as she went to assemble an enormous sandwich.

Lowerson had really come into his own during the course of the last year and because of it he was able to override Phillips' desire to drive the short distance to MacKenzie's house. He bundled the sergeant inside his nifty Fiat and gunned the engine like a pro, covering the ground at speed.

Phillips sat in the passenger seat pressing 'redial' on his mobile phone although there was still no answer from Denise. His face was ashen with shock and he wore the distant, expressionless look of one who was living through a nightmare.

The journey from CID Headquarters to Denise MacKenzie's house could not have taken more than five minutes, but by the time Lowerson came to an emergency stop at the kerb outside, it felt like they had traversed a great distance.

Phillips sprang out of the car as soon as it reached the kerb and banged a fist on the front door. The porch lamp was switched on and shone a greenish light over his clammy, anguished face.

They had both noticed that her red Fiesta was not on the driveway where it should have been.

"Denise!"

There was no reply, but his voice awakened her immediate neighbours and Lowerson noticed their windows light up.

"Denise!"

Phillips groped for the house keys but could barely see past his overwhelming fear and he swore as they fell into the shrubbery beside the path.

He didn't bother to root around for them.

"Get back," he told Lowerson, before planting his boot against the front door. With two hard kicks, the lock broke and it fell open.

The hallway beyond was brightly lit. MacKenzie's jacket hung on the peg where she always left it and her tan leather satchel hung beside it.

And there on the hallway table was propped a small cream card which read:

CATCH ME IF YOU CAN

EPILOGUE

Keir Edwards thanked the taxi driver politely and made sure to give him a small tip. Not too much, not too little to be memorable, then stepped out onto the pavement at the bottom of the street. He moved lightly and, thanks to his new pilot friend, was dressed smartly in a navy suit which was only slightly too small across the chest.

He had bulked up a bit over the past few months in prison. There was little else to do, and he had always been a great proponent of maintaining a healthy diet. As a narcissist, he was also preoccupied with the importance of his own image and had taken great pleasure in sculpting his new, stronger form.

Now that he was free, he could be philosophical and admit that prison had taught him a thing or two. For a start, it had given him the time and thinking space to relive his past exploits in infinite detail. He had come to the conclusion that Ryan had only managed to overpower him at the last moment thanks to a small physical advantage, probably brought on by a surge in adrenaline induced by fear. The kilos he had gained in pure muscle would compensate for that in the future and, next time, there would be no room for failure.

There was a time when the two men might have been mistaken for brothers. Both were tall and dark, both what society might consider handsome. Their backgrounds were not dissimilar, either. Both were middle class, well-educated men who had entered respectable 'professions'.

That was where the similarity ended.

He wondered whether Ryan would recognise him on the street. Gone was the polished, expensive hair cut; it had been replaced by a short, cropped military style and he had grown a full beard. His arms were no longer lean but hard and thickly muscled, as were his legs.

He began to stroll down the street, happy as a peacock, until he found the number he was looking for.

MacKenzie replaced the receiver and quickly towelled herself off. Images of Anna lying dismembered on the floor of her cottage spurred her into action and she moved quickly around the room pulling on clean clothes. She didn't stop to worry about hair or make-up; it didn't enter her mind. Her feet pattered down the stairs and she tugged on her boots, eager to get back to CID where she could be of use. She was about to scoop up her car keys when there came a knock at the front door.

She automatically assumed that Frank had come to meet her and had forgotten his keys. Grief and worry made her careless and she opened the door.

MacKenzie recognised the eyes, which were black and filled with malice.

"Hello, *Ruth*. Have you missed me?"

An instant later, his hand shot out and her world went dark.

AUTHOR'S NOTE

Although this murder mystery story depicts fictional characters belonging to the Catholic faith in the North East, it is important to make clear that I believe wrongdoing is a human behavioural trait and not a religious one. People of all religions, as well as people who do not identify with any religion at all, are equally capable of the kinds of deeds I have set out in this book. Therefore, no offence or slight is intended towards anybody belonging to the Catholic faith; my intention is to explore the manner in which a disturbed person could take its teachings and manipulate them for his own ends.

LJ ROSS
2nd August 2016

ACKNOWLEDGMENTS

Thank you to all the readers who have joined me in discovering new adventures for DCI Ryan over the past eighteen months. I can hardly believe that my pipe dream to become an author is now a living, breathing reality but I owe it to every one of you who has taken the time and effort to read the books and to get in touch. You are a wonderful driving force for me to carry on writing, all the time striving to write even better stories!

Similar thanks go to all the lovely book bloggers who have read and supported the series, your kind words have meant so much and I know that you have been pivotal in helping to spread the word about Ryan's exploits up in the beautiful North East.

I am grateful to Jon Elek and Millie Hoskins of United Agents, who have offered their valuable insights and advice and who continue to be wonderfully supportive as I grow as an author and embark upon new challenges. Likewise, the teams at Amazon KDP, Amazon Crossing and

Audible Studios, who have enabled me to release this series and make it possible for everybody to read it, listen to it and (hopefully) enjoy it for years to come.

The love and support from my family and friends is always humbling. My husband, James, has been a consistent source of encouragement and his unstinting praise tempered with sound practical advice and technical know-how has been invaluable. Without it, I imagine I would still be working in a profession that didn't suit me, wishing I had taken the leap. To my mum, my dad and my sister, thank you all so much for your positivity and for giving me the self-belief to try in the first place. Tallulah, Katie, Alex, Lauren, Kirsty, Kirsten and all my friends: thank you for offering me strategic glasses of *vino tinto* when I needed it most!

Finally, to my son, Ethan. Thank you for being the little bundle of sunshine which brightens up my day. I hope that you will like reading my books when you are older and have grown out of *Thomas the Tank Engine*—but don't grow up too fast, you're only three but almost as tall as me.

ABOUT THE AUTHOR

LJ Ross is an international bestselling author, best known for creating atmospheric mystery and thriller novels, including the DCI Ryan series of Northumbrian murder mysteries which have sold over five million copies worldwide.

Her debut, *Holy Island*, was released in January 2015 and reached number one in the UK and Australian charts. Since then, she has released a further eighteen novels, fifteen of which have been top three global bestsellers and twelve of which have been UK #1 bestsellers. Louise has garnered an army of loyal readers through her storytelling and, thanks to them, several of her books reached the coveted #1 spot whilst only available to pre-order ahead of release.

Louise was born in Northumberland, England. She studied undergraduate and postgraduate Law at King's College, University of London and then abroad in Paris and Florence. She spent much of her working life in London, where she was a lawyer for a number of years until taking the decision to change career and pursue her dream to write. Now, she writes full time and lives with her husband and son in Northumberland. She enjoys reading all manner of books, travelling and spending time with family and friends.

If you enjoyed reading *Angel*, please consider leaving a review online.

DCI Ryan will return in

HIGH FORCE

A DCI RYAN MYSTERY (Book #5)

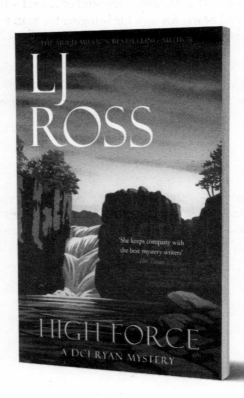

Hell has unleashed a demon – and he's coming for you...

Detective Chief Inspector Ryan's worst nightmare has just become a reality. Notorious serial killer *The Hacker* has escaped prison and kidnapped one of his best detectives from her own home. His brutality is the stuff of legend – Ryan lost his sister and nearly his own life bringing the man to justice first time around. Can Ryan do it again to save his friend?

There's a nationwide manhunt underway but the trail has gone cold and fear spreads like a virus. Ryan and his team must find *The Hacker* before he takes another life

– but are they too late?

The clock is ticking...

Murder and mystery are peppered with romance and humour in this fast-paced crime whodunit set amidst the spectacular Northumbrian landscape.

HIGH FORCE will be available in all good bookshops in July 2020!

If you like DCI Ryan, why not try the bestselling Alexander Gregory Thrillers by LJ Ross?

IMPOSTOR

AN ALEXANDER GREGORY THRILLER (Book #1)

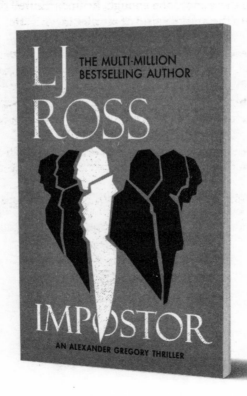

There's a killer inside all of us...

After an elite criminal profiling unit is shut down amidst
a storm of scandal and mismanagement, only one
person emerges unscathed. Forensic psychologist Doctor
Alexander Gregory has a reputation for being able to step
inside the darkest minds to uncover whatever secrets lie
hidden there and, soon enough, he finds himself drawn
into the murky world of murder investigation.

In the beautiful hills of County Mayo, Ireland, a killer is on
the loose. Panic has a stranglehold on its rural community
and the Garda are running out of time. Gregory has
sworn to follow a quiet life but, when the call comes, can
he refuse to help their desperate search for justice?

Murder and mystery are peppered with dark humour in this
fast-paced thriller set amidst the spectacular Irish landscape.

IMPOSTOR is available now in all good bookshops!

LOVE READING?

JOIN THE CLUB...